A Lime in Time
Charming Mysteries

Joann Keder

ISBN: 978-1-953270-13-9

Edited by: Amber Richberger, Exemplary Editing

Cover art by: Molly Burton

Be the first to hear about new releases! Sign up for my newsletter here:

http://www.joannkeder.com

Characters

Gemini Reed—co-owner of Kindred Spirits Detective Agency and local sleuth

Feather Jones—co-owner of Kindred Spirits Detective Agency and paranormal investigator

Leo Reed—Gemini's husband

Tug Muehler—owner of Tug Bars and Feather's boyfriend

Olive Thomas—retiree and employee of Tug Bars

Howard Beachmont—Gemini's neighbor

Tandy Jones—Feather's living great aunt

Candy Jones—Feather's deceased great aunt

Daisy Dune—Feather's inventor ghost friend

Jayden Ko—Feather's mentor

Lucinda Lime—client of Kindred Spirits and Leo's cousin

George Mint—Lucinda's neighbor

Millicent Playmoor—Feather's young ghost friend

Trent— Leo's nurse
Jasper Montgomery—client of Kindred Spirits
Mick Everson—son of Leo's neighbor
Nylah—massage therapist
Elmer—Olive's boyfriend

PROLOGUE
PRESENT DAY

Feather

"Aren't you excited, Gem? This is our first public outing with our joint detective agency! I just wish—"

Gemini pressed her finger to her partner's lips. Feather Jones, paranormal investigator, nodded.

"It's okay to be excited though, isn't it?" The twentysomething young woman was practically a fountain of excitement.

Gemini, her partner, was one for calm, but Feather's energy was infectious. "Of course. This is what we've both dreamed about for months! It's all going to work out swimmingly, I just know it."

She fanned their business cards embossed with "Kindred Spirits, Paranormal and Normal Detective Agency" in a half-circle on top of the purple vinyl tablecloth and set some of her orange dream cookies on a plate off to the side. Her setup duties were complete.

The warehouse Gemini had purchased for their office had come with some leaks and unexpected plumbing problems, but now, in addition to their office space, Tug Bars was officially occupying the factory floor. In the front of the building, she and Feather occupied a spacious area with two desks, a break room and two big couches where they could sit with new clients. Kindred Spirits Detective Agency was officially up and running, and now they were attending their first local event as a business.

When she retired from life as a legal secretary, she never dreamed she'd find herself on this path. "Our plans don't matter to the universe, Gem," her husband Leo would always remind her. At least he did, before the stroke that left him in a semi-comatose state.

Feather paused. "These are the same feelings I had before I took over Feather Works Hair Salon. It's all just self-doubt. Tug says that's the quickest way to talk yourself out of success."

"He's right, dear."

A mother and two brown-haired girls approached the table. "Look, Mommy! Ghosts!"

One of the young girls picked up a sticker.

"Take one for your sister too!" Gemini said, enjoying well-behaved children.

"You investigate... ghosts?" the mother asked timidly.

"We do." Gemini could tell the woman wasn't

comfortable discussing paranormal problems in public. It wasn't unusual, especially given they lived in such a small community. The last thing anyone wanted was for the neighbors to laugh at them or think they were crazy.

"Take a brochure and read about our services. You're welcome to come to our office and discuss it any time. We are very discreet."

The woman nodded and quickly looked away.

The cool, early morning air caused Gemini to shiver. Even though she'd brought her peach-colored sweater and her long-sleeved windbreaker, she was chilled to the bone. When she got up this morning, she planned on warmer weather. It was unusual for this time of year, but the last three months were a weak example of Pacific Northwest summer glory. As soon as the woman and her children left, she wrapped her coat around her tightly.

"Sorry to be such a wimp." She plopped down in the foldable chair, placing her hands in her armpits for warmth. She glanced at her watch. *8:55.*

"You're not a wimp," Feather replied, handing a blanket to her friend. "We purchased these Kindred Spirits branded blankets for a reason."

The blankets featured two superhero women with decidedly different bodies—Feather's slight build and Gemini's taller, more muscular form—in purple leotards. Their faces were fierce and strong. The company logo, a ghost-like apparition, was displayed on their chests.

Feather frequently reminded Gemini that she'd never encountered a ghost who looked like a walking sheet.

"Ah, yes. Superwomen. That we are, dear." Gemini tucked the blanket around her legs and took a sip of the hot ginger lemon tea she'd brought in an insulated thermos. She tucked a strand of silver hair behind one ear and smiled at her friend.

"I'm worried about you, hon. You're still having nightmares about... the incident. I thought once you'd solved the case, your dreams would return to their previously peaceful state." Gemini cleared her throat, uneasy about her next statement. "These dreams you've had for months are affecting your waking world. Making you... paranoid, even."

Instead of being upset, Feather nodded in agreement. Gemini studied her friend with concern. Feather was a spiky, bright green-haired, combat boot-wearing hair stylist and the least likely candidate for a friend for someone over seventy. Yet the retiree and the spunky twentysomething bonded like they'd been together all their lives and now shared their most intimate secrets. The dark circles under Feather's eyes and her obvious weight loss were not good signs.

Feather and Gemini rarely argued. Even though they were several decades apart in age, they were definitely "Kindred Spirits."

"Tug says I'm torturing myself. He's worried I'll continue until I'm permanently damaged. Unless—"

"Unless what?"

"Unless I see a doctor. A psychiatrist."

She and Gemini exchanged serious glances before simultaneously breaking out in laughter. "Can you imagine what a professional would say about my ability to talk to the dead?"

"You'd buy yourself a one-way ticket to Charming Psychiatric Hospital."

Gemini didn't want to let on, but Tug—Feather's tall and muscular boyfriend—had confided a very serious side effect of her troublesome dreams.

"She's been sleepwalking, Gem. Two nights ago, I got up to get a drink and when I returned, the covers were off. She was standing at the window, trying to get it open."

Feather's red-rimmed eyes darted back and forth. "Three months is too long for this problem. It's interfered with our business and my life. I want to go back to who I was before."

"You will, dear. The universe works in its own time," Gemini replied, smiling with confidence she didn't feel.

Feather nodded. "I'm going to do my best to push it to the side today. Kindred Spirits Detective Agency has its moment on the stage, and we're going to shine brightly!"

Tug Muehler, Feather's tall, chiseled boyfriend, was another unlikely match for Feather. Luckily, he saw past the stares of those who observed them together and professed his undying love for his soulmate.

"I found the sandwiches in the backseat," he said, unusually breathless. He squeezed Feather's shoulder and winked at Gemini.

"Can't say as I've ever known you to be out of breath," Gemini commented.

"I had to move the car." He cleared his throat before stating, "There's some kind of police activity going on and they've blocked off everything in this area."

"Great," Feather grumbled. "Now people won't be able to get here."

Just as Feather sat down next to her friend and business partner, a voice screeched, "Isn't this the hoon-doggiest darn thing! We've got us a tent!"

The other vendors paused and glanced up. A portly woman with short orange hair practically bounced to their tent. She was sporting a bright blue t-shirt that read "Tug Bars, Tug-n-Olive's Creations." Olive Thomas, also a retiree, was Tug's business partner. They often clashed over Tug Bar flavors, but Olive was a hard worker.

"Olive, you can take it down a notch," Feather responded with irritation. "I see you didn't take my advice." She pointed to Olive's dirty rust-colored hair. "I tried warning you that the red color you got from an off-brand box was a mistake. It looks like you took matters into your own hands."

"Pssht. It looks just fine. The gal next door found the color at a discount store. Only expired three months. Couldn't get an appointment for you to change it, Miss Too Busy For Her Friends," Olive replied dismissively. "Besides, my new man friend thinks I'm sexy as-is."

"You know I told you I'd be happy to change it, once it recovers from your last home-color-experiment-gone-wrong," Feather protested.

"We're glad you're enthused, dear!" Gemini added, trying to lighten the mood. She didn't dare ask Olive about her man friend again. It was always followed by an uncomfortable conversation about their private activities. "Feather's feeling nervous is all."

"Haven't your spirits told you things is gonna be fine?" Olive asked, inserting her chair in the inches of space between theirs. Both women scooched to make room.

"The opening bell is in one minute!" a woman's voice boomed over the speakers.

"Count down with me now. Fifty-nine, fifty-eight, fifty-seven..."

All three women enthusiastically joined in.

"Miss Feather Jones?" His bark caught them all off guard. A tall man wearing a heavy jacket ducked inside the tent, his head barely clearing their colorful purple-and-orange banner. As he stepped closer, Gemini could see his police uniform. She felt a sick feeling in her stomach, thinking about what lied ahead.

"Miss Feather Jones?" he asked again with a forceful tone that sounded more like an announcement than a question.

She glanced worriedly at Tug. "That's me!"

"Thirty, twenty-nine, twenty-eight..."

He walked around the table and commanded, "Please stand and place your hands behind your back, ma'am. You're under arrest."

Tug sprang up and stopped just short of attacking the officer. "For what?"

Gemini quickly grabbed his arm before things escalated. "Officers, my son-in-law is an attorney and we know our rights. What is it you're arresting her for?"

"Murder."

CHAPTER ONE
THREE MONTHS AGO

Feather

For the past week, Feather had felt off. To start, she was visited nightly by a spirit with no face. She couldn't tell if it was a man or woman, but it was definitely in pain. Every time it appeared, her hands ached.

In addition, when the spirit was present, she sensed the strong scent of caramel corn cooking. Wracking her brain to come up with an entity who routinely carried that delightful scent, she found no one.

Tug rolled over and pulled her in close, burying his face in her spiky green hair. "Do we really have to get up today?" he murmured.

"Not unless you want to make money," she replied. Feather pulled the covers off her legs, exposing long scratches.

When she gasped, Tug bolted upright. "What? Did something happen?"

"It's nothing." She attempted to cover her legs again, but he prevented her from taking the covers.

Tug leaned over to see what she was seeing and he, too, gasped. "Who did this? I'll take care of them right now."

It was her turn to grab the covers. "It's not a who but a what. Do you remember me telling you about the visions I've been having?"

"Most people just call them dreams." Tug chuckled. "Yeah, you mention that every time I ask why you have dark circles under your eyes. And the whole popcorn thingy."

"Caramel corn," she corrected him. "This entity wants to make sure I listen. I'm not sure what the smell has to do with—" She snapped her fingers before swinging her legs over the side of the bed. "I've got to make a stop. Will you tell Gem I'll be late?"

Tug let out a frustrated huff. "Why are you cutting me out? We share everything, don't we?"

She turned and ran her fingers across his rough, stubble-filled cheeks before gently kissing his lips. "I will. I promise. Just as soon as I make sure I'm not in the wrong. I don't want to say it out loud until I'm positive."

"And the scratches? Can you at least tell me about those?"

Without responding, Feather pulled her black pajama top over her head and dropped it on the floor.

Luckily, her usual attire of jeans, a plaid shirt and combat boots didn't require much forethought. After combing her hair and forgoing makeup, she gave Tug a second kiss and headed out the door, ignoring his forlorn look.

It was a short drive across town. So short, in fact, that she chastised herself for not going sooner.

She knocked on the fluorescent green door of 1240 Peabody Circle, tapping her foot in rhythm. *Tap. Taptaptap.* The door swung open and a droopy, haggard face greeted her. Only a few streaks of the family dark hair remained, consumed by the mess of wiry grey strands. She had the distinct look of a skunk.

As soon as a look of recognition crossed her face, her features softened. "My great-niece Feather? I can't believe my eyes!"

"Hi Aunt Tandy. May I come in?"

The old woman nodded and Feather stepped inside the modest home. When the door was shut, she remarked, "Haven't seen you at a family reunion for years. There were rumors you were dead."

"You know that isn't true, Auntie. I did your hair last spring."

Her aunt shrugged and sat down with a thud, causing the plastic-covered couch to squeak in protest.

"What brings you here? I can't believe you even remembered my address."

Feather swallowed hard. "I know. I struggle trying to communicate with family. Now that I'm out in the open with my gift, I—"

"Gift? Is that what you're calling it?" She chuckled dismissively. "Those that don't think you're dead say you've been locked up in a mental facility." Tandy's fingers made small circles around her ears. "I can see why."

Feather purposely avoided these conversations when she styled the hair of anyone in her family. Luckily, they didn't bother to visit her salon often.

"Your house still smells like caramel corn," she observed, abruptly changing direction. "When your sister was alive, the two of you made caramel corn every Friday for the neighborhood kids."

Tandy's eyes twinkled. "I suppose we did. Your Aunt Candy always said we never had children of our own so we could spoil others."

Every Christmas, Feather and her brothers watched out the window, waiting impatiently for the old green sedan to pull into the driveway. Every time, her father would scurry out to help them. "Who are these presents for?" he would ask as he came through the door. He was unusually cheery on those days.

They were filled with a multitude of gifts, candies and cookies. "You shouldn't spoil them," Feather's mother would admonish, though Feather knew her mother secretly loved that her children were doted on.

"It's not spoiling if I do it," Tandy would always insist.

Tandy coughed until something came up that she spat in a previously hidden tissue. "You came today for caramel corn? I haven't made it in at least a decade. Doubt I'd know the recipe anymore."

"You're going to have to believe in me, just for a few minutes," Feather said quietly. She took a deep breath and let it out slowly, running her palms up and down her worn jeans. "I have to tell you something that may be hard to hear."

"Okay."

Tandy clasped her hands, gnarled by arthritis, and set them on her lap. Feather remembered how she did this every time someone talked about the family secrets.

"I've been contacted by a spirit for a week now. They've been very insistent—"

Aunt Tandy leaned forward and whispered, "I've seen those television programs before. You need a priest and a bucket of holy water to get rid of 'em."

There was no use in being upset. No one in her family had any idea what she did, and that wouldn't change today.

"You don't have to worry about that, Auntie. This is more of a nudge. This spirit wants my attention. And they've been offering the scent of caramel corn."

Tandy's eyes widened and she maneuvered her way off the couch, grunting and groaning in time with the squeaking sounds of loose skin against plastic, until she was in a standing position. "I've heard just about enough. Trying to involve me and my dearly departed sister in your nonsense is low. Everyone in the family always says, 'Stay away from Feather unless you want her to involve you in her malarkey.' You need to leave before I call the police."

"But I just wanted to confirm—"

"Out the door you go." Tandy pushed on Feather's back until she was standing at the threshold.

"I was hoping you would want to solve a mystery," Feather said helplessly. "I guess I was wrong."

Tandy nodded. "Guess so. Be on your way now. Don't darken my doorstep again."

She opened her front door and gave Feather one more brisk shove, slamming it shut behind her.

Feather's body didn't hurt from the unexpected movement off the porch. Her heart, however, was another matter entirely.

It wasn't something that normally upset her, but all the way to the warehouse she felt lost. No one in her family supported her gift, and only two cousins came regularly to get their hair done at her salon. Most days, she was fine with her family of choice taking the place of the large Jones clan. But some days, like today, she let the hurt get to her. Tears poured down her cheeks and she allowed herself to fall into an all-too-familiar darkness. The kind spirits she'd met over the years were all there, some offering encouragement.

You don't need them, Feather. They're your past, not your future.

"Daisy?"

Daisy Dune was an entity who came to Feather while she and Tug were picnicking at the beach. Tug left her alone momentarily while he ran back to the car for his binoculars. She was startled by the sound of someone laughing.

Looking down at her feet, she saw a woman dressed in a long skirt and a wrinkled white blouse with her hair haphazardly clumped on the side of her head. Once she'd ascertained that it was in fact a spirit and no one living, Feather studied her hair. It was full of twigs and—was that a dead bird?

"Name's Daisy. Don't wear it out."

She turned out to be the most entertaining entity Feather had met.

In 1881, Daisy Dune was working in the Charming General Store when she found her unfortunate end. Mr. Zappum, store proprietor, warned Daisy that if she were late again, she would be out of a job.

Daisy read in the newspaper about a lamplighter who used a ten-pound rock tied to his alarm clock. He placed it on the shelf beside his bed, so that when the alarm clock went off, the rock would fall onto the floor.

Though she had a history of poor decisions, beginning with her idea to start a fire in her father's barn to warm the mice, she was certain that this time, Daisy Drum, inventor, had found the perfect invention.

The first two nights it worked splendidly. Mr. Zappum was pleased at her early arrival. On the third night, Daisy was trying to figure out how she could create furniture that moved on a turntable, like the train she'd seen in Seattle. After several stern taps on her floor (which was the ceiling for her downstairs neighbors), the boarding house matron knocked on her door. "Go to bed, Daisy. Save your crazy ideas for the hours when folks aren't trying to sleep."

Resigned to the fact that she'd have to save this invention for another time, she went to bed. The next morning, the alarm clock went off as expected. But unlike her previous experiences, she'd forgotten that the furnishings were in different spots. When the rock fell, it landed squarely on her head.

"Morning, Daisy," Feather said with little enthusiasm.

"You don't have to feel sad, Feather Weather. Your dead friends are here for you."

Feather glanced in her rear view mirror, where an apparition fluttered in and out. She noticed that today, Daisy's hair was full of butterflies.

"What's got you in the dumps? Do you need me to tell you about one of my inventions?"

Feather shook her head. Most days when Daisy appeared, she loved hearing her stories. "My family hates me."

Daisy giggled in a high-pitched tone that always made Feather's ears ring.

"Feather Weather, you don't need them." Daisy

swooped into the front seat in a rush of hot air. *"Do you want me to haunt those suckers until they cry?"*

Daisy was thrusting her fists in the air, and the butterflies surrounding her head had disappeared. Now there were kittens swirling around her almost-translucent skull.

"You couldn't haunt if your very death depended on it." Feather pulled into her parking space and shut off the engine. She blew her nose and reached for her purse. "Thanks for the chat, but I've got to get to work."

"Okay," Daisy replied in a sad voice. *"Tell Tuggles that Daisy says hello!"*

Feather smiled as she always did when she read the sign Gemini placed in front of her parking space when they opened: Parking for Feather Jones, Master Paranormal Detective.

Wiping her face with the back of her hand, she jumped out of the car, pushing the darkness aside. Feather readied an excuse for her reddened eyes. "Allergies. The ragweed must be bad today."

The light beep of a car horn made her jump. She was surprised to see her mentor, Jayden Ko, parked next to her. Jayden exited her vehicle, adjusting the Lycra legs of her black-and-white striped cat suit.

Jayden was not only the leader of the local paranormal group PINK but also a successful business woman, running Ko Industries. For her to join Feather on a business day was extremely unusual.

"Hi, doll!" Jayden's deep voice cooed.

Feather took comfort in Jayden's tone. It was always soothing but was especially appreciated today.

Feather hugged Jayden and kissed her on either cheek, something she reserved for those she felt a deep affection. "What are you doing here? Don't you need to be at work? Important boss and all."

"That's the best part about being the important boss. I can come and go as I please. And the message I got this morning was too important to wait."

It was curious she hadn't just picked up the phone. "Come on in and I'll make you a coffee," Feather said, moving toward the glass doors.

"No, we need to talk in the car. It's not that I don't trust your friends, but this is too delicate. Please." She opened her passenger door and motioned for Feather to hop in before moving around to the driver's door.

The smooth grey leather interior felt like butter against Feather's legs. "Ooh. This is nice, Jayden!"

"You like? I bought myself a present after our last board meeting. The company has doubled in revenue under my leadership!"

Jayden applied a layer of berry lipstick before turning to Feather. She was always exquisite in her presentation, taking more time each day to put on her makeup and maintain it than Feather did in an entire week.

"There's an entity I speak with on a daily basis. Just like your Millie."

"The kid only comes around when she feels like it."

Feather clucked her tongue. "She's just a little kid, I guess I can't fault her."

Recently, Feather had been visited by a young spirit named Millicent. She was a precocious child who had perished as a result of the 1918 pandemic. The child was at times exasperating but usually a good source of information. As long as Feather had plenty of time and patience, she could extract something important from her.

"That's probably why my frequent visitor, Genesee, has been so persistent. She says you've been having some bad dreams."

Feather stared at Jayden. It wasn't that she expected this to be a secret, but for an entity other than one of her own to mention it was downright odd.

"She's been watching you. She's worried because there is someone carrying a grudge against you, and they have the propensity toward violence. Those scratches on your legs are a serious sign."

Feather unconsciously rubbed her legs. She'd forgotten all about them. It seemed like so long ago now.

"And what about the caramel corn smell?"

"You've got me stumped there, doll. Are you smelling it often?"

"No, it was just once," Feather fibbed. "Forget it, I'm sure it's nothing."

Jayden looked out the window and waved at one of the factory workers arriving at the Tug Bars factory.

"I received a call yesterday from a former member.

He'd been in contact with his grandmother. She was fit to be tied. She said there's quite an uproar in her world because someone from the living world has been trying to bring an entity back from the dead. Playing both sides of the fence, so to speak."

Feather's eyes widened. "Someone in our group? Can't we call a special session of PINK and just ask?"

She'd been reluctant to join the group, but ever since she passed her initiation, Paranormal Investigators of the Northwest, Level K, had been nothing but kind.

"What is the "k" for?"

Jayden took a deep breath. "We've had some missteps as an organization. Phoebe over there," she pointed across the room to a tall, thin woman, whose makeup portrayed a white tiger and whose braids swirled around the top of her head, "told a family she'd banished their ghost. That's a level L skill and she only wishes she was there. We're stuck on 'K' for the time being, I'm afraid."

"That would be too easy, wouldn't it?" Jayden smiled and patted Feather's arm reassuringly.

"How do I know who it is, then?"

It occurred to Feather that the fact that Jayden had driven all the way out to the warehouse to talk to her didn't bode well. "It's me, isn't it? Someone thinks I've been trying to raise the dead, just like the horror movies!"

Jayden chuckled again. "You always make me laugh, even on the days when I think there's absolutely no reason for levity."

Always the people pleaser, Feather felt a sense of satisfaction. "Is it me?"

Jayden shrugged. "Just because someone brought up your name, doesn't mean that—"

"Jayden! I know the rules. No hocus pocus with the other world. They are there for a reason. Besides, that would mean I was doing something behind your back. I'd hope by now you know I would never do that."

Jayden patted her arm. "I didn't for one second think it was true. My feeling is that this particular former member heard your name within the context of the conversation and missed important parts of the message."

"Who else knows about this? Will I get kicked out of PINK?"

Jayden frowned. "It's my turn to ask why you haven't learned yet that you can trust me?"

Feather fidgeted with two fingers, half-covered in black nail polish. "I'm sorry. You've been my biggest champion and best support since I began using my gift."

Jayden sighed a long, luxurious sigh. "As I was saying, you and I will have to do our own investigation. At this moment, I have no idea why your name was brought up. But for the time being, I'd prefer you don't tell your friends."

Jayden always had the answers. If she didn't know, the answers didn't exist.

"Why don't you want me to tell Tug or Gemini?"

"Because we don't know who the person is in our world."

Feather opened her mouth to protest, but Jayden raised her hand.

"I know, I know. They are completely trustworthy. But what if it's someone they communicate with regularly? What if they accidentally spill the beans? With help from the other side, this person could plot your dear ones' demise. No, it's safer to keep your friends in the dark." Jayden shook her head. "That way you don't have to worry about any slips of the tongue."

She hated the thought. *Keeping secrets from Tug?* That wasn't the way their relationship worked. And Gemini—she would know. She had a special gift of her own. She called it a mother's intuition, but Feather knew there was more to it.

"What if they guess? Can I tell them at that point?"

"That's up to you, doll. Just remember, it's your job to keep your family of choice as safe as possible. Your emotions this morning weren't because of the family you lost. They resulted from the perspective you've gained. You're no longer that forlorn little girl, and you want to hold her tight."

Feather nodded, fighting the tears that crept into her eyes.

Jayden brought her bejeweled phone case to her face before it rang. Her ability to see the future always fascinated Feather.

"Thanks. See you soon." Jayden hung up and

glanced at Feather with concern. "You gonna be all right, doll? You look like I just stole your favorite toy."

"I'm lost without Tug and Gem. One is my right hand and the other my left. How am I going to keep something this important from them?"

"It's not forever. It's just for now. Contact that little friend of yours. Millicent, was it? She might offer some suggestions."

Feather wasn't so sure, but she nodded.

"I've got a board meeting in an hour. I have to bounce."

Feather opened the car door and turned to gaze at her friend. "This is going to be so hard. Will you keep working on it? Let me know as soon as you can who this double agent might be?"

"You know I will." Jayden turned the ignition switch as Feather shut the door. Feather watched her drive away, wondering just how difficult this was going to be.

Chapter Two
Gemini

"Mavis tells me you've been giving her a hard time when she brings in your nighttime meds."

Gemini squeezed her husband's hand. Leo still possessed steely blue eyes and the movie star face that reminded her of James Dean. Since his coma caused by an unscrupulous nurse and her boyfriend, Leo had been under the care of the Charming Waves Care Center. While he showed improvement from his early days, he was still unable to speak. His eyes stared straight ahead, and though he would thrash about in unpredictable episodes, he was still—for all intents and purposes—comatose.

"You have to take those pills or you won't sleep at night. We've talked about that before, dear."

She'd grown comfortable with the silence. At first it was hard, carrying on a conversation by herself, but she grew to enjoy their solitude too. She could feel his spirit in the room, his undying love. That was all she needed.

"Good morning, Mrs. Reed." Gemini looked up, surprised by the interruption.

"Oh, Edith. I've been meaning to bring you some cookies." Edith Morning was Leo's across-the-hall neighbor. She was like the neighborhood busybody who kept an eye on the comings and goings of every house. Living in a care center was no exception.

Edith leaned forward on her walker, resting her elbows awkwardly on the handles. "Leo's had a visitor. Pretty lady. She's been here twice now." She smacked her lips and gazed at the pictures of their grandson Taurus adorning his wall. "That one's crooked," she remarked, pointing to the picture in the middle, the one taken after Taurus's first karate lesson. In the minutes following the photo, Taurus threw a fit and kicked the instructor in the jaw, causing the poor man to go through six excruciating months with his jaw wired shut.

"I never check the visitor log anymore. I wonder who that could be?"

She went through her mental list of usual visitors. Tug and Feather usually asked ahead of time if it would work okay to visit Leo. Olive came once in a while, but she would have left a card or a Tug Bar. Leo's nightstand contained only his plastic pitcher and cup.

"Oh, are you thinking of our daughter, Sophia? She's young and—"

"I know your daughter!" Edith snapped. "I'm not dense. This one's closer to our age."

"Oh." She was relieved that Sophia hadn't been in town without telling her.

"Never know, this old gal may be after your man," Edith warned. "I've been reading in the *Snoopz* magazine that women are doing that sort of thing now. They come into nursing homes and sink their claws into a poor old coot without much left upstairs." She knocked on her skull for emphasis.

Gemini bit her tongue.

"The next thing you know, bam! His bank account is empty," Edith continued, oblivious to Gemini's suffering.

"Those *Home and Happy* magazines I brought you weren't enough? I keep telling you, *Snoopz* isn't a reliable news source."

Edith pressed her hands against the walker until her body was in an upright position. "Snack time. Butterscotch pudding cups and sugar cookies today." Edith pivoted her walker and moved away from Leo's door. "Check on that mystery woman!" she called over her shoulder.

"Should I be worried that you're interested in another woman, Leo?" Gemini giggled. She watched, as she always did, for any signs of comprehension. He blinked once.

It was a beautiful summer day with a gentle breeze, a respite from the unrelenting rain. Gemini stood and opened the window so they could both breathe in the healing ocean air.

As she was finding her chair again, there was a knock on the door frame. It never made any sense to her why people knocked; they already moved halfway in the room to reach the door.

"Gemini Reed?"

Gemini turned around to find a statuesque woman with short silver hair and bright red lipstick. This must be the woman Edith warned her about. There was something familiar about her face.

"Do I know you?"

She hated feeling protective, and hated it even more that Edith may have been right.

"You don't recognize me?" She glided closerand leaned in beside Gemini, almost nose to nose. "I've had a little work done since the last funeral, but who hasn't?"

Gemini studied her. Strong jaw, piercing green eyes, the trademark Reed dimples. "You're... Leo's cousin? I thought you were dead!"

She laughed softly. "Rumors of my demise... you know the rest. I'm sure there are people who wouldn't mind seeing me under my incredibly expensive headstone. Now I'm going to embarrass you further and see if you can remember which cousin I am, exactly."

It felt more like a cruelty than an embarrassment. She knew every one of his cousins by name. They all attended their wedding, but that was decades ago. She remembered stuffing cake in Leo's mouth and his mother "accidentally" spilling red wine on her dress, but that was the extent of her memories of that special day, unfortunately.

Leo had a very large family that wasn't close. When she made out the wedding invitations, Leo warned her that sending an invite out of kindness wouldn't be met with the polite refusal she planned. The Reeds showed up, en masse, for every wedding, graduation, baptism and funeral. And then they never spoke again, until the next event.

"I'm sorry. Your name isn't coming to me. Can you refresh my memory?"

The woman sighed with irritation. "You've gotten a Christmas card from me every single year. Lucinda Lime."

She studied the woman again before a look of recognition passed over her face. "Oh! Lucinda! The one who spends every Christmas in some quaint ski village. Your cards are beautiful."

"You and Leo missed Scorpio's medical school graduation and Ashley's baby shower. We've felt somewhat slighted."

She couldn't tell if this was said with sarcasm or anger. Gemini was doing her best to curtail her mounting frustration with this stranger. That's what she was—a stranger. No doubt Lucinda heard about the multimillion-dollar settlement they'd received from the hospital after Leo's mistreatment. She wanted her slice of the pie.

"Leo and I have missed more Reed gatherings than

we've attended," she replied, trying valiantly to keep her emotions in check. "And we've been a little busy of late. I hope you didn't come all the way to Charming to berate us. If so, kindly see yourself out. Leo and I have our routine and you're interfering."

Slowly, memories of Lucinda and her husband Lyle filtered into her head. "You own the family cabin. I remember now, we received a Reed Family Newsletter that said you were planning to sell it. That place has been in the Reed family for generations, Lucinda. You won't make any friends in the family by getting rid of it."

Lucinda stepped back slightly and brought a slender hand up to her chest. "You're insulted, I can see that. The reason I made this trip was to ask for your help. I've come more than once hoping to make contact with you. I'm happy to pay for your services."

"What?" Gemini turned her head sharply. "What services are you referring to? I can't imagine what the Reed rumor mill has picked up about me. I'm no longer at the law firm, so I can't offer a good deal on an attorney."

Lucinda found the only remaining chair in the room and scooted it over to Gemini's side, avoiding Leo altogether. "We've heard amazing stories about your detective agency. I'm here to hire you for some sleuthing."

"Oh." Gemini hadn't even entertained that possibility. She was shocked and a little flattered. "What—or who—do you want me to investigate?"

"You probably remember, or maybe you don't, my husband Lyle. We've been married for thirty-eight years this Friday."

"Congratulations," Gemini replied without emotion. She squeezed her husband's hand. It always brought her strength.

"Yes, I wish it were a reason to celebrate." Lucinda sighed. "But my Lyle has disappeared. He was on a business trip a month ago. He was in Chicago for a conference on ethoesium, a wonderful new product with many uses."

"I thought he sold insurance?"

"He does. Lyle likes to invest in up-and-coming businesses too." Lucinda attempted a smile, but her lips barely moved. "That evening, he called to tell me he'd ordered a pizza," she continued. "That is how we do things on his trips: he tells me about dinner, I tell him about dinner, sometimes we eat at the same time."

Lucinda paused and breathed out slowly. "His usual routine was watching the eleven p.m. news before going to bed. The next morning, he didn't show up for his meeting."

Gemini turned to look Lucinda in the eye. "You must've been beside yourself!" She'd lost sight of her intent to stay neutral. "Where was he?"

"I still don't know. His boss called when he didn't show for the meeting and half-jokingly asked if he'd run off to a tropical island. You see, my Lyle was planning to retire this week. We were going to travel together—"

"Did the police intervene?"

Lucinda nodded. "They went up to his room and knocked. When no one answered, the manager opened the door. The pizza, uneaten, was sitting on the bed. Lyle's suitcase and his wallet were gone. 'He's run off. It's not uncommon.' That's what they told me." She stared at Gemini plaintively. "Can you believe it? No investigation at all."

Gemini scooched her chair around, so that she was facing Lucinda, and took both of her delicate hands in her own. They were smooth and soft, as though they hadn't been used once in her lifetime. She would later explain it to Leo as "fresh from the box hands, darling. You should have felt them!"

"We wives have a sixth sense about these things, don't we dear? What do you think happened?"

Lucinda's mouth twitched just slightly. "At first, I believed what the police said. It was the easiest explanation, and the one that required the least thought. I was just furious. I tore our room apart, every dresser drawer, everything that man ever touched ended up on the floor. That's when I noticed this."

She reached into her bag and pulled out a large manila envelope, handing it to Gemini.

The first thing Gemini noticed was that the envelope was worn, like someone had handled it several times. There was an address on the front:

Lyle Lime

4785 Blueberry Circle

"Is this your home address?" she asked.

"Yes, it is. But you'll notice there is no postage on the front, so it was hand-delivered."

Gemini stood and moved to Leo's bed, where she opened the envelope and poured out its contents.

A folded up newspaper article, a box of Bittersby Chocolate Hard Candies and a gold button landed in a heap.

"Read it," Lucinda urged.

"Local man wins invention contest." Gemini looked at the picture. A distinguished-looking gentleman with broad shoulders and a bushy mustache held a certificate while shaking the hand of a man in a black suit.

Her gaze traveled to the caption and read the names out loud. "Lyle Lime, inventor and Earnest Buckley, mayor." She paused and glanced up at Lucinda. "That's something to be proud of. I can understand you would be disappointed that he didn't—"

"Look at the date!"

Gemini picked up the article again and gasped, bringing her hand to her mouth. "It's a misprint, surely!"

"I wish it was. My husband has time traveled back to 1924."

"Cheese and crackers!" Gemini exclaimed. "There has to be a reasonable explanation for this, Lucinda. Have you checked his credit card receipts? Spoken with acquaintances? I hate to ask, but is his secretary still around?"

"I've done all of the above. His assistant, Ben, is still showing up for work every day." She smirked. "There's been no activity on his credit cards. None."

"That's peculiar, I'll grant you. What about this button?" Gemini picked it up and examined it. There was an inscription on the back, so tiny she wasn't sure she could read it. "A.E."

Gemini squinted, allowing a moment for her eyes to readjust to her surroundings. "I fail to see how this means your husband is cheating."

"Lyle belongs to a group of time travelers. One month before he disappeared, I received a phone call. The voice on the other end said Lyle was making frequent trips to see his lover, A.E. When I asked why they were telling me, the voice on the other end said Lyle was in trouble. The caller ID was blank."

"How would that whole process work? A machine? A vaporizer?" Gemini stole a glance at Leo without thinking. He would say, "Gem, you've been watching too much television. Your mind is stuck in make-believe."

"I've given it some thought," Lucinda began. "I believe he had a portal door of some kind, just like a door that goes outside, only this one leads to another century. He was going through with ease until this last time. Something locked the door and now he can't return."

Never one to judge, Gemini had learned during her short time in the business that nothing was out of bounds.

"It sounds like you have put a lot of effort into this," Gemini replied, studying her with skepticism. It wasn't like the Reeds to play practical jokes, but she didn't know this couple well. Lucinda's smooth face didn't reveal any of the telltale signs of a liar, such as rapid blinking or other facial tics.

"My Lyle had a group of friends—I never took their conversations seriously—they always talked about time travel. What I put together came directly from their mouths."

"I have good news for you, Lucinda. My partner is a paranormal investigator. She'll be able to help with that. In the meantime, I'll need to gather information on his life leading up to his disappearance."

Lucinda's lip curled upward slightly. "Oh, thank you, Gemini! I always felt close to you!"

Gemini smiled, wondering how Lucinda felt close to someone she'd barely known.

"Did you contact his friends?"

"I'm embarrassed to say I don't know them. Lyle and I have led separate lives. It's what kept our marriage afloat all these years."

This wasn't Gemini's first challenging case, but it was going to be an unusual one.

"Can I ask that you don't share this with the rest of the family?" Lucinda continued. "You know how gossipy they can be."

Gemini drew an X across her chest and said, "Cross my heart. No spilling of the time traveler's secrets."

"We're having a service for Lyle this Saturday. It's

more about closure for me than anything. All of the Limes will be in attendance, and of course the Reeds. You mentioned the family cabin and you must not have gotten the follow-up email. My husband was adamant that we keep it, and the Reed family agreed." She sighed. "I'm hoping that by providing this closure for everyone, they'll be more receptive to my plans to sell. I just don't want the burden of upkeep anymore."

Gemini nodded sympathetically. "Lucinda, one more question, if I may."

"Yes, thank you for reminding me." She opened her purse and pulled out four one-hundred-dollar bills, handing them to Gemini. "That should get you started, right?"

"It will, thank you." Gemini didn't share the information on her large hospital settlement with anyone. It always changed relationships. "That's not what I was referring to. Did Lyle have any enemies?"

Lucinda stared at the ceiling. "Not to my knowledge, but just as with our friends, the identities of our enemies were never shared."

Chapter Three

Feather

"Are you sure we shouldn't wait for Gemini?"

A new client, Gemini's next-door neighbor, squirmed in his seat. Feather couldn't understand why he came in at the exact time he knew Gemini was with her husband.

"Howard, if you'd be more comfortable, we could wait until Gemini is here. She said to expect her by one." Feather glanced up at the spy glass-shaped clock Tug bought when they opened. 11:15.

"She'll be here in two hours. Do you want to wait? Or join me and Tug for lunch? We're trying out that new place, Tickled Egg."

Trying to hide the pain in her hands, she placed them under her desk, where she could massage them unnoticed.

"No, I used to be a businessman myself." Howard leaned forward and tapped his well-manicured nails on the desk. "I know how valuable your time is. Let's get to things right now."

He pulled out a letter and slid it across the desk. "This is the second one."

Feather opened the crinkled envelope, unusual for the usually neat-and-tidy neighbor of Gemini.

"Dear Mr. Beachmont," she began. "It's come to our attention that an item you recently insured, one Prestler pocket watch, may need further information in order for us to process your claim."

Feather glanced up at him. "I'm sorry you lost your watch. Why do you need a private investigator?"

"Keep reading," he urged, sliding one more letter across the desk.

She opened the second letter, dated a week ago. "Our records indicate that another client has already submitted a claim for the same watch. We've notified local authorities. We take fraud very seriously here at Big Rock Insurance, Mr. Beachmont. We have no alternative but to contact the authorities and let them sort this out. Until such time as ownership of said watch is determined, we are suspending your insurance."

"They think I'm a thief," Howard said, his voice shaking. "My great-grandfather's watch, the one that's been in the family for almost one hundred years, and they think I stole it!"

Feather's mind whirred. Was this the person Jayden had warned her about? Reliable Howard, Gemini's neighbor? *Doubtful.*

"What made you decide to insure your watch now, if I may ask?"

"It's always been insured," he snapped. "I'm very conscientious in all areas of my life. I've been doing an extensive remodel of my home. The company I hired for the work accidentally knocked over the glass case where this was stored. Just an accident. The case was dented, so I took it to a jeweler to be repaired. That's how this all came about."

Feather wrote down everything he said. She and Gemini would go over it later, as was their current mode of operation.

"Before you even ask, this painting company is licensed, bonded, and comes highly recommended. There have been no reports of incidents with the company before."

Feather nodded. She paused before her next sentence. "Have the police come to your home? I'm not accusing you of anything, I'm just asking if the insurance company reported it as stolen."

He shook his head. "No, but they'll be coming soon, I'm sure. I have several other items stored in that case. I'm just fit to be tied about this, and I can't bring myself to get them checked out as well." His chest heaved and Feather could feel his pain. "I've only come up with one plausible scenario. A neighbor convinced me to host the Annual Tulip Society meeting three weeks ago. Although the cabinet was locked, it's possible one of the attendees found out where I kept the key and helped themselves."

Feather's eyes widened. "You think these people planned a theft? Where do you think they found the fake watch?"

Howard folded the letters up and placed them in his breast pocket. "That's where you and Gemini come in. You need to get to the bottom of this ASAP. It can't just be me. There has to be someone else who has been victimized."

Howard reached in his shirt and pulled out a chain with a key and two rings. "For now, I'm keeping my parents' wedding rings with me at all times. And of course the key to the cabinet where the rest of my most precious family heirlooms are stored."

"Do you have any proof this is your watch? That's the first thing the police will ask."

Howard stared at her as if she'd just asked if he was a murderer. "Of course not! When great-granddad was gifted this beautiful piece, he didn't think about a receipt. It's not how things were done back then."

She nodded sympathetically. "I'll see if I can make contact with your great-grandfather. He may be able to shed some light on this. If you're not opposed to that?"

"Whatever it takes. I just want this to go away." Howard stood and zipped his jacket. "Tell Gemini it's pureed squash tonight."

"What is?" Feather asked, wondering why he would need a coat on this warm summer day.

"The soup I'm making. Tuesdays we share soup. This week, it's my turn."

She watched him leave and wondered how she

would make any progress on this puzzling case if her spirit friends weren't able to help.

When the phone rang, she was in another zone, thinking about Howard. After four rings, she picked it up.

"Feather Jones?"

"That's me. How can I help you?"

"Meet me at Troubled Tom's Gas in thirty minutes. I've got information you need to hear."

"What? Who is this? Hello?"

She hung up and searched quickly for caller ID. There was none.

It would take almost thirty minutes to get back into town from the warehouse, so she had no time to think about it. Instead, she sent Tug a message:

Had to run an errand.

Get burgers from Paul's Burger Cave and bring them here. I'll be back in time to eat with my handsome boyfriend.

Love you!

Everything in her screamed that this was a horrible mistake, but she couldn't afford to miss an opportunity. As she was driving, she tried to place the voice. Was it a man? A woman? She couldn't be sure. Was this person old? Young?

"You're quite the detective, Jones," she chided herself out loud.

They'd recently had a slew of clients who thought their spouses were cheating, only to find out they were all attending the same twelve-step meeting. In a town the size of Charming, Oregon there wasn't much anonymity.

There was a Peggy, no Pearl. She couldn't remember exactly. Pauline?

Lost in thought, she didn't notice the figure crossing her path until it was too late. When she swerved to miss it, her car plowed into a giant fir tree.

Her last conscious thoughts were of Tug. How would he survive without her?

CHAPTER FOUR
GEMINI

"You haven't been here since the remodel."

Howard gestured around his formerly dark, paneled living room. The crew he'd hired removed the paneling, replacing it with sheetrock and pale grey paint.

Gemini stepped out of her soggy shoes. Normally it stopped raining by the end of May, but this year it just kept coming.

"I like it! I'm surprised, though, that you allowed people into your home for an entire week."

She drank in the rich smell of soup and fresh-baked bread.

Howard grinned. "You know me well, Gemini Reed. This company came highly recommended from a college friend. M and E Painting and Restoration, if you ever need someone. Very professional. On the last day, they left some tea for me, knowing how much I enjoy it."

Howard walked to the refrigerator and opened the door. He returned with a small glass. "Here."

Howard handed the glass to her. "It's an acquired taste, but they left it with a note stating it was an old Indian combination of herbs. Designed to make you feel ten years younger."

It was all she could do to keep from spitting it out. "That's the most vile thing I've ever tasted, and I've had my daughter's lasagna!"

He shrugged. "I've grown fond of it."

Changing the subject, she continued, "Sophia is always telling me my place looks like old lady 1975." Gemini sniffed. "At least she didn't suggest an earlier century."

"It suits you, that's all that matters. Wait right here."

Howard disappeared. When he returned, he was carrying an old photo. "This is a prized possession. One of them. It was the reason I met with Feather today."

It concerned her to see that his hand was shaking.

"Howard, when did this start?" she asked.

"Not long ago. I have an appointment with the doctor in a few weeks. Nothing to worry about, I'm sure."

Gemini put her readers on and studied the photo. The watch that Feather told her about was rather small, with intricate details. Sensing her straining to see it, Howard handed over a large magnifying glass.

"Lovely swirls around the edges, and such detail with the leaves," she commented. She noticed two people sitting in chairs, obviously on their wedding day. The woman, a beautiful large-eyed girl of no more than twenty, was wearing a simple lace veil and a white button-up dress. The man, sitting much shorter, shared Howard's sharp jaw and long nose. They both looked dour.

"Your great-grandmother is beautiful, Howard. Was there any engraving inside? Do you have a picture of that too?" she asked, doing her best to avoid mentioning Lucinda.

Howard's scowl made her realize she'd hit a nerve. "If it's too personal, you don't have to tell me."

"No, that's fine. I'm flattered you would ask. It was a gift for my great-grandfather's retirement from Beachmont Fine Furniture. A family business that ended with my father, unfortunately."

Howard pursed his lips for a moment. "Did you know, that man never took a day off? Never. My dad had the same work ethic. He said a family business meant his name was in everyone's home. Dad took that seriously. Unfortunately, the Depression made new furniture a luxury that most people couldn't afford."

"I'm so impressed. Leo's grandfather was much the same. He had a hardware store that he handed down. In fact, Reed's Hardware and Paint was in the same location for fifty years."

She sighed, thinking about the long days mixing paint and matching odd-sized screws for customers. At the time, it was a labor of love with her husband by her side. Despite that, she didn't shed any tears when they closed it and retired. It was too much work.

"You asked about the engraving?"

"What?" She was embarrassed to have been caught deep in thought. "Yes, if it's not too painful, can you tell me what it said?"

"Yes, it said, 'thank you for a lifetime of service.' All of the other businesses in town chipped in to buy it."

"Oh."

"You sound disappointed. Were you hoping for something more scandalous?" Howard seemed a little hurt that Gemini wasn't more impressed.

"My mind is elsewhere, if I'm being honest." She paused for a moment, wondering if she should burden him with this when he had his own mystery to solve.

"Don't worry about me, Gemini. We'll discuss my worries over dinner. Tell me what has you so distracted."

She smiled appreciatively. Next to Leo, Howard was the only person her age she could confide in. "Well, since you asked, I've got to tell you about this case that fell in my lap." She proceeded to tell him all about Lyle's disappearance. He listened, nodding at the appropriate moments.

"Howard, believe me when I tell you, it was the most bizarre conversation I'd ever had, and I've had some doozies."

She took a sip of the lavender infused iced tea Howard made each year. "Mm. You've outdone your-self again, friend."

"It's not your ordinary case, I'll grant you that." Howard sat back in his tall leather chair, bringing his glass with him. "You say she's Leo's cousin?"

"Yes. Leo hadn't seen her for... at least a decade." She looked up at the complicated designs, almost like a maze of wood on his ceiling. He once told her that when he was bored, he liked to count the lines. She was glad that hadn't been updated.

"No, that's not right. One of their uncles passed away three years before we moved to Charming." She diverted her gaze to Howard. "How could I forget about dear old Uncle Buzz's funeral? He wanted his lifestyle guru Rahani flown in from India. The man showed up to the funeral sans shoes and a good bath." She chuckled to herself at the memory and the stench. "I do wonder why Lucinda didn't mention that."

Howard shrugged before bringing his glass to his lips. "Many reasons. Too painful, too complicated, too—"

"Too suspicious," she added. Gemini snapped her fingers. "Now I'm remembering more about the day of Uncle Buzz's funeral. We brought Sophia with us, and our daughter insisted we return in time for her evening cycling class. Leo was actually relieved she'd given us an excuse to leave early. When we got in our car, we discovered another vehicle parked inches from ours. Someone was in the driver's seat but they weren't moving, keeping us trapped. Sophia, being a woman of little patience, reached through the seats and honked.

A man and a woman got out of the car. It was Lucinda and her neighbor, George Mint."

Howard squinted. "And this didn't seem odd to you?"

"We were always doing our best to keep Sophia in check. I think Leo said they were planning a surprise party for Lyle, or something like that. I never gave it another thought, until right now."

Howard leaned forward and scooted a plate of perfectly cylindrical pastries across the table, toward his friend. "Strawberry cannoli. Seems like sacrilege to confuse a perfectly good cannoli with a fruit, but Phyllis over on the next block brings them to me every year."

Gemini took a cannoli and placed it on a napkin in front of her. She knew Phyllis from the community yard sale. It was obvious she thought her not-so-discreet shoulder touches and overly-excited laughter would gain her Howard's favor.

"She's hoping her pastries will work like a magnet and suck you into her web," Gemini teased. "As long as I've lived here, it's not been a secret that she's on the hunt for her next husband. Number eight by my count."

Howard's jaw dropped. He glanced down at the plate then back up to Gemini. "It never even occurred to me. Now I'm regretting that I allowed her to have the Tulip Society meeting here. What should I do? Throw them away?"

"No, just enjoy them. I shouldn't have said anything."

"I'm glad you did. To think I've invited that woman in all the times I have and she had ulterior motives. No wonder she was so interested in my dishes! She wanted to make sure they matched her décor."

"Now, Howard, you can't jump to conclusions," Gemini chided. She took a bite of the cannoli, which was actually quite tasty.

"Phyllis did tell me she wanted to see if our patterns matched," he insisted. "She just didn't mention the rest of that."

Realizing that she'd made him feel flustered, she quickly changed the subject. "The reception after the funeral was held at the family cabin. It was Uncle Buzz's favorite place to think. Quite a lovely place, with high, finished wood ceilings and seven bedrooms."

Gemini stood and walked over to Howard's large picture window, where the rain was coming down so hard she could barely see the street. The lawn service he'd hired was cutting his grass, despite the drippy weather. When one of the hardworking men noticed her gaze, he waved heartily. She returned the favor before turning back to Howard.

"These memories are suddenly tumbling out! The day of the funeral held more than one surprise."

"Don't keep me in suspense, Gemini," Howard said as he bit down on another cannoli.

"You know how picky my Sophia can be when it comes to food," she continued.

"And clothing, and anything else," Howard grumbled. "I don't know how you put up with it."

"That day, she surveyed the table of casseroles and announced she would be eating none of it. Pedro, the son of Lucinda's brother Larry, happened to be in the room. Pedro said he worked for a health food store that sold a line of vegan snacks. He'd brought some along. I'm skeptical that he actually worked there. Rumor has it, Pedro has never had a real job. At the last funeral, I overheard people speculating that he is selling drugs or something. I've tried to keep an open mind."

"What does this have to do with Lucinda?"

"I'm getting to that. We'd been watching the time carefully so Sophia would be back in time to attend her cycle class, as I already mentioned. Well, at the agreed upon time, we couldn't find her anywhere."

"And? Was she in the attic, eating ice cubes?"

"Howard, don't tease. You know she's very self-conscious about her body. If only I could adhere to her strict rules. Anyway, after we'd scoured the house, we were shocked to find her under the deck, deep in conversation. She and her cousin Pedro looked like the cat that swallowed the canary."

Gemini swallowed hard, disturbed by the memory. Her daughter, newly engaged and putting every effort into pleasing her fiancé's wealthy parents, seated on the cement slab. She refused to sit on the grass, let alone cement.

Howard furrowed his brows. "That doesn't sound like your daughter at all, Gemini."

"That was our feeling as well. While we were driving home, Leo joked that she and Pedro must have been discussing matters of national security. Our daughter stared in the mirror, waiting to catch his eye. When she did, she said, rather cryptically, 'The Reed family has secrets. Dark ones. Right, Daddy?'"

CHAPTER FIVE
FEATHER

The shock of waking up with an airbag in her face took some time to absorb. Feather couldn't tell if she was injured; the enormity of what had happened was still seeping in. Wedging her door open just far enough to get out, she stood and waited until her wobbly legs were steady. At least that part of her was working fine. *Unless she was dead. Was she?* Making her way across the tall grass, she made it back to the road. It was eerily quiet, with the exception of her heart beating so loud she thought it might burst out of her chest.

What had transpired was coming back to her. The phone call. "Meet me at Troubled Tom's Gas in thirty minutes. I've got important information."

Her distraction. The shadowy figure crossing the highway.

She was frightened by the prospect of what she might find. When she reached the spot where she'd veered off the road, she clenched her teeth. Whatever wrong she'd done, she would make right.

Except there was no evidence she'd hit anything. Other than two black skid marks, the road showed no sign of injury or death. Though she was relieved that no one was hurt, Feather was frustrated thinking that no one would believe her, least of all the insurance company.

She bent down and touched the asphalt, at once thankful it was a cool day and upset she hadn't worried before touching it.

Immediately the hairs on her arms rose. Instead of one person, there were many, screaming her name. They were in pain or angry or both.

"Stop! Stop now!" She stood and covered her ears. It didn't matter, the sounds were in her head and weren't about to stop.

"Meet me at Troubled Tom's Gas in thirty minutes. You fell for it!"

It was the same voice she'd heard on the phone, that one and many more. They were mocking her. She'd never heard of spirits who could make phone calls, but maybe this one was especially gifted.

One thing she knew for sure—she wasn't going to the gas station until she had a full understanding of what had just taken place.

Shakily, Feather returned to her car and searched for her purse. After several minutes, she gave up and tears ran down her face. "Why? What have I done to deserve this?" she cried.

She felt a tapping on her shoulder. Knowing she was in the middle of nowhere, she spun around quickly, ready to defend herself. Instead of seeing a person, Feather discovered a flurry of angry bees.

The last thing she needed today was a bee sting. Cursing her bad luck once again, the tears flowed. At that moment, the bees all lined up in formation, their yellow bodies making an arrow.

She realized they were pointing to her purse, lying unscathed under the tree. "I know that's you, Daisy! Thank you!"

Luckily, her phone was still inside. Dialing quickly, she started to call Jayden but changed her mind.

"Tug? Please try not to panic. I'm just fine, but my car isn't."

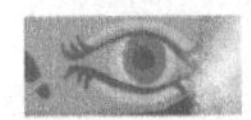

It had been a week since someone jumped in front of her car. At least she thought it was a someone. Just as in her dream, something or someone burst out in front of her. She swerved and her car hit a tree. Every night she sat up in a cold sweat, unable to sleep any more.

Other than some nasty bruises, her body was fine. Her car, on the other hand, wasn't as fortunate.

Tug encouraged her to take her car to a "guy he knew" to get it fixed instead of taking it into their regular auto body place, where questions would be asked.

"I'm not going to act like a criminal," she replied. "I did nothing wrong."

Tug squeezed her rock-hard shoulders. "You didn't. But people who walk around without your gifts won't understand. You have to function in their world, unfortunately." He continued massaging her shoulders until she could feel them loosening slightly. She knew he was right, but after she'd waited so long to be herself, it felt like a betrayal to step back in the shadows.

Finally, she relented and allowed Tug to have her car towed to "the guy he knew." Chip regularly spoke to his dead grandfather, so he understood how the accident happened. He agreed to be discreet and tell anyone who asked she swerved to avoid a deer.

Because Chip had a small operation, it would take at least a month for the repairs. The next day, they went out and found a rental car. Her insurance wouldn't let her choose which type of vehicle she got, so when she was handed the keys to a large four-wheel drive, she was hesitant to drive it. "I don't know how to drive something the size of our apartment," she said.

After some gentle coaxing by Tug, she agreed to follow him home. It turned out to be the right kind of car to overcome her feelings of insecurity. She felt powerful in the high seat, like she could do anything.

There wasn't much cause for her to drive, however, since her friends insisted that she stay home from work. No matter how much she protested, Gemini and Tug wouldn't allow her to come into the warehouse. They didn't understand how it was home to her and they were her family.

"You and these tight shoulders need some love," Tug said after massaging her tight muscles for the hundredth time. "You did just hire a new massage therapist."

"Nylah? I don't know."

The newest employee of Feather Works Salon was a frail-looking young woman who came to the salon on one of the two days a week Feather still worked there. She looked like a cat who'd been set out in the rain, with hair that hung in wet waves around her tiny face and a body that trembled constantly.

She showed Feather her impressive credentials and asked if she could set up a massage room in the back of the shop. It just so happened that Chair Number Five was vacant, due to Tanya's surprise pregnancy. She and the new owner of the salon, Stevie—formerly The New Girl, decided to section off the back of the salon for a massage table.

Everyone who'd received a massage from Nylah raved about her magic hands.

"I guess I could see if she has any openings," Feather said hesitantly. The more she thought about it, the more she liked the idea.

"Great! I took the liberty of booking you an appointment. Nylah wants you there by ten."

Feather glanced at her watch. "I've got forty

minutes!" she protested. "When were you going to spring this on me?"

Tug shrugged sheepishly. "I wanted to make sure you got out of bed first."

It was true. Since she wasn't allowed back at work, she'd had trouble rousing herself from bed. Her mind was on constant replay: the call, the voice, hitting the tree. Sleep was her only respite.

"I've also taken the liberty of laying your clothes out in the bathroom and making your favorite oatmeal."

Feather grabbed him impulsively, pulling him in tight. "You're too good for me, Tug Muehler."

"We're evenly matched there, Jones," he replied, tussling her spiky hair.

She felt relief when she walked through the doors of the salon. No one there had any idea of the trauma she'd been through, and that was just the way she wanted to keep it.

Nylah, still appearing as though she'd been placed under a faucet, greeted her with a smile. "Hi Feather! I'm ready for you!"

Though she'd asked other girls in the salon to do her hair, Feather had never been in such a vulnerable position with an employee. "Do you mind if I keep my—"

"Clothes on? My clients come in all state of undress." Nylah giggled. "You don't have to worry about me. I don't massage and tell."

Feather was relieved when Nylah shut the door so

she could undress. Feeling a little silly about her earlier modesty, she removed her top and laid on the bed.

"Ready?" Nylah asked.

"Ready!"

"Do you care if I light a candle?"

"Sure."

"The other girls have been telling me about your amazing abilities. My side job is reading palms. I did one for a group of business men not long ago and they tipped me three hundred dollars!"

"Mm." As interesting as this topic may have been on another day, Feather really just wanted to close her eyes and forget about the world.

"Since it's just us here, I'll admit that I went a little beyond my capabilities. They wanted a séance and I thought, what the heck?"

As Nylah rubbed her back, Feather drifted off. Her stress seemed to melt away with the candle wax. Nylah truly did possess magic hands. Though she felt like she should remain professional and carry on small talk, her body released and she fell asleep.

Feather was back in the car, driving down the road and listening to her favorite song. She was singing so loud her eardrums were shaking. In an instant, someone jumped in front of her. She got out of her car with a sick feeling in her stomach, knowing this had happened before. When she reached the front of her vehicle, Tug was lying in front of her. Though he'd been gravely injured, he reached for her.

"Feather! Why did you do this to me? All I've done is love you!"

"I'm so sorry!" So sorry!" she cried as she bent down to help. The moment her hands touched Tug, he grabbed her and said, "Why aren't you paying attention?" She withdrew her hands and saw that they were in flames. Feather wanted to scream too, but the scent of caramel assaulted her like a poisonous gas and she couldn't breathe.

"Feather? Are you okay?"

She opened her eyes and looked up groggily. "Where am I?"

Nylah giggled. "You're getting a massage, silly! I'm good, but I've never knocked the memory out of someone before."

Feather wrinkled her nose as she tried to re-acclimate. "What's that smell?"

"It's my favorite scent—caramel corn calmer. You said it was okay if I burned a candle. You can roll over now. I'll hold up the sheet and—"

Feather threw the covers off her body and jumped up without any concern for modesty.

She pulled her shirt over her head and picked up her combat boots before opening the door. "I have to go."

"Wait!" Nylah called. "We haven't done any lower body work!"

"Give the rest of my time to another customer," Feather called over her shoulder. "I can't be here."

When she reached her car, she realized she was

sweating. Her body shivered at the same time, the way it did when she had a high fever. Shakily, she somehow managed to place her key in the ignition and start the car.

By the time she arrived in the industrial area, where their warehouse was located, her sweat and trembling had subsided. This was home and she didn't care if she wasn't wanted, it was what she needed.

Feather could hear Tug, Olive and Gemini engaged in a lively conversation before she even opened the door.

"What did I miss?"

They all paused, and the excitement in the air dissipated like a popped balloon.

"Are you sure you should be here, hon?" Gemini asked with concern in her voice. "You've been through a terrible experience."

"Positive. I've got to tell you all something."

They stared at her. Not with annoyance but with love. "I promised Jayden I wouldn't, but maybe that's part of the reason for these nightmares."

Gemini pulled out a chair and patted it. "Sit. We're all ears."

Feather proceeded to tell her about Jayden's dire

words and how she needed to figure out why she was being placed in the middle of this.

"You're the bridge? Like an actual bridge?" Olive asked, scratching her head. "Sounds to me like you have an allergy to metal and bolts."

"It's not that kind of bridge, Olive," she explained, now wondering if this was the right thing to do.

Tug rubbed her shoulders, which were considerably looser than they were before this morning. "Why haven't you contacted Millicent?"

She turned around to look at him. "You know how she drives me nuts. I guess I was hoping I wouldn't have to."

"How can we help you?" Gemini asked.

"I wish I knew. Just telling you made me feel better." Feather wiped the tears that had formed in the corners of her eyes. "Now, what was it you were buzzing about before I walked in?"

Gemini glanced at Tug, who nodded his approval.

"Olive was just telling us about an end-of-summer market in Charming City Park. They have spaces for fifty vendors," Gemini began.

Feather could tell when Gemini was excited; her voice rose an octave. "We were talking about sharing a tent. You and I would hand out information on Kindred Spirits and—"

"Me and Tug would hand out Tug Bars along with a discount coupon. That way, we can attract everybody." Olive smiled with satisfaction. "I thought that up on my way in this morning. Elmer, my next door neighbor, is selling his candied almonds and gave me the flyer."

"Is this the man who's sweet on you, Olive?" Gemini asked.

"Sure hope so. He hasn't asked me on a date yet, but who can resist this dandy body?" Olive stood and twirled, with one "Whoop!" and a cat call whistle.

"Do you really think this is a good idea, Gem? People are already wary of us. If we are in public, someone may decide to make an example of the..." Feather paused to make air quotes, "kooky investigators."

Gemini patted her friend's hand. "Not to worry. We'll show them all we're the friendliest ghost hunters on the entire Oregon coast."

"Let's do it, Feath!" Tug urged. "We've been talking about what we could do to promote our businesses, and if this one goes well, we could do all of the Charming markets next summer!"

She still wasn't sure this was the best idea, but glancing from one hopeful face to the next, it was hard to say no. "Okay. You've worn me down."

"It's settled then!" Gemini clapped her hands together. "I'll order a nice banner and a tent, maybe blue, and of course I'll make cookies!"

The hairs on Feather's arms rose. *What?*

This is a mistake. Bad luck will follow you, Feather Jones.

She nodded vigorously. "I can't wait!" she replied.

Chapter Six
Gemini

"I wouldn't ask unless I absolutely needed you," Gemini snapped at her daughter.

She knew how Sophia hated doing family activities, at least Reed family activities. She didn't seem to have the same issues when it came time to get togethers with Brandon's side.

4785 Blueberry Circle was a flurry of activity, with cars parked in every spare space as well as all the way down the block. People were coming and going, laughing and talking to each other.

"You remember everything we discussed?" Gemini asked as she applied pink lipstick, carefully wiping the corners of her mouth.

"Mother, I'm offended. You act as though I've never had ulterior motives in my life." Sophia adjusted her black lace dress on her bony shoulders. "If you knew half of the stories I told you growing up, just so I could go out and—"

"Enough!" Gemini slapped the visor shut and glared at her daughter. "This isn't the day for those kinds of stories. This is an investigation, Sophia. I asked you to accompany me for a specific reason. We have to find out exactly what these relatives know about Lyle. And you and Pedro have a close relationship." She paused, hoping her daughter would confess their secret from long ago.

Sophia pressed her lips together tightly, as if the words might escape.

"Oh, come on. Out with it! You don't need to be coy. When we went to Uncle Buzz's funeral, you and Pedro were huddled underneath the deck. What were you talking about?"

Sophia was stoic. It wasn't Sophia's normal behavior. She liked to dispense information in a trickle, just enough to make Gemini crazy. With this particular topic, there wasn't even a droplet.

"I'll have to ask Pedro if it's all right to share. I don't want to tell you anything until I know for sure." She hesitated before opening the door. "You know Pedro is a gossip, right? I've never been able to verify his stories."

Gemini opened her mouth to protest. Sophia held some kind of power over her father for years. Leo never revealed what the secret might be, no matter how much Gemini pleaded with him. They didn't keep things from each other, but after some time had passed, she forgot all about it. Now that Sophia was suggesting it was all a ruse, she didn't know whether to be upset with her daughter or angry at her husband for holding on to a mere rumor.

Lucinda appeared on the porch, waving vigorously. She was dressed as though she'd walked out of an Audrey Hepburn movie, with upswept hair and an off-the-shoulder pale blue dress.

"Cousin Lucinda doesn't act like she has a dead husband," Sophia remarked through gritted teeth, waving back.

"We all deal with loss differently, daughter," Gemini said, still seething over Sophia's revelation, though she had to agree. Lucinda was dressed for a trip to the society ball, not her husband's memorial.

When they reached the porch, she and Lucinda embraced before Lucinda took Sophia's arms and held them away from her body.

"Look at our little Sophia. When was the last time we saw you? You must've been in high school because I remember the braces."

Sophia gave her a stern look. "I had braces right after Taurus was born. I was far beyond those childish years."

"Your cousins are scattered everywhere, Sophia. Why don't you go in and find some food and join a conversation?" Lucinda gestured toward the large living room where at least twenty people were milling around.

When Sophia disappeared, Lucinda took Gemini's arm. "I want to show you something," she whispered.

They walked to the far side of the large home,

through a lovely tunnel with floor-to-ceiling windows and giant plants. The entire jaunt took longer than Gemini's morning walks. Their home was at least the size of the Charming Entertainment Center, where she and Howard attended musicals.

Lucinda stopped in front of a set of double doors. "This was—is—I don't know how to say it. The room is an office, the one Lyle used. I want you to feel free to open every drawer, look in every cabinet, do what you need to do. All I ask is that when you find something shocking, and you will, you don't share it with anyone outside of your investigation. Oh, and please don't take anything. My shaman says whatever has befallen Lyle may be attached to his possessions."

Gemini furrowed her brow. It opened up a whole host of new questions she would have to address with Lucinda later.

Lucinda handed Gemini the key and left her.

It occurred to Gemini that she may have trouble finding her way back to the other part of the house. She could always call Sophia and ask for directions, a sure way to irritate her daughter.

She giggled at the thought as she stuck the key in the lock and turned it. Gemini gasped when she entered.

What Lucinda described as an office was the size of the apartment she lived in right after college. Gemini's parents thought a two-bedroom apartment far too extravagant for one young woman, but she liked having extra space.

The two-story "office" was lined with bookshelves. She breathed in the scent of old books, remembering the smell of the library when she took Sophia for story hour. Closing her eyes, she took another deep breath. *Caramel. How odd.*

She wandered through until she reached a bathroom, complete with a sauna and large shower. There were French doors leading to a bricked patio, where four chairs and a pecan-colored picnic table sat.

Pulling out her Hearex 220 phone, the one Tug convinced her to buy on the company card, she began snapping photos. She wasn't sure what she needed, but later she could look them over. Gemini found with each investigation she honed her senses and even bought herself a large magnifying glass to study photos.

She walked around, snapping indiscriminately until she reached a massive desk. Pausing to make sure there were no unexpected visitors, she opened the top drawer. What would have seemed like an invasion of privacy earlier in her life became a necessity in her current world. Inside the drawer were Bittersby Hard Chocolate Candies, just like the ones in the envelope Lucinda showed her. Underneath that box was another newspaper article, yellowed by time. She snapped another photo.

Carefully, she removed the newspaper from the drawer and placed it on the desk, opening it up to a photograph. The first thing she noticed was the brittle yellowed pages. It wasn't the type of paper used in the modern world, nothing from this century at least.

Though only four pages, the print was tiny enough a person could spend much of their morning reading each article. On the front page was a story about a little boy who had been kidnapped. The grainy photo showed a dark-haired toddler staring somberly into the camera.

On the next page was a large photo with the caption "Local Inventor Makes it Big" underneath.

She squinted as she brought the picture up to her face. It was Lyle, no doubt about it. He had the same sneer on his face she remembered from the last funeral. His hair was even cut in the same modern style with a part on the left.

That was where his present-day look ended. He was wearing a dark suit with a vest underneath and a black top hat. Perched on his cheek was a small round glass, the precursor to the modern-day reading glasses. It was on a chain attached to his breast pocket.

Gemini perused the article. "Mr. Lyle Lime has invented a device to slice bread. He calls it the Lime Loaf and it makes a woman's chores a breeze. In addition, he made a clever substance and placed it on the back of small squares of paper. These can be 'stuck' on any hard surface. Mr. Lime assures us there is no trickery involved."

Gemini put her hand up to her mouth and continued reading.

"Because of his ingenuity, our lives have been made

better. Today the mayor gave him a key to the city and next week he'll be given the prestigious Medal of Innovation by the governor."

"Cheese and crackers! How is this possible?"

She photographed everything and then carefully refolded the article before placing it back in the drawer.

Making her way around the room, she found another curious item. On the bookshelf sat a coin purse.

Gemini picked it up to examine and dropped it on the floor. Numerous pieces of jewelry spilled out, as well as a tiny glass ornament that shattered. Removing the aqua scarf she'd added to her ensemble at the last minute, she bent down to sweep up the shards of glass.

Her phone buzzed and, when she looked at the screen, she saw Sophia was calling.

"Hello?"

"Mother, where have you disappeared to?" Sophia hissed. "I'm stuck with these mouth breathers and I've developed a migraine because of their foul smells."

"I'm sure you haven't eaten or drunk a thing. Why don't you have a nice glass of ice water? I'll rejoin you soon."

Sophia huffed, not used to her mother telling her no.

"I'll be in the kitchen. Hopefully none of them will pester me. Don't keep me waiting!"

She hung up abruptly.

CHAPTER SEVEN
GEMINI

Hesitantly, she stuck the coin purse and its contents in her large bag. It wasn't like her to steal, even if it was for an investigation. Once she had Feather check for any otherworldly attachments, she'd bring it back. "No harm, no foul," she said, hoping whatever the shaman thought was going on wasn't attached to the coin purse.

Before pulling the doors shut, Gemini took one last look around. There was something very odd about this room. Besides being spacious and dark, the room had a sharp breeze, causing a whistle. The doors to the patio were closed, so it wouldn't be coming from there.

Scouring the space, she was ready to admit defeat when her eyes fell upon a large square on the floor. Gemini bent down and put her hand close to the top, where she felt the air.

She pushed and then tried to pry the door up with

her fingers, but nothing would move it. Once again her phone buzzed, and once again it was Sophia calling.

"Always poor timing, daughter," she lamented. "I'm coming. Go lock yourself in the bathroom if you need privacy."

Knowing her daughter wouldn't wait much longer, Gemini squinted, trying to see what might be there. She moved her body slightly, placing her weight on one corner. The trapdoor lifted on the other side. A light turned on when she opened it and three bags were visible. "Property of HOO," she read.

A buzzing noise alerted her to the fact that she'd been caught. Quickly she closed the hatch, standing and wiping dust from her pants.

With only two wrong turns, she found her way back to the group of mourners. Lucinda was enjoying a conversation with a red-faced man. He was her age, at least, with curly grey hair and a curvy mustache. They were laughing and touching each other's arms with too much intimacy. She recognized him now.

"Gemini! Did you find what you were looking for?"

She tilted her head to the side, puzzled that Lucinda didn't remember she was the one who suggested Gemini investigate.

"For now. Thank you for showing me Lyle's office. I'd like to come back and do a little more investigating."

Lucinda's face tightened.

The man extended his hand to her. "I'm George Mint. Also known as the next-door neighbor."

"Yes, I remember you from the car." It just slipped out. "I mean, I remember seeing you many years ago. You must be a long time neighbor!"

She let out a sigh of relief, glad she'd avoided potential embarrassment.

"I've lived next door to the Limes for over two decades." He beamed, nodding to Lucinda. "These folks are like family to me. I promised Lyle I would take care of his special gal if anything ever happened to him."

I'll bet.

"Gemini, before you leave, please stop at the donation table and leave what you can. It's Lyle's favorite charity."

"Of course."

"Would you excuse me for a moment?" George asked. "Lovely meeting you... again?"

When he was out of earshot, Lucinda glared at Gemini. "Why did you mention you were investigating in front of George? I told you to keep this quiet!"

Gemini's cheeks burned bright red. "The way the two of you were carrying on, I didn't think you had any secrets."

It was at that moment that Lucinda did something entirely unexpected. Instead of being angry, she grinned and opened her arms, gesturing for Gemini to hug.

When Gemini didn't reciprocate, Lucinda lurched

forward and pulled her in close. As Gemini struggled to get away, Lucinda whispered in her ear, "No one needs to know about George. I know you have money. Lots of it. Make a big donation today and I won't tell the rest of the family. You know how they'd want their share."

She released Gemini, still smiling. "Dear, dear cousin. I'm so glad you came," Lucinda said loud enough for the entire room to hear. Everything stopped and the attendees stared at the two women.

"I... um, I'd be happy to make a donation. Can you tell me the name of Lyle's favorite charity?"

"Yes, of course, dear. It's his little time travel group. I'll get the name for you." Lucinda chuckled uncomfortably. "The many mysteries of Lyle Lime."

CHAPTER EIGHT

GEMINI

For once, she and Sophia were on the same page. They needed to leave. Now.

Lucinda took Gemini's elbow and guided her into a hallway where the din of the living room was lessened. "Were you able to find anything of importance in Lyle's office?"

Gemini studied her face. She could see similarities between Lucinda and Sophia. The same brow line, the same tight lips and slight build.

"A few things. I'll have to go back to my office and talk to my partner about them." There was no way she would share her findings with Lucinda. At least not right now.

"I've got a confession to make," Lucinda started with more humility than she'd shown the entire day. "George Mint and I are starting a new business in Charming. I'm sorry I haven't contacted you when I'm in Charming—it was rude of me to avoid you. To be truthful, I didn't want to see Leo as..."

"As an invalid? You might be interested to learn that my friends have all been to see him, some coming every week. They understand his temporary limitations and meet him where he is. That's all it takes, Lucinda." Gemini pivoted, more than ready to track down Sophia.

"Gemini, wait!" Lucinda called after her. "You need to know one more thing!"

She paused, not sure if it was worth turning around. "What?" Feeling very little patience, she may have yelled louder than required for the room. She kept her feet planted across the room from Lucinda.

Lucinda's eyes darted back and forth to the friends and relatives whose eyes were wide with interest in the unfolding drama. She rushed to Gemini's side and whispered in her ear. "You didn't take anything from Lyle's office, did you? We don't want the shaman's words to come true."

Gemini huffed and pulled away from her. It was time this nonsense ended. Now. "I'm going to find my daughter."

When Gemini reached Sophia, her daughter's posture made it obvious a storm was brewing.

"Mother! How nice of you to join us!" Sophia said with a fake enthusiasm that always made Gemini cringe. Sophia usually reserved it for those she felt were of her stature but held no interest for her. "You remember cousin Pedro?"

A young man who shared Sophia's slight build and small chin smiled at Gemini. "Hello, Auntie! I haven't seen you since—"

One of the numerous things that irritated Gemini about family events was how every woman over forty was considered an "auntie." It was a term of familiarity that didn't sit well with her, given these people were all strangers. Pedro had aged, moreso than Sophia. He already had the suggestion of grey hair. His eyes were rimmed red.

"Probably your Uncle Buzz's funeral." Gemini turned her body away from him, having little interest in small talk. "Sophia, I'm ready to go. Gather your things, please."

Sophia's face displayed a mixture of surprise and relief. "I'll find our coats."

When Sophia was out of earshot, Pedro whispered, "I know why you're here. It's this crazy time travel idea. Auntie Lucinda is out of her gourd."

"Why do you say that, Pedro?"

He tugged on Gemini's sleeve until she realized he wanted her to follow him. Pedro led her to a secluded hallway before releasing her.

"You never can tell who is on your side in this family," he remarked.

"I can't argue with that. But I'm interested in your knowledge of time travel. Lucinda thinks—" Gemini caught her tongue. She'd promised Lucinda she wouldn't share with anyone in the family. "She's very concerned about Lyle's whereabouts."

Pedro smiled. "Yeah, I know all about the," he made air quotes with his fingers, "affair."

"You don't believe it? Why not?"

"Oh, I didn't say that. Uncle Lyle has been keeping secrets from his wife since I was a kid. He's always been like a father to me. That's why today has been so hard."

Thus the red eyes.

"One time, he was out behind the family cabin talking to some of his buddies. I think it might have been after Great-Uncle Tip died. You guys weren't there."

Gemini nodded. How in the world would he remember who was and wasn't in attendance? With dozens of family members at every event, she could hardly remember who she spoke with, let alone who came.

"What happened?"

"It was the one and only time he was ever angry with me." Pedro sucked in his bottom lip. "He was whispering to the other men about a business idea. That's all I heard. I was hiding from them in the trees, but George Mint made sure my presence was known. 'You'd better get the boy, Lyle. He's likely to tell someone.' Well, Uncle Lyle had to make a showing, so he picked me up by the collar and carried me inside. He scared me to death. He threatened to hurt me if I told anyone."

"That is peculiar, especially since you were so close. Is there anything else? You mentioned to Sophia that the Reed family has many secrets."

Some children playing hide-and-seek ran down the hallway. "Come play with us, Pedro!" one of the girls begged.

At that moment, Sophia appeared with their coats. "There you are! At your age, you shouldn't wander off, Mother. I'm likely to think you've developed memory problems."

The young girl was tugging insistently on Pedro's arm. Neither of them had an excuse for more conversation.

"Nice to see you again, Auntie Gemini," Pedro said before he was pulled off to play with the children.

"You look mad. He must've told you," Sophia said, helping Gemini fit her arm through her coat sleeve.

"Let's discuss this in the car," Gemini replied, moving with purpose toward the door.

"Don't we need to tell Cousin Lucinda goodbye?"

Gemini shook her head. When the two were safely seated in the car, out of earshot of Pedro and Lucinda, Sophia put the keys in the ignition and turned her seat heater on high. She leaned back and crossed her arms. "I feel like there's something you need to tell me, Mother."

There was no reason to be ashamed, but Gemini felt like telling her daughter made her somehow culpable in Lucinda's little game.

"Lucinda wanted me to help her with something completely bonkers. I don't know why I fell for her story." Gemini shook her head. It would take some time to come to terms with why she was so gullible.

She remembered the coin purse in her bag and felt even more shame for stealing it.

"That's not even the worst of it," she continued. "She neglected to tell me that she's been in Charming opening a new business. Never once did she come and see your father."

Saying it out loud made her feel better. She wasn't in the habit of tattling, but this was a grievous misdeed.

"That's so rude," Sophia agreed. "Pedro says she's been acting strangely for some time now. He thinks Lucinda killed Lyle and hid his body in a storage shed."

"Whaat?" Her daughter's nonchalance about things that should have been worrisome always caught her off guard. "Why does Pedro think that? Doesn't he get along with Lucinda?"

"His family has been fighting with Lucinda and Lyle over some property for two years now. And did you notice none of Lucinda and Lyle's children were there? Don't you think that's odd, given this service was about honoring their father?"

"Tell me more about Pedro. Why is he suspicious of Lucinda?" Gemini had once overheard a conversation about the Lime children. They all hated their parents.

Sophia took a deep breath and squeezed the steering wheel tightly with both hands. She started the engine and drove away from the Lime residence, her tires squealing as she swerved on to Blueberry Court. "I'm paranoid, I know. But with what Pedro told me, I can't be too careful."

"You're being very dramatic, dear," Gemini remarked, instantly mad at herself when the words fell out of her mouth.

"Mother, may I remind you that I'm only here because you forced me to come? And you gave me strict instructions to obtain information from my cousin? That's just what I did, and now you think I'm being dramatic? I never!"

Gemini knew from experience that it was better to give things a minute before replying. After they were out of Lucinda's neighborhood and safely removed from fancy cars, potential targets for her overly-emotional daughter, she said, "You're right. I apologize. Please continue. Lucinda has been acting strange?"

Sophia clicked the blinker and they merged onto Highway 101. "Pedro says she and Lyle couldn't come to an agreement about the family cabin. Lucinda wanted to sell it, but Lylea felt it was important for it to stay in their branch of the family. Then Lyle joined some weird organization—"

"It's probably the time travel group. Lucinda told me about that. And why on earth would Lucinda want to sell the family cabin?"

"Because they were having financial difficulties. Lucinda is trying to start a new business and she goes on all of these extravagant trips. That's why Pedro thinks she killed him and stuffed him in the shed."

Sophia stuck her tongue in her cheek, as she always did when she thought she was the only one in the room with a secret. "Did Lucinda happen to mention that one of Lyle's friends is under investigation for murder?"

Gemini turned in her seat to face Sophia. "No!"

"They think he killed his wife. She's been missing for six months. Her husband insisted she time traveled back to the turn of the nineteenth century and he had newspaper articles to prove it."

"I've been had," Gemini said softly. "I found one in Lyle's office that showed him receiving some award. It never occurred to me that he wasn't the only one performing this sham."

"Maybe or maybe not. This woman hasn't been found. There's no trace of her. Car keys, wallet, everything important to this woman is still in her home. Just like Lyle."

"What else did Pedro say?"

"That Lyle had all sorts of gadgets he said came from time travel. He showed Pedro an old gun and some boots. Lucinda knew all about it."

Gemini frowned. "How odd. So, what Pedro believes is that Lucinda decided this old-timey woman was having an affair with Lyle. And further, he thinks Lucinda... killed him for the affair? She's made quite an elaborate ruse, if that's true."

She started thinking about the reception book at Charming Acres. *What if Lucinda signed in to give herself an alibi?* Gemini stared out the window at the angry sea. A storm was visible just over the horizon.

"Maybe Feather and I should trail Lucinda and see where she goes."

"Mother!" Sophia gasped. "That's too dangerous!"

"It's a few hours of driving time, Sophia, not armed combat," Gemini replied dryly. "The other thing I need to do is talk to Feather about Lyle. If he's truly in another time, she may be able to contact the other people in the photo. They could tell her if he's been there."

Sophia's phone played "You are so beautiful..." and she pushed the button to answer.

"Mrs. Floris? Your son wanted to say hello."

"Thank you, Martine. Put him on, please."

"Mama?"

"It's Grammie, sweet boy!" Gemini said enthusiastically. Though he could be a little stinker, she loved her grandson with such gusto she sometimes wondered if it were normal. "What are you doing with your nanny today?"

Sophia shook her head. "We don't call her a nanny," she whispered. "She's his *au pair*. It sounds much more prestigious, and besides, he's learning French."

Gemini shrugged. "Tell me what you're doing today, Taurus!"

"I'm painting with my hands. I made a blue sky and—"

"Is Mommy's little boy using his special painting apron?"

"It's stoop-ed-o."

Sophia huffed. "Put your au pair back on, son."

Gemini braced for the embarrassing dressing down that was about to take place. She felt sorry for all of

Sophia's hired help; her daughter treated them all as if they were placed on this earth only to serve her.

"Yes, Mrs. Floris?"

"Martine, I expressly told you to keep him clean. We've been working on hygiene and—"

While trying to find something to occupy herself with, Gemini attempted to pull down the visor to check her lipstick. When it stuck (she later realized the culprit was an old piece of chewing gum), Gemini glanced instead at the rear view mirror.

"Sophia!" she gasped. "Step on the gas!"

CHAPTER NINE
FEATHER

Feather Jones was nothing if not good at remaining calm in sticky situations. Today was no exception.

"I didn't mention this sooner because I knew you would freak out, but I went to see my Aunt Tandy," Feather announced between bites of toast. She'd kept this secret for far too long.

"Oh?" Tug dropped his fork full of scrambled eggs, his cheeks bulging. "Why, Feath? She doesn't believe in your gift."

"She's in the majority there," Feather replied, rolling her eyes.

Tug grabbed her hand and squeezed it. "You should have told me. I would have gone with you, babe."

"I'm eternally grateful for you, Tug Muehler, do you know that?"

They both leaned in, lips meeting in the center of the table.

When their embrace ended, Tug proceeded to scrape purple jam from a jar and slather his toast with it. "Now that you've spilled it, why did you put yourself through that torment?"

"Because I've been hearing her sister, Candy. Well, not so much hearing as smelling."

He laughed and quickly covered his mouth, but not before crumbs flew across the table. "Sorry," he said through a full mouth.

Tug attempted to rise, but Feather stood and placed a hand on his shoulder. "I'll get it. You finish eating," she insisted, bringing a dish cloth from the sink to wipe the mess.

"The smell of caramel corn has been with me now for weeks. Every time I have this dream, there is a faceless person trying to tell me something. I thought it was my Great-Aunt Candy because she used to make caramel corn. I was convinced of it until my accident."

"I'm really confused. Tandy is... dead? We've never been to that funeral!"

"She's not dead. It's her twin sister, Candy. I've never mentioned her because she died when I was still a kid." Feather scooped the crumbs off the table and into her hand. "Candy was a kind woman, unlike her sister. Always making treats for the neighborhood kids."

Tug wiped his mouth with his napkin and smiled. "I'm glad there are a few Jones family members who aren't nightmarish."

"Hey!" she protested.

'"You know what I mean. Was Tandy able to give you any answers?"

Feather thought back to that day, standing on the porch as the door slammed in her face. *"Don't ever come back, Feather!"*

"She wasn't in the mood." She licked her lips, hoping Tug wouldn't ask any more. It was too painful to relive.

"This scent is everywhere—in my dreams, in my massage, even when that person jumped in front of my car. All spirits have a different way of communicating. I think this is Candy's."

"Wait, what?" Tug scrunched his face in confusion, a look that always made Feather's heart melt.

"Your great aunt jumped in front of your car, causing you to wreck it, something that could have ended your life." He paused as he contemplated his words for the first time since her accident. "I could have lost you, babe!" Tears welled up in his eyes.

"It's okay, really," she whispered. "Jayden thinks someone is trying to reach me through alternative means. They are jealous or angry, I didn't figure out which."

It felt good to tell him, even though she knew she shouldn't.

"And how do we protect you?"

"You don't. At least not now. I've got to keep my eyes peeled. Whatever or whoever is coming for me, I have to be ready."

Tug glanced up at the clock with two scissors as arms. "I'm Olive's ride today. If we don't take off soon, she'll start calling my phone in two-minute increments."

Feather's car was still being repaired, so she and Tug shared a ride in the morning and evening. So far, it was working out splendidly.

Feather shook her head. "You're not exaggerating. Last week, you were talking to a new client and she started calling me when you didn't answer!"

Usually on the way to work, they chatted about the shows they were watching, how one villain was faking his actions and a hero was too sincere in hers. Today, though, they were both silent.

As they rounded the corner to Charming Arms, Luxury Retirement Communitythey both spoke at once.

"We have to—"

"Go ahead, Feath," Tug urged as he put the car in park.

"I was just going to say, you don't have to worry. We've gotten through rough situations before. This is no different."

Quickly, she hugged her middle to avoid Tug's view of her arms. If he saw the hairs standing at attention, he would know immediately that she was getting a message from beyond and ask what it was. Feather hated lying to him and avoided it at all costs.

Before either of them could say anything further, Olive banged on the window.

"Can I sit in front?" she asked, carefully mouthing each word as though they couldn't decipher her yelling.

Feather opened the door and got out.

"I forgot about your vertigo, Olive."

Olive had a not-so-secret crush on Tug. So much so that she would become irritated when Feather took *her* seat beside him. Olive's vertigo only reared its ugly head when Feather was too chummy with Tug.

After they were situated, Olive turned her sturdy body around. "Okay, spill it you two. I'm sensing a real heaviness today. Do we need to stop at the drug store for gas pills on the way to work?"

Feather leaned up between the seats. "I think our digestive systems are fine today, Olive, but I appreciate your concern." She squeezed Tug's bicep and added, "We *both* appreciate your concern. Right, sweetie?"

She leaned back without waiting for a reply. Tug glanced in the rear view mirror and frowned. "I had a troubling conversation with a spirit is all."

"Seems like more'n that to me," Olive objected. "You have those ghostie problems every day. Doesn't stop you two from giggling about something you saw on television."

Sensing Olive wouldn't give up, Feather created a story on the spot. "I guess we can't keep secrets from you."

Tug tapped his fingers on the steering wheel.

"There is an entity who has been telling me the Date with Olive bar still needs some work. He says if you don't wait to release it, your online ratings will go down."

Feather knew Olive was pushing to have this particular bar released. She wanted to brag to her new boyfriend that she was a successful entrepreneur. When Feather and Gemini tested it, however, it tasted bitter.

"Oh boy. I've done it now. Do we need to prepare to meet our maker? I was hoping I would be wearing my black slacks and beige top. I've been told they make me look like a babe in her sixties."

"No, Olive. Nothing like that. You'll just have to delay the release. You don't have to worry."

Feather glanced at Tug once more. His mouth tilted up in an adorable half-smile.

They pulled into the parking lot of the dual-use factory building and Tug hopped out. Olive waited patiently for Tug to come around and open her door. He usually opened Feather's too, but today she was in a hurry.

"I've got to talk to Gem." She stood on her tiptoes and kissed Tug. "I'll see you at lunch. Love you!"

Tug reached in to grab her coffee from the cup holder and handed it off. "Love you too!" he called over his shoulder as he helped a dramatically crippled Olive from the car.

Feather entered their office only to find she was the first to arrive. It was unusual for Gemini to show up to work later than her partner; she was the most punctual person Feather had ever met.

She felt her phone buzz in the pocket of her jeans and immediately worried that something had happened to Gemini.

"Gem? I was so—"

"You should get in the habit of checking to see who's calling before you answer, doll."

"Jayden?" Her stomach lurched. The last time they spoke, Jayden had warned her of danger from an unknown source. She'd also warned Feather not to tell her friends.

Jayden's throaty laugh brought her comfort. "You have other catsuit-wearing friends? I'm insulted!"

"Just you, Jayden."

She breathed a sigh of relief. If Jayden knew Feather had confessed her secret to her family of choice, and it was likely she did, she wasn't telling.

"You don't have to worry, Gemini is getting out of the car as we speak. Tell her I said hello and that shade of rose really makes her skin tones pop."

It was uncanny the way Jayden could picture a situation in her mind as it was happening. Her gifts seemed to have no boundaries.

As if on cue, Gemini entered the office sporting a blush-colored short-sleeved blouse.

Feather pointed to her phone and mouthed, "Jayden."

"Hiya, Jayden!" Gemini called cheerily.

"We're going to do the Charming Fall Market." She hoped by changing the subject, Jayden would forget to yell at her. "Just to meet people and hand out our cards."

Jayden was silent.

"Jayden? Are you still there?"

"Do you think that's wise? Those who haven't used your services might be offended by your gift. It's harsh, but I don't want you to set yourself up for a big fall."

"I have thought about that." Feather glanced at Gemini, who was humming a nursery rhyme from her grandson's school while she typed on the keyboard.

"It's going to be a group effort. Tug may even bring his Tug Bars. I think all of us working as a group will prevent too many negative people. Besides, have you seen my boyfriend? A person would have to be crazy to challenge that muscled man."

"Okay. You've thought this through, so I know when I'm defeated." Jayden chuckled again. "You're probably wondering why I'm calling. I had a visit from an entity last night that you'll find interesting."

Feather wasn't used to entities coming to her through Jayden. "Oh really? Someone I know?"

"I think so. She whispered your name over and over. And then she scratched me."

"I'm so sorry!" Feather replied automatically. "I mean, it should have been me! Could you figure out who it was? Why didn't they just come and torture me?"

Jayden laughed. "Just like the living, the dead have hangups. Maybe Miss Something is concerned you'll be upset with her."

Jayden cupped her hand over her phone, stifling a muffled conversation.

"Feather? Sorry about that, doll. I've got a client emergency. Still have to pay the bills and all that. We've got a big merger happening soon."

Feather knew very well that Jayden was the president of her company and could easily delegate tasks, but it wasn't worth it to argue. "Was there anything else?"

"As I told you before, this particular entity isn't messing around. Please, please be careful, okay, doll?"

Chapter Ten
Gemini

"Gem, that's terrifying! Are you and Sophia all right?"

"We were shaking all the way back to Charming."

Feather was wide eyed as Gemini explained almost being run off the road the night before.

"Why didn't you call when you got home? I would've come over!"

Gemini's normally pink complexion became progressively more ashen. "I couldn't think straight. It was all so scary. One minute we were talking to Taurus on speaker and the next, someone was trying to ram us off the side of the cliff."

She shuddered, obviously shook from reliving the experience. "It's a good thing Sophia has annoying sounds on her car. You remember me telling you about that odd purchase, don't you?"

Feather wrinkled her nose. "No, I can't say that I do."

"Brandon convinced my daughter that she needed more protection when she was out alone, so he bought her this fancy noise package to go on her car. With the touch of a button, she can play sounds like, 'screaming woman', 'fire truck' or 'police on megaphone' over a speaker. She used 'authoritative voice.' It did the trick."

"What does that sound like?"

"A man says," Gemini cleared her throat and lowered her head. "Your license plate has been sent to local authorities, along with your photo. They will arrive momentarily. Whatever you do from now on is being recorded." She smiled. "It repeats, getting louder each time."

"So, this noise happens, and then what? Did it scare them?"

"They hightailed it out of there. Sophia and I stayed until we had our wits about us." Gemini shook her head. "All of this felt a little too coincidental. Lucinda had me search Lyle's office, maybe knowing I would take something, and then we're run off the road. Sophia's cousin thinks Lucinda killed Lyle."

Feather took another drink of her coffee and cocked her head. "Why would she do that? Seems like a lot of work with no benefit."

"That's what we need to figure out."

Gemini reached into her purse and removed the items she'd taken from Lyle's office, handing them to

Feather. "There are thirty dollars' worth of coins and two hundred dollars in bills. Oh, and this button."

Gemini handed the large, polished brass button to Feather. On it was engraved the letters "H.R."

Feather picked up the button, examining it closely. "And you're thinking this cursed you?"

"Cheese and crackers, Feather. I'm not that easily swayed. But I do wonder if there was a camera in Lyle's office and someone was just waiting for me to take something."

Gemini rose and found a teabag for her current favorite, blackberry mint tea. She poured hot water in her mug, the one inscribed with "Senior Detective, I've got age and brains on my side!" that Tug and Feather had gifted her.

When she sat back down at her desk, she was disappointed to see that Feather was typing on her computer. She appeared to have little interest in the items Gemini brought.

"The only reason I took these things was so that you could spend some time holding them and see if you get any reading."

Feather turned away from her computer. "Oh! Sorry, I have lots on my mind today, Gem. Give me a sec."

She picked up the button and squeezed it in the palm of her hand. As her eyes closed, Gemini watched with fascination.

The office was so still that the sound of the refrigerator kicking on jolted them both.

Feather closed her eyes again. Within a few seconds, she jumped up, dropping the button on her desk. "Ow!" She grabbed her hand and rubbed it.

"What happened? Who is it?"

"I felt... I felt burning. It was so hot."

She uncurled her fingers to reveal a round red mark in the center of her hand.

"I've got some salve for that, give me a minute."

Gemini rushed to a long set of cupboards, bending over and rummaging until she found a large metal box.

"If you'll recall, I felt it was worth the rather extravagant price to get a first aid box containing everything but the kitchen sink."

She opened the burn ointment and rubbed it gently on Feather's palm.

"You were right, Gem. I don't know why I ever bother arguing with you."

When they were calm again, Gemini asked, "What do you think caused the burn? Something evil?"

Feather shrugged. "I don't think so. It felt more like a child, someone testing their limits. I'll take this home with me tonight and ask Millicent."

"Oh, the sweet girl who can't stay focused? She's a dear but doesn't help much when you need hard evidence."

Feather nodded. "I've been putting it off for too long. Jayden encouraged me to talk to her about the faceless spirit a while back. I need your patience with small children."

Gemini folded her arms across her blouse. "I had

more patience when Sophia was little. Now, I'm often ashamed of my quick temper with Taurus."

"Well, you must've been born with an understanding of wild kids, because I definitely don't have the skill at any level," Feather said. "I forgot to ask about the memorial. Besides finding these mementos, did you come away with anything else?"

Gemini leaned back in her Relaxo 900 Premium Leather office chair and crossed her legs. "The memorial service was odd. We've been to many Reed memorials. They're all a big party, but this one was different. Very somber."

"Why do you think that is?"

She hadn't given herself the time or space to ask that question. She was still shook up after their experience, though she would never tell Feather. The poor child would worry too much, and she had enough on her plate already.

Gemini leaned back against the padded headrest and thought. It occurred to her that Sophia was uncharacteristically tight-lipped all the way home. It would have been more like her to express outrage and threats of lawsuits. Instead, Sophia grasped the steering wheel as though it would fly off. She barely put the car in park to drop Gemini at her home before continuing on to her home.

Gemini spun her chair around to face Feather. "There was one thing Sophia told me when we reached my place. She said her cousin Pedro overheard Lyle talking about a business scheme. When Pedro was discovered, Lyle hauled him away quick. The other thing I learned was that Lyle and Lucinda were at odds over the sale of the family cabin. Don't you find it peculiar that she and her husband were both so determined? One to sell, one to keep?"

"Very."

"I was thinking we might take a trip out to the cabin tomorrow, a field trip of sorts. I was trying to look at the schedule while you were talking to Jayden."

Gemini returned to her computer. She used her finger to follow the lines across, something she knew drove Feather crazy.

"Just use the right arrow, Gem. Then you won't have to clean your screen so often."

Finding the next day's clients, Gemini said, "You have a client tomorrow morning, but we could go afterward?"

Feather stared at the ceiling. "It's not coming to me."

"It's something about a man with a ghost in his refrigerator."

CHAPTER ELEVEN
FEATHER

"I know you're there. Come out and talk to me." She bounced a small ball between her legs as she sat crossed-legged on the spare bedroom floor.

Millicent Playmoor was a five-year-old girl who died during the Spanish influenza. Her parents, grief stricken and unable to find a mortician who would take her remains, buried her on their property. The land happened to be where, in modern day, Feather and Tug's apartment building stood.

She began appearing the day Feather stayed home from work with a migraine. Feather felt a small hand on her cheek and, when she looked up, a girl with blonde ringlets and a starched white pinafore stood in front of her.

"I'm ever so worried about you, Feather dear."

Millicent sat beside Feather that day until Tug came home. Though she wasn't a fully formed entity (her legs weren't visible), Feather sensed her comforting presence as she suffered through the powerful headache.

Feather thought Millicent was going to be a great resource. The next time they met, however, Millicent's full personality was on display. The precocious child bounced around the room and rarely answered questions. After consulting Gemini, she realized this was normal behavior for a child of that age.

"Millicent! Please come out! I've got a very important question to ask you."

When that received no response, she added, "If you'll sit on the floor with me, I'll read you a story."

A small hand appeared on the doorframe followed by a young girl with long curls and a big flat bow on top of her head. Her dress had a lace collar around the neck and her face was round and cherubic.

"Hello, dear Feather," a squeaky voice said.

Entities' voices often came across as radio reception did: crackling, muted or crystal clear. High and intermittent, Millicent's voice always sounded as if she were broadcasting from the other realm.

Feather patted the floor beside her. "Come sit down."

The girl skipped into the room and flopped on the floor. Her legs weren't visible, but the sound of her shoes tapping against the oak floor made it seem as though they were.

"Is that puffy man here? I like it when he tickles me."

Tug had graciously agreed to partake in her meetings with Millicent when the young girl mentioned she'd been observing him too. Millicent had been in awe of Tug's physique, calling him the "puffy man."

"No, he's not here today. But he sends his regards." Feather smiled so hard she felt like her cheeks might fall off. Gemini told her little kids related better to adults who smiled a lot.

"What is ever-so-important, my dear, sweet Feather?"

Feather opened a small box containing the button and showed Millicent.

"Oh, that's from my time!" she squealed.

"Tell me who wore it," Feather insisted. "I bet it's someone special."

Millicent looked up and put a finger on her chin. "Hm. I'd like to, but..." She directed her gaze toward Feather. "I'm not supposed to tell."

"What? You've never kept secrets from me before!"

Feather, feeling defeated, remembered something else Gemini told her. *You can bargain with children. You can't give them candy, but promise something else.*

"I'll read you a story from my time! Silly Milly is feeling Chilly."

Gemini recommended it so she found it at the library.

Millicent contemplated the offer for a minute. "Do you know what's black and white and red all over?"

Feather sighed with enough exasperation to wake even the sleepiest entity from the other side.

"Tell you what," *bargain with the child, Feather.*

"I'll listen to your riddle, but first you have to whisper in my ear the secret of the button. I'm a good secret keeper."

Millicent crossed her arms over her tiny chest and looked as though she might throw a fit. Feather's body tensed, unsure of the proper way to handle a screaming ghost child.

Suddenly, she felt a gust of cool air around her head.

Captain Horatio's lost his thread, he's upset but also dead. Return it to its rightful place before his story is disgrace. Naughty, naughty.

"Is this naughty person in my world?" Feather asked.

Millicent stood and skipped in a circle around Feather. *"Naughty Nat, ate his hat, lost his bucket in a vat,"* she sang.

This wasn't going to work, so she'd have to pivot and ask about another pressing subject. "I have an important mission. I suppose I could ask someone else. If you're not interested." Feather turned her head away.

Millicent immediately halted. "Why?"

"Because you're not listening. This requires someone who is serious about spy work. Do you know anyone like that?"

Millicent jumped up and down. "That's me! I received a spy glass for my last birthday, but I was never able to use it."

"Well, I'm trying to find someone who doesn't understand that you have your world and I have mine.

They think they can just go back and forth whenever they please." Feather paused, her face tight and serious. "And they'll probably keep getting away with it too. Unless..."

"Unless what?"

"Unless I have a super spy who will help me find them."

"Oh." Millicent's voice dropped. "I'm not supposed to leave my house. You know, what's your house now."

"I know that, sweetie. If you could just ask your family and maybe your neighbors? See if they know of someone going back and forth?"

Feather constantly had to remind herself that this was a young girl and her knowledge and ability to listen were severely curtailed in her short life. "If you do that for me, I'll come with five new jokes next time."

Millicent clapped her hands together and bounced. "Really?"

Feather made an X across her chest. "I promise."

"Do you know what's black and white and red all over?" the girl asked again, an impish smile covering her face.

Feather smiled. "No, I don't."

"An embarrassed zebra!" Millicent dissolved into giggles. "Isn't that funny?"

The young girl's head turned abruptly, as though someone were calling to her. "It's time for my supper of baked ham and boiled potatoes, Feather. I shall come and visit you when I can report on my mission!"

CHAPTER TWELVE
GEMINI

"Jasper Montgomery, age sixty-five. Certain he's seeing his dead grandmother in his refrigerator. He refuses to open the door now in case she is there, insulting him for gaining weight. We're here to... remove a spirit from a pickle jar."

Gemini dropped her phone to her lap. "Do you think it's wise to play along? Shouldn't we phone his relatives instead?"

They were parked in front of a 1920s Victorian-style mansion, painted pale blue with a neat white picket fence in front. It didn't give off the vibe of someone lost in their delusions.

"His next-door neighbor is the one who hired me. During our initial phone call, Jasper laid out his very specific rules. He wasn't going to allow me inside unless I signed a document, stating I would follow every single one."

She scrolled through her phone until she found it and handed her phone to Gemini. "Read these."

Gemini cleared her throat and read, "I don't like people in my home, so I'm granting you a very special favor. I shall mark the areas you can walk and you mustn't deviate from the path laid out for you." There were many more.

"Well! That's a new one! Asking YOU to sign an agreement!"

"I'm so glad you're coming with me. It should only take a few minutes to visit grandma next to the pickles." Feather rolled her eyes.

Gemini got a kick out of Feather's clients. Not the "please spy on my cheating spouse" type of mysteries she was used to dealing with as a secretary/detective at Floris, Fealgood and Flem.

"Do you want me to wait in the car? I'm still a little shaken from my experience after the memorial and I'm not up for any otherworldly surprises."

Feather frowned. "I'm worried about you, Gem. You're usually unflappable. But you can do what makes you the most comfortable. I promise, there are no entities in this man's refrigerator."

"This got to me because I was in the car with my daughter. If he would have succeeded in pushing us off that cliff and into the ocean..."

Feather reached over from the passenger seat and hugged her. It took everything in Gemini not to let the waterworks flow. She knew it wasn't safe to go down that path, especially when they had so much on their plates today.

"Thank you, hon. I needed that. You are the dearest friend and the best business partner I could ask for."

Feather blushed and turned away, biting her fingernail as she gazed out the window. She didn't take compliments well, no matter how often Gemini dished them out.

"I'll go in with you. A refrigerator ghost might be just what I need to nudge me out of this funk."

They climbed up the steps of the formidable home, only to find the door ajar when they arrived at the top.

Gemini paused. "This is how every single horror film begins. Should we call the authorities before we go any further?"

"No, it's okay, Gem. Jasper doesn't like the doorbell to ring. Rule Number Seven. When he knows someone is coming, he leaves the door open so we can enter quietly. I tried explaining that he could disconnect his doorbell, but he told me that was more information than he could absorb."

"I can understand that."

Gemini often called Howard over to help with new electronics. It wasn't that she couldn't figure them out on her own, it was more of a lack of interest on her part.

They entered quietly. Once her eyes adjusted to the

dim light, Gemini glanced around the living room. It was full of antiques—a Victrola record player, a Queen Anne sofa and glass lamps, to name a few. If Jasper weren't so afraid of human contact, his place would make the perfect bed and breakfast for antique enthusiasts.

Feather motioned for Gemini to follow her to the kitchen. When they reached the threshold, Feather held her arm in front of Gemini to prevent her from moving any further.

"There's a board that makes a loud creaking sound right over there." Feather pointed to a nondescript spot in front of the oven. "We have to avoid that spot because Jasper is unnerved by the sound. He sent me a picture with the spot circled. Rule Number Eight."

"Why doesn't he just get it fixed?" Gemini asked.

Feather shrugged and motioned for Gemini to follow her.

They crept through the large kitchen, stepping carefully on the squares of paper trash bags marked STEP HERE until they reached the refrigerator.

Feather laced her fingers together and stretched them in front of her, cracking her knuckles.

"How does Jasper know you're here, ridding his refrigerator of evil?" Gemini whispered.

"He's watching us on a camera up in the corner."

Gemini tilted her head back, trying to find a camera.

"Don't look up," Feather hissed. "He gets freaked out by dead-on stares. Rule Number Twelve."

"I hope you're making good money on this," Gemini remarked.

Feather slowly opened the refrigerator door and pulled out her phone, pushing the record button. "Milk, most likely well passed its date, grapes beginning to shrivel and a pickle jar. Now moving pickle jar one-quarter inch."

She paused and stood, glancing back at Gemini. "Rule Number Five. I tell him what I move or I don't get paid."

Gemini stifled a giggle.

"You hoo, Mrs. Montgomery! It's Feather Jones," she said in a slightly sarcastic tone. "I know you're trying to scare Jasper. You've got to leave."

Gemini stepped back one step, causing a creak she hadn't anticipated. "Sorry!" she mouthed when Feather stood and glared.

"I'll go wait in the living room," Gemini whispered.

Feather nodded and continued on.

Though she wasn't certain which of Jasper's rules pertained to his antiques, Gemini could tell he took great care with each and every one. There wasn't a hint of dust on anything. Tiptoeing across a maroon Egyptian rug, she found something on an antique secretary, a tall roll-top desk with a fold out writing area, across the room.

Leo made her one the year she started working for her son-in-law. He thought it was funny to give a secretary a secretary, but more than that, he was proud of the craftsmanship.

Leo had met her at the door with a twinkle in his eye. "I'm going to blindfold you, dear."

"Oh, Leo. I've had a particularly hard day. I'm not really in the mood for—"

"Please?" he begged.

Since he didn't plead with her often, it was a sure way to soften her up. "Okay. Blindfold me. But lock the door this time. Sophia said she needed three extra therapy sessions after she walked in on us last month."

Leo tied the cloth gently over her eyes and led her by her shoulders through their home. She could smell Leo's famous goulash simmering on the stove as they passed through the kitchen. Gemini felt a twinge of guilt that she was more interested in dinner than anything else he had planned.

When they reached the bedroom, he removed her blindfold. "All right, my dear. Open your eyes!"

She opened her eyes and sniffed. It smelled like fresh wood and a finishing glaze. Glancing around, Gemini discovered a beautiful piece of furniture sitting in the corner. Made from white oak, it stood shoulder height and intricate swirls were carved on the front of each of the four drawers.

"Oh, Leo! This is wonderful! A new dresser!"

"It's actually a secretary, for my secretary. Watch."

He walked over to one of the "drawers" and pulled it down instead of out. "It's a flat surface to write on. These were very popular in the late 1800s."

She walked over and touched each section, feeling the love he put into each part.

"It's perfect, my love."

Gemini kissed him passionately before Leo showed her every single nook and cranny.

Today, as she examined Jasper's secretary, she was amazed by the knickknacks sitting on top. Being tactile in nature, she had to run her fingers across the surface. Not nearly as smooth as the one Leo made for her. It needed sanding.

She carefully opened the large drawer, which was transformed into a writing spot in the one Leo made. Jasper's secretary had an additional set of tiny shelves, each one holding an antique of some kind. There were miniature salt-and-pepper shakers, a thimble and— "Cheese and crackers!"

CHAPTER THIRTEEN
FEATHER

Pausing the required thirty-four seconds, as per Jasper's instructions, Feather returned to her vantage point amongst the spoiled food. She wasn't feeling a bit guilty for charging him double her normal rate.

Feather Jones!

Feather stuck her head in deeper, trying not to inhale the suspect food smells. "What?"

Look at me.

There was absolutely nothing to look at. On a whim, she turned the pickle jar slightly. To her surprise and horror, a face appeared. The eyes were barely open and it had saggy jowls, like a cartoon hound dog.

You are the bridge. Don't give up until you make the connection.

"I've been told. What can you tell me about Jasper? How do I get rid of his mother?" she snapped.

This is a trap. Leave now before he locks you in.

She pulled her head out of the refrigerator so fast that she banged it on the way out. As she rushed toward the living room, she grasped the throbbing spot. There was no attempt on her part to place her feet on the assigned squares.

When she reached her friend, Gemini was admiring the antiques.

"We have to go! Now!" Feather hissed.

"Cheese and crackers!" Gemini gasped, forgetting to use her whisper.

"He's going to lock us in!"

The two women made a beeline for the front door, neither concerned with the squeaks they were making. When they were safely in the car with the doors locked, Gemini placed her hand on Feather's arm, running her fingers up and down in order to spot the telltale standing hairs.

"No entities right now," Feather said. "This one is bizarre, even for me. Let's get going and I'll explain as best I can on the way. I don't know what other games Jasper has up his sleeve."

She'd experienced more than her fair share of people who thought they had entities in their home. While most were earnest in their request, there were the odd few who had a fascination with the other world and hoped Feather could uncover something that wasn't there.

Jasper was neither.

She started the engine of her ridiculously large rental SUV. "You are precious cargo, babe," Tug had assured her when she complained about the size.

Glancing once more at Jasper's home, she spotted her client. In a second-story turret, he was peeking through some lace curtains. His steely gaze gave her the chills.

"This is too creepy, even for me."

Gemini nodded in agreement.

One of the many wonderful things about their relationship was that each understood the other's need for solitude. Instead of explaining what she'd heard, she enjoyed the view on the way up to Lyle and Lucinda's cabin. The narrow, winding road was lined on either side with tall pine trees, at times so thick the sky wasn't visible. She opened her window and breathed in the fresh scent of pine.

"Here we are!" Gemini said cheerfully as they pulled up to the gate. She gave Feather the code and the massive iron gates opened. The beautiful log cabin-style home was three stories tall with windows that stretched all three stories.

"Wow! This is like something out of a magazine!"

"It's been in the Reed family for decades," Gemini explained. "Lucinda's family came up here as guests of the Reed family for years before she and Lyle became an item. When Lucinda and Lyle bought the place, they added on to the back. If you can't already tell, they're loaded."

Feather suppressed a giggle. Gemini was worth several million since her settlement with Charming

General Hospital, but she was still of the mindset she was a retired hardware and paint store owner.

"When all of our kids were little, we used to meet up here for picnics. Always preceded by a funeral, of course."

"What happened? Why did it stop?"

"Oh, I don't know." Gemini opened the lid of a green cookie jar on the porch and pulled out a key before unlocking the door.

"Our kids grew up and they all went their separate ways, I suppose." She held the door open and motioned for Feather to enter. "When Lyle and Lucinda took ownership, they set up a strict occupancy schedule. Unless you have applied for and received approval to stay, you aren't allowed to be here."

"Will this get you in trouble, Gem?"

Gemini shook her head. "We're not spending the night. Just doing a little snooping. We'll be in and out before anyone even knows."

Feather was amazed by the inside. The logs were a rich blond and, in addition to the large windows in the front of the cabin, there were three huge skylights. A spiral wooden staircase climbed three floors, each one opening to the living room below.

"Can I get you something to drink?"

"Sure. Sparkling water, if that's okay."

Gemini huffed. "Course it is! Remember? They're loaded!"

Feather sat down on a wood-framed couch with

bright green pillows. She tilted her head back in order to appreciate the spiral staircase and the skylights above it.

Suddenly she became dizzy. She leaned forward, placing her head in her hands as she tried to steady herself.

We're all here! Nobody knows what we've hidden!

The voices were swirling in her head just as fast as the room was spinning. She felt Gemini's cool hand on her back.

"Would some fresh air help?"

Feather nodded, though she was afraid to open her eyes. Gemini guided her outside. Once she heard the door shut behind them, she opened her eyes and breathed in the mountain air. Her headache, and the voices, were gone.

"There were so many voices. I can't tell if they were all people who passed here, or my presence brought them from all over."

"You're a popular girl," Gemini replied. "Let's walk to the fire pit. We can relax there while you get your bearings."

It was a short walk on a mulch-covered pathway to the fire pit. There were padded chairs, logs and swinging benches on which to sit. Feather chose a padded seat.

"You know, the first time we came out here, Leo and I had been dating for two months. I don't remember who died—probably an aunt because the

Reed aunts were bountiful—and I became over-whelmed by all the new faces. Leo walked me over to this very fire pit. He told me he understood his family was a lot. 'We don't have to talk, Gemini,' he said to me. We didn't. That was when I knew he was The One."

Feather nodded and smiled. While she was reas-sured by Gemini's story, her chest felt heavy.

"What's wrong, dear?" Gemini, always perceptive, asked. "Is your headache coming back?"

Feather shook her head. "Either I've developed some new allergies, or there's something really bad out here." She glanced down at her forearms, where the hairs were still flat against her.

"No spirits yet. I would have thought with this extreme sense of heaviness in my chest that one would be nearby. I can't get over the idea that we're being watched. Let's talk about something else. Once I've moved on, I bet my mind will too."

"Are you going to tell me what happened at Jasper's place? I've never seen you so spooked by a refrigerator!"

Gemini's deadpan made it unclear if she was making fun of her or serious.

"I heard someone. In a jar of pickles."

Gemini rolled her lips inward and held them there until they were white.

"It's all right to laugh. It's very weird."

Gemini let out a big whoop. "I'm so sorry. That's not at all what I was expecting. Tell me more!" She wiped away the tears that had formed in the corners of her eyes.

"The entity said I was the bridge, which I've heard before. And then it told me that crazy old Jasper was planning to do something to us. It was all his orchestrated trap."

Jasper hadn't made her uncomfortable the way he did other people. In fact, she likened his peculiarities to her own. Her family thought she was a nut and Jasper's neighbor didn't understand his quirks either. Somehow, she overlooked the dangerous part of him. How she missed this, and any spirit warning about him, was a puzzle.

"That's it!"

"What? Is someone here? Should I call the police?" Gemini dug furiously in her purse, searching for her phone. It was unlike her friend to be so jumpy, and she blamed herself for dragging her into that house.

"No, nothing like that. We are perfectly safe here. I just figured out who the face in the pickle jar was. You know when they're green and made of liquid, it can be a challenge."

Gemini stared. "Don't keep me in suspense—who is it?"

"It's Augustus Treadwill. His family lives two blocks from Jasper. I spoke to him in March, and he promised me he would leave the premises. Now he's apparently taken up residence in Jasper's pickle jar!"

"What a relief!" Gemini clapped her hands together, as excited as Feather was with the news. "And now that you've made that wonderful discovery, I have a confession to make." Gemini reached into her pale lavender pants pocket and pulled out something. Feather reached for it, but at the last minute, Gemini retracted her hand.

"Why did you do that?"

"Because I just remembered how you were burned the last time I gave you a button."

"You found another button? Where?"

Gemini stared at the ground. "I may have... stolen it from Jasper's home."

Feather burst out laughing, causing Gemini to jerk her head up.

"That wasn't the response I was expecting," Gemini replied solemnly.

"Sorry," Feather said, putting one hand over her mouth. "This whole day has been kind of bizarre, don't you think?"

Gemini chuckled. "You're so right, dear. I just thought it peculiar that Jasper had the exact same—"

They both looked up when they heard the sound of rustling in the tall pine trees surrounding them. When nothing appeared, Gemini smiled. "Probably an animal of some kind. Us city folk aren't used to that."

Feather stood and rubbed her hands on her jeans. "I'd like to go for a walk. I do my best thinking when my feet are moving."

Gemini followed suit. "I'll go inside and see if there are any more random buttons lying around."

They gave each other a knowing glance and went their separate ways.

As Feather walked on a worn path through the trees, she took in large breaths, enjoying the strong pine scent. As she'd expected, the hairs on her arms rose.

"You've been here all along, haven't you? You didn't need to be scared of my friend. She's very kind." She closed her eyes and concentrated. "Are you Lyle?"

No. But I know him. He's dangerous.

"Why do you think he's dangerous? Isn't he dead?"

I'm here to warn you, nothing more.

She took a deep breath and let it out, not wanting her mounting frustration to scare the spirit away.

"Tell me about you. What do you remember of your life on this side?"

Picnics. Boats. Grandchildren. My darling sons.

"It sounds like you had a long and fulfilling life!"

She felt the heaviness in her chest once more.

I'm the cause of this heartache!

"I'm sorry. I didn't mean to—"

Feather felt dizzy again and struggled to stay upright. "What do you want from me?" she screamed as she lost her vision.

Right my wrong.

In what felt like a minute, she opened her eyes. This wasn't a pathway in the woods. She could hear beeping and the sounds of lots of conversations. As she continued to awaken, she realized Tug was stroking her arm.

"Where am I?" she asked, attempting to sit up. When she did, a wave of nausea overtook her. Both Tug and another set of hands helped her back to the prone position.

"You scared us, sweetheart!" It was Gemini's soothing voice. *The other set of arms.* "The doctor said you have a condition called vasovagal syncope that may be causing you to pass out. It occurs when you faint because your body overreacts to certain triggers, such as the sight of blood or extreme emotional distress. You've had no shortage of stress, my sweet girl."

Tug reached for her hand and she squeezed his when she felt his comforting touch. "It's probably why you're having those terrible dreams and you ran into that tree. You fainted because your body is overreacting to stress. From now on, we're treating you like glass."

She wanted to argue and tell them that she knew an entity when she saw it, but her head hurt and she felt like she'd just run a marathon, so she smiled and closed her eyes again.

"We can take you home as soon as the doctor comes back to release you," Gemini continued. "This settles it. I'll be handling all cases from here on out."

CHAPTER FOURTEEN
GEMINI

"I'm fit to be tied, Leo. I'm no closer to finding out what happened to Lyle, and my neighbor Howard is facing criminal charges if we don't get to the bottom of all this."

Gemini took the towel in his lap and gently wiped the corners of Leo's mouth. She'd been feeding him pudding, something he'd recently begun to swallow.

"Our conversations always guide me in the right direction. This time though, we may have met our match, eh?"

Leo's doctor told Gemini when he was first brought to Charming Acres Assisted Living that she was to speak to him as though he was fully functional. There was no indication that his brain wasn't working. It was the part that connected his brain to his speech that caused the issues.

"One of these days, he may well respond when you talk and you want to make sure you've told him everything there is to know about you," her doctor said with a smile and a wink.

She found it easier to solve cases when she was able to do all of the talking anyway.

"I've been writing down all of my communication with Lyle. I remember them attending our wedding. Lucinda told me I should have chosen a more flattering dress. Can you believe that? I don't think I ever told you. You said they'd grow on me."

She reached in her purse and pulled out one of the hard candies she'd confiscated from Lyle's desk. It was a smooth milk chocolate that tasted like chocolate pudding. "Then there were the endless weddings and funerals. I think some of those family members came from another family, dear. Especially Aunt Louise. When I saw her in that casket, I swear it was the first time I'd ever laid eyes on her." Gemini chuckled at the memory.

"Good morning, Mrs. Reed!"

It was Gemini's favorite nurse, Trent. He always spent time reading to Leo in the afternoons when he wasn't busy.

"I brought you some carrot muffins. Over on top of my coat." She gestured behind her without looking.

"Something's got you worked up today. What is it?" Trent removed the lid and sniffed. "Oh, Gemini, these smell even better than the last time."

"This case is a real head scratcher. My client, let's call her L, believes her husband, let's call him Y, has time traveled to another time to have an affair."

He sat down on the empty chair, laughing. When he realized Gemini wasn't joking, he placed his hand on top of his head. "I've heard some crazy stories working here. There's a night nurse who believes drinking owl's blood will help him see better. You told her she's nuts, right?"

"No, I couldn't. I owe..." She glanced at her husband, who stared straight ahead. "It's a family matter. That's why it's so important. In addition to this story, my neighbor's been accused of stealing watches from the same time period. They are related, no doubt."

"Hm. You get some interesting cases, Mrs. Reed." Trent wrapped his massive hands around his knees, the action he used to signal he was thinking. Gemini found most often his thinking involved video games and the attractive woman who lived in the apartment above him.

"You know, I had a kid in one of my classes in high school who thought he came from another time. We all made fun of him, but he was convinced he didn't belong in the present day. He went to great lengths to prove himself."

Gemini scooted her chair around so that she was facing him head on. She stood and moved Leo's recliner, with Trent's help, so they all faced the same direction.

"Tell me more. What did he say or do to prove his point?"

"Oh, lemme see... Well, one time he brought in

candy that came from fifty years ago. He told us he got it on one of his visits. My mom said there are specialty shops where you can find that stuff, so it was easy to prove him wrong. But then, he showed up one day wearing rings that supposedly came from a king. That one took some time."

She thought about the hard candies she found in Lyle's desk drawer. Easily explained. "And? Obviously he didn't get the rings from any king."

Trent shook his head. "Nope. Me and a coupla other kids went to the pawn shop and described the rings. The guy showed us in a book how much those went for—thousands of dollars. But there were fakes floating around for less than one hundred dollars."

"Your chum had that much money?" Gemini raised one brow. "That still seems very elaborate."

"He found all of it in his parents' bedroom. Poor kid just wanted attention. They didn't even notice it was gone until a bunch of concerned parents, mine included, had them drug into the principal's office. They were running an online theft ring, and every-thing he brought to school was stolen."

Gemini brought her hand up to her mouth. "Oh no! The poor dear. What happened to him?"

"I never found out. As soon as his folks were arrested, we never saw him again."

A muffled voice called for Trent over the loud-speaker.

"I'll be there in a minute," he replied. "I... shouldn't be telling you this, but—"

Gemini cocked her head to the side. "But? You've got a resident here doing some time travel?"

"Marv Everson's son. He has an organization of time travelers. I'd be glad to introduce you, if you like."

"It would be most appreciated. I'm not one to discount anything until I've thoroughly researched it."

He stood and grabbed the plastic tub. "Thanks for the muffins. I won't tell you how many days it takes me to eat them. Less than two."

"You're over six feet tall, Trent. That requires more calories to maintain than the average person. Eat at your own pace!" she called after him.

Looking at the clock, she realized her time with Leo was almost over. She stood and kissed his cheek. "Till tomorrow, my love," she said in his ear.

As she exited the building, she received a call. The caller ID said it was the Charming Police. It always gave her an ugly feeling in the pit of her stomach.

Raising the phone to her ear, she steadied herself for whatever news she was about to hear. "Hello?"

"Mrs. Reed? This is the Charming Police Station. We have a gentleman here who asked that we call you."

She ran through the list of people she knew who might be in trouble. "Is it Seven?" He was Howard's son who seemed to find trouble wherever he went. "I thought he was doing—"

"No, it's not a number, ma'am. It's a person. Mr. Howard Beachmont. He said you were his neighbor?"

"Howard?" Her voice rose two octaves. "Why is here there?"

"He was out in the middle of the street, yelling. Several neighbors phoned us, concerned about his well-being."

Nothing about that sounded like Howard to her. "I'll be right there."

The police station admittance desk was tall and imposing. A throwback from the early days of Charming, it was made of dark wood and stood at least six feet tall. The officers working the desk had a small step stool to assist them to their perch.

Gemini imagined all of the hardened criminals whose days of hardship and poor choices ended them right where she stood. They waited to be processed, to have their lives changed, some for the better.

She glanced over at the row of folding chairs behind the desk, where Howard sat. He was wrapped in a green blanket with the words "Charming Corrections" stamped all over. As if the blanket itself were a punishment.

Her wise neighbor looked lost and forlorn. He brought a cup of tea to his lips and glanced down at his hands. It hurt her heart to see him in this condition.

"May I see my friend?" she asked. It occurred to her that this policeman must see people at their worst every day. "I don't envy you your job. I'm certain they don't pay you enough."

The officer looked up, surprised by the question. "You're right about that. Every day we're dealing with nuts, and—" Realizing he'd spoken about Howard, he rephrased, "the people who are brought in have chal-lenges in life."

"Officer—" She squinted to read his badge. "Officer Klump, I see you and appreciate your hard work."

He smiled and hit a button that buzzed and simul-taneously opened the gate. "You know the magic words, ma'am."

Howard was sitting in an almost trance-like state. His hair hadn't been brushed and he was still wearing his pajamas.

"This isn't like you, Howard." She placed her hand on his arm and he jerked it away. Gemini didn't move from his side, waiting patiently until he felt comfortable.

When Howard actually turned to see who it was, his expression softened. "Gem? They called you?"

"You told them to, Howard," she said quietly.

"Can we go home now?" he asked in a forlorn voice.

"Yes! Let me check you out first." She wasn't sure how things worked here, but kindness was never a bad thing.

"Officer Klump, I'd like to take my friend home now." She gestured toward Howard.

Officer Klump stopped shuffling papers and stared hard at her. "You realize he was brought here because he was shouting in the middle of the street? Doesn't seem safe for a woman of your—"

"I'll ask you not to finish that sentence," she replied firmly. "He's my neighbor. Howard used to be a hospital administrator and is one of the smartest men I know. I'm sure there is a logical explanation for this."

Officer Klump looked back down at his papers. "Just because I like you, I'll find his paperwork." He winked at Gemini. "Here we go... a woman called to say he was harassing her. Someone by the name of Phyllis Buckley."

Gemini gasped. "Oh my!"

Officer Klump glanced at her before continuing. "When our officers arrived on scene, Mr. Beachmont was yelling and standing in the middle of the street in front of her home. He refused commands to stop, so he was tased. Not pretty, but you asked. And as soon as you pay his bail, he can go home with you."

Immediately, she opened her purse and pulled out her wallet.

Officer Klump viewed her with pity. "I've seen this a million times. A little old lady thinks she's doing the world a favor and as soon as the perp is sprung, he's in the wind, along with her bail money."

Gemini shook her head. "I know Howard. He's in a state. Yes, admittedly, he shouldn't have acted the way he did, but when he has time to reflect, he'll come to his senses."

She removed a glittering gold card. "If I don't help my friends with my money, what good is it?"

Now she had Officer Klump's full and undivided attention. He raised his eyebrows in surprise. "You sure? This will tie up your funds for—"

"I don't need a lesson in finance," Gemini replied

curtly. "Just give me the okay to take my friend home." Feeling embarrassed by her abrupt words, she added, "I'll be back to see you, Officer Klump. I'll bring you my famous brownies."

"That's awfully nice of you, ma'am. We don't normally take food from folks, but if you'll include your name and address with them, I'll take some!"

After the paperwork had been completed, the officer motioned for Howard to come to the desk. When he didn't move, Gemini went over to help him. "Come on, dear. Let's get you home now."

Gemini took one of Howard's arms and coaxed him into a standing position.

He frowned as she did. "I'm not an invalid," he growled.

"You are not. But you are acting quite childish. This is beyond you, Howard. If I didn't know any better, I'd think it was Sophia in front of me instead of my scholarly neighbor."

Howard stood and placed his plastic cup on the floor. He followed her like a lost puppy outside of the small gate and the three of them made their way to Gemini's car.

After they'd buckled in, Gemini pivoted in her seat, half-viewing Howard.

"Spill it. What's going on?"

Howard let out a long sigh. "This whole experience has me unsettled. I've spent my entire life being a law-abiding citizen, and suddenly I'm accused of something like this out of left field. It's not the identity I've cultivated. But that's beside the point. I have no idea what happened tonight."

Gemini thought about all the ways he'd helped her with cases. Most were illegal.

"I was at the table, examining my family jewelry under the light. The next thing I remember, I'm standing in front of Phyllis's home, serenading her with a song about her strawberry cannoli."

Gemini giggled. "That's one way to tell her you're not interested."

"Don't tease. You know I'm not the type to make a public display."

"Of course. I'm sorry." She started the engine and pulled out of the Charming Fire, Rescue and Police Station. "Let's try and figure out exactly what happened. Did you feel odd at any other point in your day?"

Howard leaned his head back against the headrest. "Come to think of it, I've been feeling odd for several weeks now. I may have mentioned I made an appointment with my doctor."

"Yes, you did. You also mentioned that the appointment isn't for some time. It may be wise to call them tomorrow."

"I'll concede that maybe you're right."

"Do you have any of that casserole I brought over left? If not, we can stop at a drive thru on the way home. You're not leaving my sight until I'm satisfied you've eaten something."

Howard leaned back and put his hand on his forehead. "I'd argue with you, but I've learned the hard way it's not worth it. Let's stop at Smitty's Burgers."

All the way home Gemini couldn't shake the feeling that there was something more to Howard's outburst. Nothing in his character led her to believe he would draw attention to himself like this, not even when he was wrongly accused of a crime.

She followed him inside to make sure there were no surprises. As he sat at the table, she poured him a glass of tea.

"You don't think it's your tea, do you?"

"What? I don't use pesticides on my produce, Gemini, you know that!"

"I didn't mean to offend you, Howard. I'm trying to cover every angle."

He wiped his face on a napkin and crumpled up his burger wrapper. "I must've blacked out. When I had clarity again, you were shaking my shoulders."

"Oh, Howard. That must've been disorienting. No wonder you scowled at me when I tapped on your shoulder."

Gemini knew he hated to be pitied, but this was one instance it was truly warranted.

Howard cleared his throat and leaned forward again. "Would you mind running one more errand this evening?"

"Of course. Where would you like me to go?"

"I need to pick up a prescription. I accidentally took two doses of my blood pressure medication last night."

Gemini had picked up his medication before, so she knew exactly which pharmacy to go to. Before she left, she had one more pressing question. "I don't want to pry, but I'm wondering. This whole experience with your insurance company and the claim, could that have led to your...?"

"Psychotic break? It's entirely possible. I guess I've never felt this helpless before. Maybe I just couldn't handle it. Don't worry, Gemini. It won't happen again."

She studied his face. He was indeed sleep deprived. There were dark circles under his eyes and he was sporting at least three days' growth on his chin.

"That's understandable. I'm going to get you some help. I promise. Tug's selling some natural sleep supplements that knock you out like a baby. I'll call and have him bring some over. You'll be asleep in under an hour."

He nodded and stood. "Are we good? I hate to think I've damaged our friendship tonight."

"Nothing has changed between us, Howard," Gemini replied solemnly. "Scouts honor."

Chapter Fifteen
Feather

Feather had followed the doctor's instructions, staying home for four days, practicing yoga, reading boring books. She watched every single show on their DVR and then read the few books she had lying around. She soon discovered that she wasn't a fan of teen vampires or *Phitness Exercises for Your Physique*. Feather understood that she needed rest, but wasn't boredom important to avoid too?

This seemed like a cruel repeat of her car accident, only this time she had no spirit to blame it on. Well, at least not one she could identify.

When Tug kissed her goodbye the fifth day, she knew she wouldn't be following his directive.

"What?" he asked, always able to read her.

"Nothing. It's just..."

He let his head fall back. "Feath, you're not going in. The doctor said you needed rest and peace this week."

"I know, but I'm just about out of relaxation. My mind needs stimulation."

"What if we go out for dinner? Pizza?"

There was no way she would convince him to release her from this round of captivity. "Okay, sure."

Waiting until she'd heard his car speed away, she felt like a criminal readying herself for the prime opportunity to commit a crime. Giddy with excitement over a forbidden experience, she got out of her pajamas and into her normal workday clothing.

It was almost too much. Should she go to the salon? Or to the detective agency? Both. She would do both.

"You're being so naughty, watty, Feather!"

If she wasn't mistaken, a shovel was digging dirt in Daisy's scalp. She tried not to stare, but it was impossible. "Not that you aren't wonderful company, but I need to talk to someone in my world."

"Hmph!" Daisy crossed her arms and attempted to storm off. Instead, she ran into Feather's bedroom wall.

"You still haven't mastered the exit," Feather mused.

"Want to see my invention?"

"Be quick, Daisy."

Daisy's image, fading in and out like bad television reception, moved to the window. She lifted her long skirt over a bike that wasn't fully visible. "See?"

"I'm sorry, what is this?"

Daisy pointed to the ground. "I've got no pedals, girlie."

"How do you get around then?"

Her image became clear and a metal contraption stretched from the handlebars to the back of the bike. She was attached by a harness at the waist. "No more cumbersome biking with pedals. Us girls need a way to get around too!"

Though it was a strange-looking thing, Feather appreciated the effort that went into it. "Thanks for showing me, Daisy."

"I'm working on something to help with your problem, Feather Weather."

Feather turned and smiled. "Thanks."

As she pulled up in front of the detective agency warehouse, she sat in the rental car and thought. *Do I really want to subject myself to all of the pitying looks and being treated like an infant?*

She loved them all—Tug, Gemini and even Olive. But maybe Tug was right; she wasn't ready. She turned on her car and pulled out of the parking lot.

When she arrived at Feather Works Salon, she hoped for a second that the news of her most recent collapse hadn't reached her colleagues there.

Nylah, looking like a drowned rat, was standing at the front desk when Feather entered.

"I'm surprised to see you again, Feather!" she said cheerily.

"Because I ran out of here like a lunatic? I'm going to try again, Nylah. That is, if you have time for me. I want to work through my... issues."

"Okay!" Nylah said with surprise in her voice. "It just so happens that I had a cancellation. I've got an hour right now."

She walked toward the back of the salon, motioning for Feather to follow her.

Feather undressed, fully this time, and waited under the sheet.

"Ready?" Nylah called from the other side of the door.

"Ready!" Feather closed her eyes and set about the process of relaxation. She heard the door open and close.

"It was the scent of my candle that set you off last time, right? I'm not going to light one today."

"Sure."

It was pure coincidence, she was sure of that now, but she wasn't going to tell Nylah.

Once more, she felt the magic hands of Nylah working out her tight muscles.

"Your back is rock hard," Nylah commented.

Though Feather did feel as though she should remain professional and carry on small talk, she could feel herself drifting off for the second time on Nylah's table.

She felt someone gently shaking her shoulder. *Was she in the hospital again?*

"You're all finished, Miss Feather," Nylah whispered in her ear. "You fell asleep right away and I didn't want to wake you."

Feather nodded. It was apparent she needed this more than she thought. "Last time I was here, you mentioned a party you attended. They asked you to do a séance?"

Nylah looked embarrassed. "Yeah. It was a little beyond my capabilities, but I went through the motions for them. From what everyone tells me, you have more talent than I do. Next time, I'll tell them to call you!"

Feather hated seances. They were campy and often spirits avoided them like the plague.

"Take your time getting dressed. My next appointment isn't for another thirty minutes."

She closed the door softly.

Feather stared at the ceiling, trying to wake up.

You are the bridge, Feather Jones.

She pulled her arms out from under the sheets and stared at the flat hairs. Nothing.

"You keep saying that. Tell me what you want me to do about it."

It occurred to her that, just like Millicent, this entity may want to connect with her before divulging any information.

"Tell me about your life. On this side. What was your profession?"

She could hear the sound of waves.

"You were a... fisherman?"

You... are... the... bridge! You... are... the... bridge!

This entity was shouting and it did no good to cover her ears because it was coming from inside her head.

"Okay! I'm sorry! Please stop!"

There was a knock at the door. "Miss Feather? Are you okay in there?"

"Fine, Nylah."

By the time she arrived back at their warehouse, she was feeling much better. The massage not only relaxed her but also cleared her mind. This was home and she didn't care if she wasn't wanted, it was what she needed.

Feather could hear Tug, Olive and Gemini engaged in a lively conversation before she even opened the door. It was like her last experience was playing on repeat.

"What did I miss?"

She pulled an office chair over to the circle and sat down.

"Are you sure you should be here, girlie?" Olive asked with concern in her voice. "We all thought the massage would be your big outing for the day."

"How did you know about that?"

Tug looked at her sheepishly. "Nylah called. She said you were talking to yourself and she was worried."

She was going to have to talk with Nylah about client confidentiality.

"I'm perfectly fine. Better than I've been in weeks. What were you talking about before I walked in?"

Gemini glanced sheepishly at Tug, who nodded his approval.

"We want to ease your burden any way we can," she began.

"The best way we know to do that is to hire another paranormal investigator," Olive said with a smile. "We'll have employees I can boss around."

Feather's eyes grew wide. "What? You're shoving me out?" She looked at Gemini and then Tug. Tears stung her eyes, but they didn't feel nearly as bad as the sense of betrayal from the people she loved the most in the world.

"No, dear heart, we're not shoving you out. We're getting you help. So you don't have to worry yourself sick. We all love you so much and want to make sure you're here for a good long time."

That didn't make Feather feel any better. "I don't need any help. I'm perfectly capable of—"

"That gal Jayden sent over some possibilities earlier." Olive chuckled. "They sure have some wacky ideas."

"Jayden knows about this too?"

Her world was crumbling around her.

"Olive is jumping way ahead," Gemini said, frowning at Olive. "Jayden sent someone over to talk to us about a potential position. We never actually reached the point of interviews."

"You..." She pointed her finger at each person in the room. "I thought you were my family. I can see I was completely misled."

She turned to walk out as Tug grabbed her arm. "Babe, wait! I can explain!"

Feather shook off his grip and stormed out.

Chapter Sixteen
Gemini

"I'm not taking any pro bono cases at the moment, Mom."

Gemini could almost feel his condescension oozing through the phone. Also, she really hated it when her son-in-law Brandon called her "Mom." It was a familiarity she didn't encourage.

"Howard is quite capable of paying you, Brandon. That's not the issue. He, or rather I, wanted to know what we could do about someone impersonating Howard online. How can we stop them? It's causing Howard great torment. I've never seen him like this before." She stopped short of telling him about Howard's arrest.

Brandon sighed. Gemini remembered from her days working at his law firm that he often made that irritating sound when he wanted to belittle a client.

"It can be tough to prove, Mom. Has he contacted the police?"

It was Gemini's turn to sigh. "Our little police department does the best they can. But cyber crimes aren't their forte."

There are lots of Howard Beachmonts in the world. Do you have any proof his item is stolen?

"Let me ask around and I'll get back to you. You know I have contacts everywhere. Oh, and Mom?"

"Yes?"

"Are you coming up for Taurus's pre-preschool graduation?"

It seemed silly to her. Why did these toddlers need to graduate from a glorified daycare when they'd be returning the following week?

"Yes, so far as I know, I can be there."

Brandon chuckled. "Got some big case you're working on? Surely it will wait."

Brandon never quite accepted that she was qualified to work as a detective. He still thought of her as a secretary at Floris, Fealgood and Flem, someone who got his coffee and nodded when he had a "brilliant" idea.

"As I said, it looks like my calendar is open right now. You'll call me back when you hear from your friend?"

"Yep."

She hung up, just as frustrated as she always was after trying to talk to her son-in-law. When Sophia brought him home, she and Leo remarked that he was much too serious and their daughter needed someone to soften her rough edges. Instead, they got the perennial knife sharpener who only served to hone her bad traits.

On a whim, she pulled out her pocket calendar adorned with scissors and feathers, with the words *Feather Works Salon* written in glitter across the top.

She opened the calendar to the day of Taurus's graduation.

"Darn it to biscuits. It's the same day as our market."

She hated to admit it, but she felt relief. She loved her grandson, but he was prone to public tantrums. Taurus was much sweeter when he was out of the public eye.

Gemini double-checked the time and realized she would be able to make the graduation if Tug and Feather would agree to pack up the tent.

It was time to research these items. She found the listing on CharmingBusiness.com and clicked on the appraiser box.

Dear Mr. Piquot,
I'd like to have a general idea of this jewelry's worth.
Can you give me some history on when and where it might have existed?
I thank you kindly,
Gemini

She stopped and erased her name. Feather told her in cases like this, it was never wise to use her real name.
I thank you kindly,

June Twin

She giggled at this clever moniker and attached the photos she'd taken in Lyle's office before pushing send.

Howard being in the state he was, she needed to make sure he was eating. Tonight's menu included ten bean soup and cornbread.

She was just about to place the cornbread pan in the oven when she heard her computer ding.

Checking her mail, Gemini discovered she already had a response from the seller.

Ms. Twin,
This jewelry was manufactured from the years 1900 to 1928. This is just at first glance, of course. If you'll bring them to our shop, J and M Antiques and Pizza, I'd be happy to give them a more thorough inspection.
Z. Piquot

When Gemini arrived at Howard's house, he was looking even more disheveled than the previous day. He was still wearing the same pajamas and robe, and his hair hadn't been combed since he slept. If he slept. The chain around his neck, holding his parents' wedding rings, made him look like a seventies movie star.

"I brought you some soup. I figured you weren't eating."

She stepped inside without waiting to be invited. Setting the cloth bag down on his table, Gemini opened the cupboard doors and retrieved plates and bowls.

"I hope you don't mind, I was planning to join you."

Howard flopped down at the table. "I don't mind."

She placed the steaming bowl of soup in front of him, along with a spoon and the certificates.

"I've been doing some research, and the jewelry I found in Lyle's office is apparently real. Maybe he did time travel?"

Gemini sliced homemade cornbread and put a piece on a plate for him, drizzling it with the honey she'd found in the cupboard.

Howard was studying the page as if it were one of his crossword puzzles. "On first glance, it does look legitimate, but I want to show you something."

He took the enlarged photo of a ring she'd placed beside him and brought it up to his face. "Do you see that?" he asked.

"No, I'm afraid I don't."

"You should see up to five marks on the inside of a ring. The sponsor's mark, the standard mark, and the assay office mark are the legally required marks. If the metal was a fair-trade item, it should also have a mark indicating this fact. None of that exists. This is a fake. And not a good one."

Gemini squinted. "Oh yes, I see it!"

"These are as fake as a four-dollar bill." Howard appeared almost giddy. "Strange that anyone would try and pass this off. Where did you say you found it again?"

"In Lyle's office."

He leaned back in his chair and smiled satisfactorily. "The next question is, how do you go about sussing out the criminal?"

Her phone buzzed and she was irritated to see it was her daughter. "I'm sorry, Sophia, but I—"

"Mother, we were able to find out who tried to run us off the road after the memorial."

Gemini stopped walking. "Who?"

"The vehicle was registered to a restoration company. M and E Restoration."

CHAPTER SEVENTEEN
FEATHER

"Ouch!"

She dropped the scissors for the third time this morning when she felt a sharp pain in her palms. "I'm so sorry. This never happens."

Feather was in the middle of cutting a new customer's hair. She'd added more days at the salon, avoiding Kindred Spirits Detective Agency altogether. Tug was sleeping in the spare room and they only spoke words like "excuse me" and "that's expired" to each other.

"Maybe you're developing early-onset arthritis," the woman offered. "My last hairdresser had to retire at thirty-six."

Gemini came rushing in from the unrelenting rain and, for a moment, Feather forgot she wasn't speaking to her.

"Feather, we need to talk."

Feather pulled auburn strands of hair from either

side of the customer's head and looked in the mirror to see if they were even. "I'm busy. Ask your new employee."

Part of her felt guilty for treating Gemini this way. She'd been like a mother to Feather ever since she came to town. But she was just as guilty as Olive and Tug of pushing her out of the business she'd helped create.

"We need to set our differences aside, dear. This is very important!"

"Gracious, Gemini Reed! Where's the fire?" Olive, who had been getting her hair done by another stylist named Sarah turned in her chair. "By the way, I'm getting the orange streaks today, in honor of our new Orange You Happy bar we're bringing to the market."

"I tried talking her out of it," Sarah said apologetically.

"I'm sure it's going to be gorgeous, Olive! I can't wait to see the finished product." Gemini bent down next to the woman in Feather's chair. "Do you mind if I steal Feather for a minute?"

"Well, I don't but my fancy hair might." She touched her hair and turned her head from side to side. "Are we done here?"

Feather smiled. "I'll be back in a minute. You make sure this is exactly what you want. I'm not much for those review sites, but they do mean everything to customers now." She motioned for Gemini to meet her in the friendship room.

"Sarah, how much longer does your product need to do its magic?" Olive asked as they walked by.

Sarah looked at her magenta watch. "About ten minutes. That's if it is still attached to your scalp."

Olive grinned, displaying her new pearly white and perfect dentures. "While you gals are back there arguing, you can get me one of those candy bars you bought from my great niece. She said you bought a whole box."

Feather disappeared momentarily, returning with Olive's favorite lemon soda and a large candy bar with the words FUNDZ FOR FANTASTIC FRIENDS written across the top.

When she and Gemini were finally alone, Feather leaned against the counter and crossed her arms. "What is it you want, Gemini?"

She saw the pain on her friend's face and a pang of guilt struck her chest. "I don't mean to be rude, but I've got a full day of clients."

"Of course. And I don't want to keep you from them, I just had a couple of things to tell you."

Feather nodded. "Go ahead."

Gemini cleared her throat and began, "Well, what you walked in on the other day was... well, it was just a brainstorming session. We were trying to come up with ideas to lighten your load. No one wants you to leave the business. Least of all me."

Gemini reached for Feather's hand but Feather kept them both gripping the counter firmly behind her.

"Olive was telling the truth when she said Jayden came in and we spoke with her. But she got things confused and we didn't get a chance to clarify before you ran out."

Feather glanced at her, angry at the tears that were forming as well as the friend who betrayed her. "So clarify."

"We were concerned about you, so we asked Jayden to come in and give us some ideas on what we could do to make things easier for you. We thought she was the best person to ask." Gemini tugged at her collar.

"But you all agreed that you were interviewing new people!" Feather protested. "Don't lie to me, Gem. Not now."

"I'm not!" Gemini replied indignantly. "Jayden sent a couple of people over to help with clerical duties. That's all. I think you should call her to confirm."

"Oh, I will."

Her anger was starting to subside, but the part of her that wanted to hold on to hurt wasn't ready to let Gemini off the hook so easily. "What else do you want? I'm busy today."

"Right. I had an epiphany while I was talking to Leo. I was telling him about my sad-looking strawberries when the idea struck me—what if someone is trafficking stolen antiques online? Maybe even Lyle? If he's stealing them and then selling them, it wouldn't take much for them to be engraved first. Kill two birds and all of that. Seems like a lesser offense than we thought."

Feather shook her head vigorously. "No, Gem. I'm

sorry, but you're wrong on this one. Cheating is the absolute worst."

Feather had been married when she was young to a jerk who cheated on her and left. The pain never went away, she reminded Gemini frequently.

"I'm sorry. That was insensitive of me. I've never dealt with either one, fortunately."

"You may be on to something though. Lyle and whoever he's working with got ahold of Howard's name somehow and they've been trafficking using his identification. It would all make sense."

CHAPTER NINETEEN
GEMINI

"They were NOT accommodating, Mother!"

Gemini was doing her best to remain focused on a conversation with Sophia. Her daughter had explained how she contacted M and E Restoration about their vehicle running them off the road.

"What did you say, Sophia?"

Sophia made the guttural sound of the offended daughter. "Why do you assume it was something I did, Mother? I told them I would be suing them for their employees' reckless behavior. You could've had a heart attack and died right there!"

Gemini rolled her eyes. "That notwithstanding, what was their response?"

"Only that the employee who was driving veered off the road due to alcohol use. He's since been fired."

It certainly seemed like he'd been deliberate in his

actions, but she didn't think it was worth keeping Sophia's hackles raised.

"I'll wait to hear what happens with your lawsuit, then."

It was time to find out more about the time traveler's group. Trent had graciously given her the name of someone who was involved with one. How many could there be in Charming?

"Knock, knock!"

She'd started knocking on the doorframe, just like the staff at Charming Acres. It drove her nuts. Why didn't they just walk into Leo's room? But here she was, doing it too.

Three heads popped up simultaneously and turned to stare.

"You look familiar." Marv had been injured in a serious car accident and, as a result, lost much of his long-term memory.

"I'm Gemini Reed. My husband Leo lives just down the hall," she explained patiently. Every time they met, the conversation was exactly the same.

Before his decline, Marv was a popular insurance agent. Gemini was told his client database included just about everyone in the county.

Trent had been reminding her every time she visited Leo that she'd wanted to meet the time traveler. Every time she'd been busy, but she was tired of his constant reminders, so today she told Tug and Olive she would be in late.

"Oh? Must've just moved in. I know everyone," Marv said.

"Yes, just moved in, Marv. I'll bring you some of my brown butter chocolate chip cookies the next time I come. A little birdie told me they're your favorite." She winked at the other two occupants of the room, one a younger version of Marv with the same heavy, round face and bushy eyebrows.

"Mick, is it? Would you mind if I spoke with you in the hallway? This will only take a few minutes."

Marv's son glanced at his father and the other man in the room and they both nodded their approval.

When they were standing outside of Marv's earshot, his son asked, "What's this about?" He folded his arms across his middle, jutting his hips forward as he stood in a wide stance. It reminded Gemini of Brandon, who assumed that position when he wanted to appear like he was listening intently.

"Trent is my husband's nurse as well as your father's. He told me you might be able to answer some questions I have about time travel."

"Really?" His voice went up an octave. "There are usually two camps: the people who think I'm bonkers and the ones who don't think I'm bonkers but think the idea of time travel is a joke."

"I've recently become acquainted with someone who at least gives the impression that he can time travel. Start at the beginning and tell me everything you know."

He chuckled. "Mrs. Reed, that would take us long

past visiting hours. I can give you the basics. Would you mind meeting me in the cafeteria in say, fifteen minutes? My brother and I were in the middle of asking our father to sell his home. I need to make sure my brother doesn't think I abandoned him."

"Of course. I'll see you there."

As she made her way down the corridor, she paused in front of Leo's room. She'd stopped to visit him first, but it was tempting to visit him again. As she approached the door, she heard his physical therapist's voice.

"There you go, good job, Leo! I see you moving that finger!"

She smiled. He was making progress. Leo's timeline was his own and she'd come to accept that. It was so much better than the alternative. He was still a living, breathing part of her life.

Continuing down the corridor, she smelled a slightly putrid smell. *Was it someone's garbage?* The closer she got to the cafeteria, she realized it wasn't garbage. Well, not exactly.

There was nothing quite as bad as the coffee in the cafeteria, Gemini had discovered. This time of day, after a meal and before snack time, the only thing available was a weak black coffee (though she wasn't entirely sure it was coffee) and some dry store-bought cookies. The coffee was a cheap instant kind. The cook once confided to Gemini that she'd used it at full strength—not the watered down, barely more than brown water amount used in the cafeteria—to scrub the toilet when she was out of toilet cleaner. It worked like a dream.

Opening her bag, she found a bag of Mint Memories tea. The hot water pot was empty, so her only other option was to drink the coffee. She could at least pretend. Pouring herself a cup of the putrid brew and settling down at a table near the window, she pulled out her phone to check her messages while she waited and another hard brown candy fell out. No sense in wasting it. She unwrapped it and popped it in her mouth.

Gemini, we have to talk. I've come across some information to help with your case. F

She felt relief that Feather was back on speaking terms with her. At least for business discussions. Maybe in time she would come to realize her friends were trying to lighten her load, not push her out.

She continued reading:

Geemi, I left a sample of a new Tuggle Bart on your desk.

"Olive," she mused. "You haven't learned a thing from my lessons on autocorrect."

"Who's Olive?"

She glanced up to find Marv's son seating himself across from her.

"You've either got a death wish or your tastebuds don't work," he said, motioning to her cup of coffee.

"Oh, thank goodness. I thought I was the only one who couldn't tolerate the coffee here. I only got it so I wouldn't appear rude." She shoved the Styrofoam cup to the far side of the table.

"I never introduced myself. I'm Mick, Marv's oldest son." He held out perhaps the largest hand she'd ever seen. When she offered her own, it disappeared within his grip.

"Thank you for taking time away from your family. Since we're working on the clock, I'll get right to it. Have you time traveled yourself?"

Mick, who had slouched down in his seat, sat up straight. "Thought we might ease into that discussion. You really do get to the point, don't you?"

When Gemini didn't reply (something she learned at the law firm, give people the space to tell their story; truthful or not, it will all come out), he reached into a paper bag and placed a silver object on the table.

"Looks like a rather large pendant to me."

"That's an unusual gift, but a lovely one." Gemini admired the square pendant with tiny diamonds forming a second square in the middle. Framing the diamonds was a symbol of some kind—what looked like three commas within a circle. "Do you know the significance of this?" She pointed to the commas.

"It's called a donan. It's common in Eastern religions. The three commas, as you called them, work in a circle that together symbolize Man, Heaven and Earth."

Gemini squinted, studying the face again.

"You can also see a star-like shape with three blades.

That means the never ending cycle of life and death. It's just how you look.

"Read the inscription," he said.

Gemini turned it over and read, "To my beloved husband, Wilfred, from your wife, O."

"Seems more like a gift given to a wife, not a husband."

"There's one more line."

She picked it up again and examined it closer. "It says April, 1846. That could be something you found in an antique store. I'm sorry, but I'm looking for definitive proof of time travel."

Mick stood so he could reach into the inside pocket of his jacket. "I carry these with me at all times, just in case I run into someone like you."

He pulled out a portion of a newspaper that had been laminated and handed it to Gemini.

She took out her readers and began, "Thank you to the anonymous person who returned my dearly departed husband's pendant. It was his most prized possession. The city of Portland has agreed to exhume his remains, so that his pendant will be at his side forever more. Orelia Johnson, 1889."

Underneath was a photo of the pendant she'd just held, with the same exact inscription.

Gemini's jaw dropped and she stared at Mick. "How can that be? If you just handed that exact pendant to me? This must be a cruel trick someone played on you. This woman's husband was buried with that pendant."

Mick shook his head. "This is the point at which you have to think beyond your comfortable mindset. My buddies and I have been studying time travel for a decade. We planned to go back in time to observe a historical event. We're history buffs, so the Gettysburg Address was our goal. It didn't quite turn out that way."

One of the cafeteria staff wiped off a table next to them and raised one brow when she was close enough for them to notice. It was clear she found this information unbelievable.

Gemini and Mick waited patiently for her to finish before continuing their conversation.

"That's the reaction I get all the time," Mick said sadly. "I'm not crazy."

"Of course you aren't, dear. Please continue. When you set your clock, or whatever it is, back to the Gettysburg Address, it didn't take you there."

"Right. We ended up in Pennsylvania in the year 1868. The Gettysburg Address had long since passed and there was nothing too exciting going on, at least where we were. But the opportunity to experience daily life—the sights and smells—were nothing like modern living. Horses filled the streets, and all of the smells that came with them. The air was thick with black smoke from the factories. It was hard not to choke. And the gals, I mean, women, were dressed in these fancy dresses and big hats. Nothing like the casual look of today."

"Do go on," Gemini urged. "What other things did you see?"

"Oh, the butcher shop on the corner, the young kid selling newspapers, every single thing was brand new." Mick leaned back, clasping his massive hands behind his head. "We found a room in a boarding house. Orelia Johnson's boarding house. That's where we found it."

"And you stole her pendant," Gemini replied with disgust. "This poor woman was obviously attached to it. How could you?"

"It wasn't me. My buddy wanted a souvenir before we left. Orelia was grieving. Her husband and son had just died in an explosion at the steel plant. She was planning the funeral and laid out all the special mementos she wanted buried with them. When we returned to present day and I realized what he'd taken, I insisted we return so that she could bury the pendant with her husband."

Gemini studied Mick. She couldn't tell if he was being sincere or not. Admitting such a heinous crime wouldn't be easy, and there was no reason he would if it weren't true. At least none she could think of.

"So you returned the pendant after the funeral."

Mick nodded. "We went back to what we thought was the next day. Only when we found a calendar, two years had gone by. Mrs. Johnson's boarding house was buzzing with people. I was relieved to see how well she was doing."

"She must've been pleased to get her property

back." Gemini didn't hide the sarcasm in her voice. "And you were celebrated as a hero."

"Not at all. We thought for sure she'd figured out we were the ones who took the pendant. We left the boarding house and the pendant left too. That's why we left it on her porch in the middle of the night, wrapped in brown paper along with a note of apology."

"How magnanimous of you. Why the mystery though? And why are you showing me the pendant now? Did you change your mind?"

"The next time I travel, I'm going alone. The pendant returned with us. We watched as Orelia opened the note and the bag and placed them back where we left them. My buddy decided that made it all right to bring home."

Even though he had been forthcoming, she wasn't sure she could trust Mick. If she didn't though, she might not get another opportunity.

"I have a relative who has been time traveling too. At least that's what they want us to think."

"Really! Tell me everything! Maybe it's someone I know!" Mick said with enthusiasm.

"His name is Lyle Lime."

Mick's demeanor immediately changed. "I see."

Chapter Twenty
Feather

Though she'd been back at Kindred Spirits for a few days, Feather wasn't any more relaxed than she had been before she passed out. There was no way she would share that with her friends. They'd have her banished to her bedroom for the rest of her life.

Not only that, the nightmares hadn't stopped. Sometimes she thought she saw the face of the person who jumped in front of her car, and other times it was an empty skull, devoid of any humanity.

"Jayden?"

"Hi, doll. What's up?"

She relaxed hearing the soothing deep voice of her mentor. It was hard to stay mad. "My friends tell me you came in for a visit."

"Oh. I should have been expecting this."

Part of her screamed, "Don't upset her!" but the stubborn part of Feather Jones remained on course.

"You told them to replace me. You even brought in potential replacements."

"Not replacements, doll," Jayden corrected her. "They were consultants. Big difference. Even with all of my talents, I bring on consultants to help me with my business. They cut through all of the bull and tell me what I need to hear."

Tears formed in Feather's eyes, as had become her daily norm. She was beginning to wonder if a person ever ran out of tears. "And what is it I need to hear, Jayden?"

"That pushing yourself harder won't solve your nightmares or your mystery. Your friends were concerned, and rightly so. The Feather I know and love is withering away. If you're going to get a handle on things, you need some support."

"Oh." Feather sniffed. "That wasn't how they explained it."

"Well, I went in with the understanding I would find them a consultant. Your cute little nose was pushed out of joint by this completely sincere gesture, so those people haven't returned. Now can we get past this nonsense and get back to why you really called?"

Feather blew her "cute little" nose and wiped her face. "Yes. Let's do that." One thing she knew Jayden had pegged was the emotion she was spending trying to figure out who or what was torturing her in her dreams. She needed to look at it as if it were a case she was working, completely detached.

"I'm really stuck. I thought this entity that ran out

in the road was someone I knew. But it's still happening, it's giving me nightmares and—"

"And you are worried you hurt someone. I get it."

"What can I do?"

"You know what? I need to see my favorite paranormal investigator. Let's meet for lunch. Say, around one?"

Feather glanced at the clock. It was 10:30 and she hadn't been out of bed yet. Feeling shame once again that her business partner was carrying the load, she threw the covers off her legs. "That's perfect. At the Tickled Egg?"

The Tickled Egg was a new brunch spot in Charming. It was getting rave reviews from everyone who went.

"I'll see you there!"

When she'd showered and dressed, she gave herself permission to quickly look in the mirror. She wasn't a fan of her reflection, but she knew that the stress she was under was taking its toll.

Sure enough, the dark circles under her eyes were pronounced enough that she looked like she had two black eyes. Her dark roots had grown out, giving her once-spiky green hair the look of wilted lettuce.

There was one thing she knew she had to do before their lunch.

She sat on the floor of the spare room, waiting. Soon enough, she felt the hairs on her arms rising.

"Who's here?"

There was the sound of giggling and the sound of a ball bouncing. Millicent.

Opening up the door to the spare room, she found her favorite small entity on the floor playing with a small leather ball. Millicent looked up when Feather opened the door and jumped to her feet.

"My sweet Feather! You came to see me!" She hugged Feather as much as an entity could hug a living being. Her small hands wrapped around Feather's waist and she felt a warmth surrounding her.

"Technically, you came to see me, but..."

There was always a reason Millicent visited, whether it was to tattle on her siblings or something more serious, like tell Feather about an entity that was causing trouble.

"Did you find an answer for me? Who is the bridge?"

Millicent shook her head. "It's a bully. Meanie Weenie."

I hate bullies. They were always making fun of me in—"

"The door is open and I'm cold."

Feather knew there was a door between their worlds. It was always open a crack, giving entities the opportunity to slip through. But now there was something more sinister happening.

"I know, sweetheart. We're working on it. If that's all—"

"DON'T LEAVE!"

The window shook and Feather swore the floor moved. She swallowed hard. "Tell me more."

"You asked me to find out who was in the wrong place. I found him!"

Feather sat down cross-legged on the floor, the way Millicent liked her to sit.

"He likes to make people sad in your world."

"What does he do to make people sad?"

"He makes up stories and then whispers them in people's ears, like this."

Millicent cupped her hand around Feather's ear and whispered, "Be afraid, girl. Evil is coming for you."

Feather jumped back as the entity, clearly not Millicent, laughed so devilishly the temperature of the room dropped. As he blew out air, frost formed on Tug's computer screen.

She ran out of the room, slamming the door. The only furniture she could move quickly was the end table in the living room. Feather positioned it against the door handle and stood back.

"That was dumb. Spirits can get through walls."

The only thing she could think of was to hurry out the door to meet Jayden. Once in her rental car, she found herself so shaky she could barely turn the ignition key. Somehow, she was able to back out of her space and squeal out of the apartment complex.

CHAPTER TWENTY-ONE
FEATHER

People were sitting on benches and standing by their cars in the parking lot of the Tickled Egg. Feather glanced at her watch, dismayed to see it had taken twenty minutes just to reach the restaurant. It was on the outskirts of town and their little two-lane highway was often overwhelmed by tourist traffic. Today it was tourists combined with excited locals, happy to have a new, trendy restaurant.

There was no way around it, she'd have to take a rain check. Feather pulled out her phone and dialed Jayden's number.

"I'm sorry, Jayden, it looks like the place is full. Should we—"

"I called ahead and got us a table. I'm way in the back."

Feather wove her way through the large crowd, some giving her angry glances as she stepped ahead of their rumbling stomachs in line. When she explained to the host that her friend was waiting for her, he smiled and motioned for her to follow him.

Jayden, looking as lovely as always in a bright blue catsuit, waved from an over-sized booth at the very back of the restaurant. "Hi doll!" she mouthed. Her silver hair was tucked behind her ears and she glowed with perfection.

Feather realized when she sat down that Jayden was on the phone.

"So we'll be signing in a week, then? Can't wait. Okay thanks again."

Jayden put her phone back in her purse and smiled at Feather. "So sorry. We're in the middle of an exciting acquisition. The chemical company that owns ethoesium will be producing for us by the end of next year."

"I'm sorry, I have no idea what that means," Feather replied sheepishly. Sometimes she forgot Jayden's world was much broader than hers.

"No one does, doll. It's a chemical compound that is quite toxic if inhaled. It comes from tenderleaf plant. But strangely enough, if it is boiled at high temperatures, the toxicity is gone. We're planning to use it in place of plastics. It decomposes in two years."

"That sounds... frightening," Feather replied honestly.

Jayden chuckled. "In the wrong hands, it is. That's why we're anxious to acquire the exclusive rights to grow the plants and extract the compound. There have already been deaths due to misuse."

"Ma'am, would you like your mimosa now? We can do any flavor you like."

Both women jumped at the sound of another voice.

Feather glanced at Jayden's glass, which was bubbling and purple. "I don't usually drink on the job," she began.

"Oh, doll, they're free! Live a little. It's a promotional thing they're doing to celebrate their opening."

Feather shrugged. "Give me one of those, I guess." She pointed at Jayden's glass and the server nodded and left.

A trickle of sweat ran down the back of her neck. Though it was the first warm day of summer they'd had, she knew it wasn't heat that was bothering her. It was nerves. "I wasn't sure if you wanted to tell me something else in person? You know, letting the other shoe drop?"

Jayden laughed a deep throaty laugh that caused the tables next to them to turn around and stare. She didn't seem bothered by it. "Oh, doll. You're always so serious. I worry that you worry too much. That's lots of worry, don't you think?"

"I'm sorry. It is."

Now she felt foolish. Of course Jayden wouldn't want to do anything to harm her after she'd spent so long training Feather as a paranormal investigator.

She took a deep breath and let it out slowly. "Okay. I was getting ready to leave when Millicent appeared. Only it wasn't Millicent at all..." Her eyes widened as she realized the potential her mentor had. "You could tell me exactly what happened! You know, don't you, Jayden!"

Jayden took a long drink and set the fluted glass down in front of her. "Sometimes. I did have a flash when you were in that accident. Like a jolt. But something blocked me from viewing the entire thing. I've been getting that a lot lately with you. Spirits, those with evil intent, are capable of doing that."

Feather slumped forward, defeated. "I've got myself an evil entity then. This is the first time I've had something this awful in my home."

"Tell me everything and start from the beginning," Jayden insisted. "Don't leave out one detail."

When Feather finished with the unsettling story, Jayden reached over and squeezed her elbow.

"Oh, doll. I'm so sorry you're dealing with this, on top of everything else. Can you see why I wanted to find a support system for you?"

Feather didn't want to think about that right now. Though she understood Jayden's reasons, she still felt the sting of betrayal. Rational or not, it was there.

"You can get rid of it, right?"

Jayden scrutinized Feather's face. Feather hated when she did that. She felt naked. Finally, Jayden replied. "Let me see what I can do." She took both of Feather's hands in her incredibly soft ones and they both closed their eyes. Feather was well-versed in Jayden's process for contacting spirits.

A server stopped at their table. "Can I get you gals a drink to start with?"

Feather opened one eye and shook her head.

"Come back in five, hon," Jayden replied calmly. When she'd left the table, they resumed their position.

Feather cleared her head and tried to leave her mind empty of everything so that Jayden could easily search her memory.

After a few minutes, Jayden released her hands and sat back.

"Well? Is the entity gone?"

"I'm so sorry, doll. This isn't like an entity that's lost. This is someone whose purposely here to cause trouble."

Feather's heart sank. Jayden always found solutions to her problems. She glanced at Jayden, who was rubbing her hands.

"Did I do that to you?" Instinctively, she grabbed one of Jayden's well-manicured hands. It was bright red and hot. "Now I've done it."

"Feather Jones," Jayden began in her sternest voice. "YOU did not cause this. I was trying to remove the block your entity has placed on me." She looked at her long fingers. "This is what they thought of my plan." She laughed her deep, throaty laugh.

"What am I supposed to do now?"

"You're going to figure out why you brought the spirit to our world."

"What?" Feather grasped either side of the table and squeezed it. "You can't be serious! The very last thing I would do is purposely bring something like that here!"

Jayden reached over and held firmly to Feather's arm. "Calm down, doll. I didn't say you did it on purpose. There is something going on with you that attracted this spirit. Something you haven't talked about that's bothering you. Because of your gift, you attracted help. Because you're still relatively new to this game, you attracted the wrong kind."

She thought about the entity that jumped in front of her car. A blur of energy without any distinguishable features. "How do I get rid of it?"

The server appeared in front of their table once more. "You gals still chattin' away, or can we get this party started?"

"Sparkling water for me," Jayden said. She glanced at Feather. "And one for my friend."

The server glared at Jayden and then looked kindly at Feather. "Cat got your tongue, sweetie?"

"No, my mentor here always knows what I need before I do. Sparkling water for me too." There was no use explaining to the server that Jayden was not only a paranormal expert, but also able to read minds.

When the server left, Feather leaned in and whispered, "Tell me what I can do to get rid of this evil thing. My poor little car can't handle any more trees."

"That's simple. Solve your problem and then tell the evil spirit you don't need it anymore."

Feather eyed her friend with trepidation. "You

already know what I'm going to say, so let's just cut to the chase."

"You don't know how to solve your problem because you're not sure it even is a problem. What you saw in front of your car was indeed an entity. You've been missing the message entirely, so the entity is going to continue appearing. The car accident was supposed to get your attention."

Jayden glanced around the room and then trained her eyes on Feather. "This will continue to escalate until you figure out what the entity wants to tell you."

"Right." Feather took a sip of her mimosa. "Oh wow, that's wonderful!"

"As is the food here. This is my third trip."

Feather gulped down the rest of her mimosa, probably a little too fast. She felt warm and fuzzy inside, and she was no longer controlled by a nagging anxiety.

"On the subject of evil entities, your little Millicent is trapped," Jayden continued. "She got the information you wanted, but unfortunately this caramel corn-smelling troublemaker found out."

Today was starting to feel like a roller coaster. Just when she was about to relax again, another piece of information made her stomach drop like a lead balloon.

"Now I feel awful. I did this to her! Before I find any answers for myself, I need to free Millicent!"

"You ready to order?" a different server asked.

"I haven't even—"

"The silly turkey with frivolous potatoes and

drunken fruit salad," Jayden said. She nodded toward Feather. "I believe that's what my friend would like as well."

Feather nodded, feeling warm and fuzzy inside. Jayden was like a loving parent, the kind who could read her thoughts without her verbalizing them.

"Please tell me there's a way to release Millicent."

Jayden clucked her tongue. "Poor dear. I've only had experience with this once before and it didn't end well." She pursed her lips. "But I do have an idea. We'll get your little girl free. That I can promise you."

Chapter Twenty-Two
Gemini

"And now you want to see if he's telling the truth?"

Mick and Gemini had been sitting in the Charming Acres cafeteria for over an hour, discussing time travel and just how Lyle might have achieved it.

"That's the gist of it," Mick chuckled. "Though it's a gist that's taken sixty minutes to relay."

She still wasn't sure if he was trustworthy. Something about Mick Everson was...off.

Mick looked at his watch. "Shoot. Visiting hours end in fifteen minutes. I'll write down my email address and you can send me everything. I'll do some investigating of my own within the Hawkite community and see what I find. We're a pretty close-knit group."

"Hawkite? Some kind of code?" Gemini asked, still suspicious of his motives and his story. This was the charity Lyle supported, though Mick didn't seem to know him.

"After Stephen Hawking. He believed in time travel and paved the way for the rest of us."

Gemini nodded. "Just tell me one thing before you leave. If Lyle is hiding out with his mistress, won't he prevent his children and grandchildren from being born?"

Mick stood and pushed his chair in. "There's still a lot we don't know. On the surface, it would seem so. But if they're all alive and kicking, then—"

"Then he's lying."

"No, that's not necessarily true. I can invite you to our next meeting. Maybe that would be helpful in your understanding of the process."

She looked at him with surprise. "Your Hawkites wouldn't be opposed to a stranger joining in?"

"Not if I email them first. I'm one of the founding members, so I get final say on who comes to our gatherings. I've got to run. I'll be in touch about the next meeting, and please send me all that you have on Lyle."

He started to walk away.

"Oh, Mick? Do you mind if I take your pendant to show a friend of mine? I promise, it will be returned to you unscathed."

He looked at her with skepticism. "I just met you. This is pretty important to me. What if you disappear like your cousin and I never see it again?"

"You have my word, but more than that, you know

where the most precious person in the world to me resides."

Mick knitted his thick brow. When he'd been quiet so long Gemini thought about checking for a pulse, he finally uttered, "That's fair." He scooted the pendant back over to her side of the table. She barely caught it before it fell on the ground.

"I'll get it back to you the next time we meet, " she promised.

"I don't have to tell you how valuable this is to Mick," Gemini said as she handed the pendant to Feather. "Though I trust you implicitly."

Feather took the pendant from her hand and set it gently on a cloth on her desk. "You have my word."

She placed each fingertip lightly on top of the pendant, one at a time. Feather closed her eyes and took a deep breath.

Gemini sat down at her desk, facing Feather. She never tired of watching Feather's process.

"Oh," Feather said in a surprised tone.

Gemini resisted the urge to ask what she was talking about. She didn't want to interrupt.

The phone began to ring, and she turned off the ringer for fear of disturbing Feather. A flashing red light alerted her to the fact that someone left a message.

She rose and found the largest movable object in the office. The 984-page *Everything You Need To Know About Your New Detective Agency* book, used daily during their first month in business, was just what they needed. Gemini opened it up and placed it on top of the phone.

She sat back down, satisfied Feather hadn't been disturbed.

"You're right, you're right," Feather said softly.

Gemini decided it was time to start taking notes, so she could ask her about each utterance when she finished.

The door to the office of Kindred Spirits Detective Agency flew open and banged against the metal trashcan.

"You gals need to answer your phones," Olive panted. She sat down in a visitor chair and fanned herself with her apron. "This is a business, after all."

Feather's eyes snapped open and both she and Gemini frowned in Olive's general direction.

"What's so important?" Feather snapped.

"We are in the middle of something here, Olive," Gemini said with more patience than Feather. "We've reminded you more than once, when Feather is in the middle of a reading, we don't disturb her," Gemini chided gently.

"Oh, is that what this is?" Olive made a circular gesture with her finger. "Thought you both was taking a power nap."

Gemini shook her head. When Olive wasn't forthcoming with any more information, she asked, "Was there something you needed, Olive?"

"Your neighbor, Howard. Charming General just called and said you were listed as his next-of-kin."

"What happened now?"

"They said he was out in the street saying crazy things. Another neighbor yelled at him to go back inside and that's when Howard decked him. The man's wife gives a self-defense class, and apparently she roughed Howard up pretty good."

"Poor Howard. Is he in the emergency room? He's got a knuckle that gives him fits. If he broke that, he's going to be in a cast for a while."

"He was," Olive leaned forward, leaning her fore-arms on her knees. "The person he hit wanted him arrested for assault. He's probably with the popo by now."

"Cheese and crackers! You might have led with that, Olive!" Gemini grabbed her purse and coat.

"I'll come with you, Gem. I can fill you in while you drive," Feather offered.

"What about me?" Olive asked. Technically, she worked for Tug making his bars. The fact that she spent so much time in their office made it seem like she was more of a floater.

"Someone has to answer the phones. You said so yourself," Gemini replied. She patted Olive's back as she walked by. "No need to worry. We won't have an adventure without you, I promise."

The two women rushed out to Gemini's car and, as

she backed out of their parking lot, Feather tapped her fingers on the armrest.

"What is it, hon? Was it that bad?"

"No, it's just a mystery. When I picked up the pendant, I got the sense that it was a fake."

Gemini had very pointedly avoided telling Feather anything about the pendant. Although she trusted her friend's abilities, she wanted there to be no question as to the validity of her responses.

"I'm not opposed to the idea that Mick is dishonest, but why would he hand it over if he knew it wasn't the real thing?"

"Most people don't believe in paranormal events. Maybe he thought I was a fraud and wouldn't know."

Gemini giggled. "A time traveler who doesn't believe in paranormal events. That strikes me as hilarious."

Feather giggled too. "Agreed."

"It was manufactured recently, but the product used to make it was a toxic substance. Something that shouldn't be used for jewelry."

"That doesn't sound like something this man brought back from his time traveling."

They pulled up in front of Charming General Hospital. "It may take me a few minutes to find Howard. Do you want to stay in the car?"

"Yeah, I'll stay in the car. Because Howard is right behind you."

Gemini turned to see her good friend, once again haggard-looking.

"What on earth happened?" she asked.

"Can we just go home, Gemini? I don't know how much more of this I can take."

"Of course, Howard."

All the way home, Howard told them the story of his blackout. It was just like that last time, but this time, fortunately, he wasn't standing in front of Phyllis's home.

"As soon as you get home, you're calling your doctor," Gemini said firmly. "There is something physically wrong with you, Howard. I will sit with you until it's done, if need be."

Howard hung his head in shame. "I will.

Chapter Twenty-Three
Feather

"What?" Feather asked. "Is that what you were told? I don't think that's what happened here. Of course, I could be wrong. My readings aren't perfect."

"Usually they are, dear."

They pulled up in front of J and M Antiques, Pizza and More and Gemini shut off the car.

"Gem, I hope you won't be offended if I ask you something."

"You'd have to work pretty hard to offend me, hon."

"Well, I was thinking we should take this pendant in with us. They can check to see if it was stolen, or even real. In our timeline, that is."

Gemini thought for a moment. "I'm with you on that. My concern is that if it is stolen, I don't want Mick to realize we're on to him until I attend his group session."

"You won't have to worry about that, Gem."

Feather, true to her word, had a plan.

The employee of J and M Antiques, Pizza and More spent over an hour on the phone with other dealers, trying to track down the origin of the pendant.

"Grandma, you promised if I brought you down here that you would tell them the truth."

Gemini stared at Feather, blinking rapidly.

Feather's pulse quickened. "You said you'd tell the nice man about where you found the pendant since you didn't want to tell me." She nodded encouragingly.

A look of recognition crossed Gemini's face. "Oh, right. That's exactly what I said." She turned toward the store employee, an elderly man wearing an unusual-for-summer thick sweater and a look of contempt.

"I found the pendant in a box in my attic. I think it may have come from my grandparents." She turned to face Feather. "I didn't tell you because I've already willed it to my favorite grandchild, Spike."

He eyed Gemini suspiciously. "What's peculiar to me is that the diamonds in the center square are real, but I'm fairly certain those around the edge of the pendant are fakes. Manufactured in the present day. Your family treasure is worth about ten dollars."

Gemini gasped and put her hand over her mouth. "Poor Spike was going to sell this to pay for his surfing career! He'll be devastated!"

"We've had a rash of these lately. All different types of jewelry coming in that has a mixture of new and old jewels." The man shook his head. "Never can tell why people spend their time and energy on things."

Feather squinted, trying to figure out if there was any other distinguishing features. "How many have you found so far?"

"In Charming? Four. We've been in contact with Blackberry Cove, just down the road. They've had three. Probably a bigger fraud ring than just our area. Could be national."

"What would be the purpose, sir?" Gemini asked. "I don't understand why this has gained popularity."

He removed his cap and scratched the top of his balding head. "They thought they could circulate them through antique stores. The dealers who aren't worth their salt probably accept them as the real thing. They'll pay out a hundred dollars or more. It won't be until they really set down and analyze the jewelry that they figure out they've been had. Luckily, we've got an ace in the hole, here in J and M Antiques, Pizza and More."

He gestured toward another man approximately his age who had just come in from the pouring rain. "This is my nephew, Zeke. He's our own expert. Never been wrong when it comes to fake jewels."

Zeke looked over the man's shoulder. "Let's take that in the back and I'll examine it in better light."

When he was gone, Feather whispered, "Isn't that the name of the person who told you Lyle's rings were fakes?"

Gemini nodded.

The women wandered around, waiting for a definitive answer. "Oh, look!" Gemini said. "This secretary is similar to the one in Jasper's home!"

Suddenly, an argument erupted between the two men.

"Do you know what they're saying?" Gemini whispered. "You have young ears, after all."

Feather shook her head. She thought she could make out "do as you're told," but it could have been any number of things.

Zeke, red faced, returned to the women. "I'm sorry, ladies, my uncle was mistaken. This is one hundred percent real."

Feather sensed heaviness in her chest. *He's lying.* She glanced around the room, noting the shape of a man dressed in conductor attire from the 18th century. Both of his thumbs were hooked in his vest and he was rocking back and forth. *Don't tolerate the liars,* he grunted.

"I'll be happy to get it appraised," Zeke continued. "Atticus, who runs the pizza half of our place, does appraisals on the side. Happy to take it and have it appraised, if you like."

"Your pizza is really good!" Feather said, feigning enthusiasm. "Tug's favorite is the pineapple and pepperoni when he's feeling naughty. And on the days he's being strict about his eating, it's Vegetable Party."

Zeke removed a small plastic bag from a drawer and slipped the pendant inside.

"No!" Gemini and Feather said in unison.

He looked up with surprise. "Don't you want it appraised? For insurance purposes? You just found it in your attic, after all."

He smiled slyly, causing Feather to wonder why.

"Grandma needs some time to process this, don't you, Grandma?"

Gemini nodded solemnly. "What am I going to tell Spike?"

"Tell him you're investing in his future but uncovering the exact worth of his inheritance."

Gemini scrunched her face and tried to look over Zeke's shoulder. "I'm worried about your uncle. He went back there and we haven't seen him since."

Zeke was stoic, but Feather knew they could out "quiet" him.

"Now I know where I recognized your face." He pointed at Gemini and grinned, his face softening. "Last month on the news they featured a new detective agency in town and the woman who came out of retirement to run it. Your reputation precedes you, Mrs. Reed. You're that local sleuth who causes headaches for the police."

Gemini stuck out her chest defiantly. "You should be happy I'm catching criminals! And I'm still worried about your uncle. Where is he?"

Feather had warned Gemini that it was a bad idea to agree to an interview, but when she saw how important it was to Gemini, being featured during Senior Spotlight Week, she backed down. Feather pulled two business cards from her pocket and handed them to the man.

"Why would you come in here with a bogus story about this pendant? I think I should hold on to it for now."

Thinking quickly, Feather reached into her purse. "These are my business cards—one for the hair salon and one for our detective agency. If you bring either of them to the salon, I'll give you a haircut, free of charge."

Zeke rubbed his balding head. "Don't have much on my head these days, but I'm sure the wife would appreciate it."

As he reached for the cards, Feather pulled her hand back. "Pendant first."

"I'm going to keep track of you ladies—both of you." He wagged a finger in front of one woman's face and then the other. "Come back and I'll make sure my uncle is out here, ready to greet you!"

"Fair enough," Feather answered quickly, pushing on Gemini's back to make their exit.

Chapter Twenty-Four

Gemini

"I call this meeting of the Hawkites to order."

Mick hit a gavel on the folding table, causing everyone's Styrofoam coffee cups to jiggle and some to spill.

"You gonna introduce her?" a grizzled man asked, gesturing towards Gemini.

Mick glanced at Gemini and nodded. "This is a friend of my dad's. Her name's Gemini Reed. She's got some questions and I told her she could come to our discussion."

Gemini cleared her throat and carefully moved her cup to the center of the table as she stood. "Yes, hi. I'm hoping you all can help. There's a—"

"We don't do heavy discussions until we've gone through all of the procedural stuff," a heavyset woman wearing a black t-shirt that read "Area 51, Just the Beginning," said. "I promise, you'll get your chance."

Gemini sat back down, her face burning with embarrassment.

"Okay, it's time for the financial report," Mick continued. "Elvis? Whatcha got?"

All eyes focused on a laptop computer set up at the end of the table. The man onscreen looked down as he spoke.

"Five of us attended last month's Timespast Con. We had a booth where we sold buttons, pins and Marilyn's book, *Last Century When I was Old*. We ended up making about four thousand dollars."

Gemini's mouth dropped open. For an organization she'd never heard about, they were doing quite well.

"Good enough. That should give us enough working capital to buy trinkets for the fall market." Mick shuffled his papers before pulling one out. "I guess the next report is the travelers themselves. Amelia Earhart? You ready?"

The lady sitting next to Gemini, who had been knitting a baby blanket, leaned over and whispered in Gemini's ear. "These aren't our real names. It's all confidential, so most of us use the names of deaths we don't believe were accidental." She elbowed Gemini and winked. "But you already knew that. Right, 'Gemini'?"

Gemini nodded, unwilling to tell her name origin story to this stranger.

"Yeah, me and Abraham Lincoln did a jump last week," Amelia Earhart began. "We set the calendometer to 1547, but for some reason we ended up in 1985. Still have that nasty hairspray smell in my nostrils."

"Gotta look into that, Elvis. It's the second time someone has ended up in the wrong century," Marilyn admonished.

Mick raised his hand, acknowledging he heard. He must be Elvis.

Amelia Earhart rubbed her nose before continuing, "I know we're documenting research, but when JFK suggested a scavenger hunt, I went with it. Following the group post directive, I picked up..." She paused as she opened a paper bag. "A chia pet!"

One woman opened her mouth and Eleanor put up her hand in protest. "Don't worry, I didn't violate the charter code by bringing back an animal. This thing is all plant."

"Pass it around!"

Dutifully, she handed it to the next person over.

"Thank you, Amelia. We'll expect a full trip report written by next meeting," Mick said. "New business?"

The room was suddenly quiet.

"That's you, honey!" the knitting lady said, nudging Gemini.

"Oh, okay." Gemini stood and smoothed her aqua-colored shirt. "Let me see." She paused a moment to collect her thoughts. "I'm a private detective and my partner and I are working on a case involving possible time travel."

She explained everything she knew about Lyle and Lucinda. Following the group's tradition, she called them Wendell and Wilma. When she finished, she clasped her hands together, waiting for snickers.

When none came, Gemini relaxed a bit.

"It sounds like you've got several things going on there, Gemini," Amelia Earhart said. "First, the guy who's missing is either faking his disappearance, or he's using a completely different method of time travel."

"Wouldn't be unheard of," knitting lady said. "Remember last year, when we came across someone who pretended to use a portal in Tellum? Thank goodness our fearless leader shut that down before it ruined our reputation." She used a knitting needle to gesture her approval toward Mick.

There was a murmur of agreement in the room.

"How do I find out? What is my next step?"

"Well, first we need to go back ourselves to the exact date and time when your cousin supposedly jumped. We're pretty good sleuths ourselves, especially Buddy Holly." Mick pointed to a tiny man who sat in the corner. He seemed nervous, continually taking his glasses on and off, on and off.

"I'll do it, Gemini," he said quietly.

"I can pay you... Buddy. For your time and your journey. Whatever you need."

There was an audible gasp in the room.

"What? Did I say something wrong?" she asked. "Again?"

"Our code of ethics prevents us from time traveling for money. We're here for the love of science and discovery. We make our money through conferences. But thank you for the offer, Gemini," Mick said.

She made a mental note to send an anonymous donation when this was all over with.

"You said there was something else, Amelia?"

"Yes, you should check to make sure your cousin isn't hiding in plain sight."

This suggestion offended her. "Are you insinuating that I don't know how to do my business?"

"Of course not. It's just that we've had some instances where people swore their relatives time traveled and once we did some investigating of our own, we discovered they skipped town. It was a convenient way to slip away from their obligations. Isn't that right, Elvis?"

Mick nodded solemnly.

"You have my contact information, Mick... er, Elvis. I've got many things on my list today." She stood and glanced around the room. "Thank you all for inviting me. I'll look forward to your report."

Walking quickly, she was almost to the door before knitting lady caught her arm. "Did we do something to offend you, honey? I'm Eleanor. Roosevelt. But you can call me Eleanor."

"No, nothing at all. I'm not used to this kind of format. I've been out of the work world for too long." Gemini dug in her purse for her keys, pulling out a note that read "graduation gift for Taurus" instead.

"I get it. We're not a bunch of kooks. Though the

jury's still out on Thomas Jefferson." She rolled her eyes.

"We'll find your cousin. Or at least prove he isn't where he says he is."

Gemini nodded.

Though the group had been very kind to her, she couldn't help but feel as though they didn't trust her. They weren't alone; she wasn't entirely comfortable with them either.

She tossed and turned all night. Whether it was arthritis or troubling thoughts about Lyle, she couldn't be sure.

At six a.m., she gave up and went into the kitchen to make herself some tea. Gemini was transferring her mug from the counter to the table when she heard a thunk against her door.

"Too early for the paper," she mused. The young boy who delivered papers on their block was slow to rise and some days his mother ended up doing most of the delivering after he was in school.

She opened the door slowly, reminded of Tug's cautionary tale about the woman whose house was burglarized when she opened the door without looking through her window to make sure it was someone she knew first.

Looking around, Gemini didn't find anyone, but she could hear Howard's front door closing. On her porch sat a basket of his blueberry cornmeal muffins and an assortment of expensive teas.

"Thank you, Howard!" she called, though she realized there was no way he could hear.

Inside the basket was a note that read simply, "Your friendship is appreciated."

Her phone rang and she answered without looking at the caller ID.

"Howard, I'm happy to help any time. That's what friends are—"

"Mother?" Sophia sounded disappointed that she'd reached her intended party. "I thought you'd still be in bed."

"I couldn't sleep."

"Is it your arthritis? Are you feeling ill? You know Brandon offered to get you in to see a specialist in Portland."

"No, but thank you." She sighed. "I'm concerned about my neighbor."

"Oh. Well, I'm on my way to hot yoga and that's why I called particularly early. I don't have time for discussion."

It was too early for this nonsense. "Just spit it out, Sophia. Then you can be on your way."

"No need to be rude, Mother. Do you remember at the funeral, when I told you that cousin Pedro wanted to give me information?"

"Yes, I do."

"He called me last night. He went up to Happy Face Lake for old time's sake. His Aunt Lucinda asked him to clean it before she puts it up for sale while he was there. He found some very peculiar things, Mother."

She paused, as she always did, for dramatic effect. Gemini pictured her daughter with her tongue in her cheek, the manner she used to display her "I know something you don't know" face. Now was not a good time to mention she and Feather had already taken a trip out there.

"And?"

"And he wanted me to see for myself."

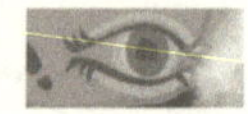

Chapter Twenty-Five
Feather

While they were eating their lunch, Jayden had explained how Feather might rid herself and Millicent of the evil entity. "You understand, doll?"

"I do." She had complete confidence in Jayden, and considerably less in herself.

Feather kissed Tug goodbye. It was the first time she'd kissed him since the showdown in the office. When their lips met, she felt like she was home.

Why had she insisted on punishing him?

"I missed this," she said breathlessly.

Tug grabbed the back of her head and kissed her back with all of his pent-up emotion. When he released her, he stared at his other half adoringly. "Let's not do this again, okay? It just about killed me."

"From now on, we talk about everything. No silent treatment," Feather agreed.

"Are you coming in to work today? I mean, you

don't have to come in. And by that, I don't mean that someone is there, waiting in the wings. But if you do—"

She wrapped her arms around him and hugged him tightly. "You don't have to worry about me anymore. I understand why everyone did what they did. I'll be in later, after I take care of this problem with Millicent."

Tug's face was pinched with concern. "You're sure? I could wait for you. Olive wanted extra time to get ready today because her new man is picking her up for dinner."

Feather took one of his hands and kissed his fingertips. "I'm positive. You won't even sit down before I get there."

Tug glanced outside, where it was beginning to rain again. "I sure wish your car was ready. My buddy promised he'd have it done by now."

"Go!" she yelled half-jokingly.

"Okay, I suppose." Tug walked toward the door and then paused. "Don't worry about dinner. I'm making my Tug-a-ziti. You told me that's your favorite, right?"

"With the garlic knots? I can't wait!"

She followed him to the door, closing and locking it when he was gone. She leaned against it for a moment, collecting her thoughts. "I'll do this for you, Millicent," she said out loud.

The way Jayden had explained it, all Feather

needed to do was show this evil entity she wasn't afraid of it and it would leave.

"You can do this, Jones. You're good at your job."

She made her way to the spare bedroom. Instead of sitting on the floor as she did every time she spoke with Millicent, she remained in the standing position. She wanted to be ready to run, if needed.

"Oh Millicent!" Feather said in a sing-song voice. "Where are you? I'm ready to play!"

Jayden told her to address the entity as Millicent because it obviously liked playing this game with her.

Her shoulders tightened in anticipation of what might come next. When nothing did, she called again. "If you're hiding from me, please come out, honey! You know I don't have much time!"

She moved in a circle, examining every space of the room. The one thing she didn't want to do was look under the bed. When she'd first become acquainted with Millicent, the little girl wanted to play hide-and-seek. Feather had the scare of her life when she had seen two glowing eyes under the bed as she lifted the skirt.

The closet doors were open, so this entity couldn't hide there. Sighing, she gave in and sat on the floor. Feather leaned forward and lifted a corner of the bed skirt. Nothing. That was a relief.

Feeling a tap on her shoulder, she turned around and said, "There you are, sweet—"

She gasped and then screamed. It wasn't Millicent, or someone pretending to be her. It was the remnants of a man. His face was half-gone, eaten off by some-thing, and his eyes glowed red. Her chest felt heavy just like it did before she got into the accident.

Standing quickly, she placed her hands on her hips in an effort to make herself look larger. *Don't let them know you're afraid, doll.*

"Who are you and why are you here?" she yelled. "Your silly antics don't scare me, so let's move on."

Was that hurt on his half-face? It was hard to tell.

Feather Jones, you're interrupting a very important operation. Cease now!

She chuckled. "You'll have to be more specific than that."

Quit investigating the origins of the jewelry and I'll return your girl.

"What?" That wasn't at all what she was expecting. "You mean the jewelry we took to the antique dealer? What does that have to do with a man whose face looks like it went through a lawn mower?"

He moved closer to her, and with that, a scent filled her nostrils. It wasn't caramel corn. *What was it?*

As he inched forward, the smell became over-whelming, causing her to cough. "Stop!" she said between coughs. "This isn't helping!" She bent over and placed her hands on her knees, trying to regain her composure.

You want something from me?

Feather stood, surprised. "I do!" She thought quickly. "Return Millicent and explain why the pendant is so important. Or... just a clue. Oh, and tell me how you're connected to my accident."

She knew it was asking a lot, but if she didn't put everything on the table, she'd regret it later.

The girl thinks she's worth more to me than she is. Instead, she only brings Saltash Luck.

"I don't understand what you're saying. Meet my demands or my friends and I will use our combined powers to remove you!"

Jayden told her she wasn't sure that would work, and it was only to be used as a last resort. Feather hoped the entity didn't know that.

A gust of wind swirled around Feather, causing the printing paper to dance in the air and her green-tipped hair to dip annoyingly in her eyes. When it ended, she heard something fall on the floor. The heaviness was gone.

As she bent down to pick it up, she heard Millicent's squeaky voice. "My dear Feather! You found me!"

Feather wasn't about to admit it, but she was afraid that it was another trick. "I'm so sorry I put you in harm's way. Are you in trouble with your parents?" she asked, keeping her eyes closed.

Millicent shook her head. "They thought I was playing hide-and-seek. Why won't you look at me? Aren't we friends anymore?"

Feather opened her eyes, relieved to see a small girl in front of her. "Who was it, this ghost who hid you?"

Millicent twisted back and forth shyly, causing her white pinafore to swish. "You know!"

Here we go again. "Millicent, I don't—"

"Mother is calling for dinner! I'll see you tomorrow, dear Feather! I love you ever-so-much!"

"Millicent! Wait!"

It was no use. The girl was gone before she could extract any more information from her. She remembered the plunking sound she heard after the half-faced man left and looked at the floor.

There, beside her foot, was a gold button.

CHAPTER TWENTY-SIX
GEMINI

Gemini was nervous.

It wasn't as if Feather and Sophia hadn't been together before; Feather and Tug attended several family dinners. Gemini made a point of inviting them when Sophia, Brandon and Taurus were in town. If she was being honest, it was a good way to water down Sophia's overreaction to every little thing. With more conversation going on, she had less time to make the color of the carrots or the number of ice cubes in her glass an issue.

It was more a matter of Sophia's insecurities. She sensed, from the very first dinner, that Sophia felt jealous or competitive of Feather. If Feather told a funny story from the salon, Sophia had a better one from her own "high-end" salon. When Feather spoke of her gym time with Tug, Sophia's yoga classes became the topic of conversation. Whatever Feather said, Sophia could top it.

Under different circumstances, Gemini might have found it humorous. At the last dinner, she spoke privately with Sophia about her love and devotion for her only child. It appeared Sophia understood, until today, when all three women were in the same car together.

"Being in the forest always gives me a sense of calm," Feather remarked as they drove down a long, tree-lined gravel driveway.

"Mother, do you remember when we planted trees out here? I was seven or eight. These trees out the window are most likely some of my handiwork."

As the car came to a stop in front of the stately home, Feather said, "Gem, someone is calling to me."

Sophia sniffed, her dissatisfaction evident.

Gemini got out and nodded to Feather. She was impressed by the self-control she showed when in Sophia's presence. Not once did she take the bait.

"I'm going to take a walk. You two go inside and I'll join you soon."

Gemini waved to Feather as she bent down to find the key. Sophia placed her hand on her mother's arm before Gemini could place the key in the lock.

"Honestly, Mother, I'm renewing my objection to her hocus pocus. I know you won't listen, but I'm going on record with my skepticism."

It did no good to try and persuade Sophia that something out of her comfort zone was beneficial. In fact, Sophia relished the idea of arguing about anything. Some days, Gemini didn't have the mental strength for the challenge.

"You are entitled to feel how you want, daughter. But let me say two things."

"Here we go." Sophia rolled her large green eyes and flipped her long wavy hair behind her shoulder. "Sophia's dumb. Sophia doesn't know anything."

"When have I ever said that about you, Sophia?" Gemini took a deep breath and collected her thoughts. "What I wanted you to know was that she's no different than that fancy astrologer you pay thousands of dollars to see every month. And—"

"Reading star signs is a science, Mother!" Sophia retorted.

Gemini raised her hand in protest. "I'm not arguing with you today. Let me finish. The second thing I wanted to tell you is that you had no problem with Feather's abilities when Taurus's teacher needed to find where her grandfather put his will."

Four months ago, Feather was called to Sophia's house to do a "thingy" where she spoke with the grandfather in question. She was given his belt and a shoe and Sophia expected her to get a reading from that.

Surprisingly, she did. The will was in the back of the freezer, behind frozen rib eye steaks. Sophia offered to pay her double her going rate, but Feather politely (and wisely) refused.

"When you lose all of this money you've sunk into this far-fetched business venture, just don't come to me or Brandon with your story of woe." Sophia gestured toward the still-locked door. "I've got a massage at six, so we need to be expedient."

"Why don't I take the upstairs while you're perusing the main floor?" Gemini said, eager for a break from her daughter. Pedro told Sophia she needed to scour the entire home, but Sophia was very mysterious as to what, exactly, they were looking for.

Gemini moved slowly up the steps, noticing her knees were a little more creaky than usual. When she got to the top, she found bedrooms on either side of the staircase.

Entering the first room to her left, she was surprised to find a bright, welcoming room with large windows and lots of light. It wasn't how she remembered it at all. The bedrooms all had a stark feeling when the cabin was owned jointly by the cousins.

There was a patchwork quilt covering a four-poster, wood-framed bed and a dresser with pictures of family members on the dresser.

Before becoming a detective, she did sleuthing work for Brandon's law office. Sitting outside someone's home and watching for them to walk out when they said they were wheelchair bound was one thing, but digging through a living person's private dresser was quite another.

Finding nothing of interest, she peeked under the bed and in the closet before moving on to the next room.

This one was almost identical to the last bedroom, except that it included a bathroom.

She entered the bathroom first, surprised to find an open bottle of lotion, a comb and a wet toothbrush. Everything else was immaculate, and it was safe to assume Lucinda paid a cleaning service to come out.

Gemini opened the curtain to the shower/tub to a shocking sight.

The tub was covered in blood—evenly coated, not splattered. There wasn't a pool of blood near the drain like someone bled out, which left her with more questions.

"Was someone killed here? Or did they leave their body here after killing them?"

She opened her purse and pulled out the testing kit she'd ordered from Detective Monthly, the online magazine for professional detectives, and a pair of plastic gloves.

Gingerly, she scraped a sample of the red substance and smeared it on the slide. She retrieved the travel bottle of hydrogen peroxide she kept in her purse and an eye dropper, dropping a few drops of the substance on top of the slide. Immediately, it began to bubble, a sign that it was truly blood. "Thought so. Too many years in the paint store means I can pick out paint at a distance."

Next, Gemini picked up the blood-covered soap.

Underneath that spot, it was perfectly clean and dry. Replacing it, she examined the shampoo bottle. *Peculiar.* There were bloody fingerprints on the bottle, so she placed it in a biohazard bag she'd brought along.

"Mother?" Sophia called. "Mother? Where are you?"

"Don't come in here!" Gemini warned. She wasn't in the mood for Sophia's hysterics. Gemini placed the test kit in its own biohazard bag and tucked it back in her over-sized bag before opening the bathroom door.

"What's going on in here?" Sophia asked, ignoring her mother's warning. She entered the bathroom as Gemini shut the curtain.

"You found something odd in the tub, didn't you?" She attempted to push past her mother, but Gemini stood firm.

"No, Sophia. This is detective work. Tell me what you found downstairs."

Sophia huffed. It was always hurtful that she didn't believe her mother was an actual detective. "You'll have to follow me." Obediently, Gemini trailed behind her daughter.

When they reached the bottom of the stairs, Sophia stopped abruptly, causing Gemini to run into the back of her daughter.

"Mother, I know you're a little... delicate. What I've got to show you may be hard to see. If you would prefer not to—"

"Just show me!" Gemini snapped.

Sophia stepped aside and followed Gemini into the formal dining room. The table was set for dinner. There were eight place settings. Gemini observed the pale green plates: each was engraved in the center with the letter L.

"It looks like someone came in and staged it for the sale," Gemini remarked. While she did find it odd that there were no plates set out on her previous visit, it was her turn to be dismissive. "I don't understand why you thought that would upset me."

Sophia said nothing, pointing to the place setting closest to Gemini.

Gemini stared at the table. When she realized what was right in front of her, she gasped in horror.

"Cousin Lucinda is a murderer!" Sophia cried. "This is why Pedro insisted I come to the house. He knew there weren't any other cousins who had the stamina for this. Brandon always says I've got a cool head when things are—"

Gemini forced a laugh. "I can see why you'd think those were real. I've seen lots of these props since becoming a detective." She smiled, but not too broadly to avoid suspicion. "Those severed fingers are nothing more than elaborate toys. Your cousin Pedro is playing tricks on you."

"Really? He sent us up here to have a laugh?" Sophia stared up at the ceiling. "If you're listening, and I'm sure you are, I'm not finding this humorous, Pedro!" Glancing back down at her mother, she said, "This has been a childish prank. I can't believe I fell for it."

For a brief moment, Gemini wondered if they were safe. Whoever did this may still be lurking around. "Your cousin went to great lengths to make sure we saw this. Are you sure he didn't say anything else?"

"Mother, I can assure you he didn't. I never would have agreed to this field trip otherwise." Sophia rubbed her forehead. "All of this funhouse horror has given me a headache. Can we please just finish this farce and leave?"

Gemini noticed her daughter was shaking. "Sweetheart, you don't have to be here. I know its unsettling. I've been at many crime scenes, so I'm used to these types of things."

"It's NOT a crime scene," Sophia scoffed. "But I do feel a little weak."

If she could remember the names of Sophia's fancy remedies, now would be the time she'd suggest one. "I'm going to take a quick pass through the kitchen. You go ahead and wait in the car. Tilt the seat back and close your eyes."

Gemini proceeded into a room off the kitchen. It was known as the Reed Memories Room, where items of significance to the family were held. This was where family albums, old pictures, clothing and old electronics were set up as if it were a museum display. She gasped when she realized a case containing old clothing was open. As she moved in closer, Gemini discovered the lock was missing and there were bloody fingerprints on the glass.

She took a quick picture and moved into the next room.

The massive kitchen had two of every appliance and a large workspace, as large as Gemini's entire main floor. She began opening drawers. What she was looking for in this house of horrors, she didn't know.

Sophia, to her mother's dismay, had followed her. She began opening drawers on the other side of the room. "Oh no!"

Gemini rushed over to the other side of the kitchen, where Sophia was pointing to a magnetic strip that held many knives. One had bloody fingerprints on the handle.

Gemini slipped her readers on and examined the knife. "Oh, yes. I do see. Someone didn't wash the knife after they cooked." She removed it quickly and placed it on the counter behind her, hoping Sophia didn't have a chance to see the fingerprints.

"Hmph." Sophia's disapproval didn't surprise Gemini. "I knew that, Mother. I was just pointing it out for you to see. Your vision isn't what it used to be."

Gemini's phone rang.

"This isn't a good time, I'm afraid."

"Didn't mean to bother you, Gemini. This is Elvis, actually Mick. Just wanted you to know that Buddy Holly was the unfortunate victim of a heart attack upon re-entry. I'm afraid he wasn't able to tell us any more about Lyle."

CHAPTER TWENTY-SEVEN

"Sorry I took so long," Feather said, breathless. She met Gemini at the front door of the two-story log cabin home, just as she was closing the door. "I've gotten some good information. It's possible that Lyle—"

"Mother and I have good information too," Sophia interrupted, joining them on the porch. "My cousin was just pulling one over on us. There was really nothing at all going on. You see? We solved the mystery and we didn't even need to talk to pretend ghosts."

Gemini rolled her eyes. "What did you learn, Feather?"

"It *is* possible someone time traveled. There is a spirit out in the woods who is related to Leo and Lucinda. He says he's been watching over the property for three decades."

Gemini coughed for several minutes and then asked, "Did you catch a name?"

Feather shook her head. "I think I've mentioned before how some spirits come through clear and others sound like an old-time radio, a faint crackling sound. It was hard to decipher. Mateo?"

"That's all you got?" Sophia sniffed. "Sounds bogus to me."

Gemini gave her a sharp look. Feather always understood Sophia's behavior, but it embarrassed Gemini nonetheless.

"He knows you, Gem," Feather continued, unfazed. "He watches every family event and knows everyone by name. That's why he was willing to open up to me. There has been lots of activity out here this year. Lyle often came out here with friends."

"How could you know that?" Sophia asked with skepticism.

Feather pulled bits of burnt paper out of her pocket. "The entity told me they sat around a campfire, talking about a business venture. I dug around the fire pit and the only thing that was legible was this paper. It's got some kind of symbol at the top and underneath are four names—Lyle Lime, Mick Everson, George Mint and Jenner Mamery. That's all that I could find that was still legible."

Sophia grabbed the torn bits of paper from Feather's hands. "Give them to me. I have excellent vision."

She squinted as she read off the names. "Lyle Lime, Mick Everson, George Mint and... it's not Jenner Mamery. It's Jasper Montgomery. It's a receipt from an antique store? J and M?"

Gemini and Feather exchanged shocked looks. "J and M Antiques! It's too coincidental!" Gemini gasped. She leaned over and stared at the paper. At the top was a symbol, what looked like three commas within a circle.

"Do you think Jasper is making fake jewels and selling them in his antique store?" Feather asked. "I got the sense there was a lot of shame on this property."

"Did another ghost tell you that? Or do you talk to forest animals too?" Sophia asked, her face stuck in smirk-mode. "We are most definitely NOT going back inside that place. I'm going to have nightmares the way it is."

"Oh, shoot. I accidentally took that ring you showed me." Gemini produced a piece of jewelry from her pocket. "I don't want to steal anything. Whatever game Lucinda is playing, I don't want her to think she's caught us removing her property. Again."

She coughed again, this time bending over when it wouldn't stop. "I'm sorry, ladies. If I'm truly coming down with something, I'll need to make my special tea before it catches hold."

Feather reached for Gemini, but Sophia blocked her hand and placed her arm around her mother's waist.

"We'll get you home, Mother. This was all a waste of time anyway."

"You guys wait in the car, I'll return the ring," Feather offered. She wasn't feeling especially enthusiastic about going inside, given Sophia and Gemini's faces as they left.

Gemini removed the ring from her pocket and reached for Feather. "Oh, shoot. I left my makeup case upstairs in a guest room bathroom."

"I'll get it for you, Mother," Sophia said firmly.

"No, I'd like to do it myself. Take one last look around, for old time's sake."

At first it looked as though Sophia wouldn't allow her mother this one last trip down memory lane. "Fine. I'll wait for you both in the car."

When they'd both watched Sophia seat herself, they walked inside.

"Take a finger from the dining room. I need to check something."

"Huh?" Feather frowned, unsure if she heard her friend correctly. It wouldn't be the first time Gemini had made an unusual request of her, but it was certainly the strangest.

Gemini disappeared up the long, wooden staircase. Feather didn't relish the thought of looking for a finger, but she trusted Gemini implicitly.

Carefully, she crept into the dining room, immediately spotting the fingers. Using a royal blue placemat, she rolled one finger inside and did her best to stuff it in her pocket. *Please don't fall out, please don't fall out.*

"Gem? Is there anything else?"

Hearing no sounds, she took it upon herself to walk around the main floor. It all looked similar to their last visit, except things were tidier. There were no books lying on the floor by the fireplace, and the couch looked like it had been steam cleaned.

She picked up a pillow and held it tight, waiting for any spirit lurking about to speak to her.

I've got the best invention, Feather Weather!

"Not now, Daisy. Please let the other spirits come through."

Feather sat in silence for a few minutes.

She jumped when Gemini appeared.

"What did you have to find? I know it's not your makeup case; it's in your fuchsia bag. It doesn't fit in the blue-striped bag you brought today."

"I want to show you something." Gemini motioned for Feather to follow her to the kitchen. When they arrived, Gemini pulled a knife from her bag and laid it on the counter. Next, she unlocked her phone and displayed a picture.

"What do you see?"

Feather studied the picture. It was a picture of a shampoo bottle with bloody fingerprints on it. The knife was also covered in bloody prints. "I see carnage. Is that what you mean?"

"No, I want you to look at the pattern of those prints. Notice anything?"

She looked at them again. This time, a light bulb went off over her head. "They are exactly the same! Same distance between the fingers—"

"No one, especially not someone who has been bloodied, takes the time to make sure their fingers are the same distance apart when grabbing an item. There's one more thing."

Gemini pointed to the picture of the shampoo bottle. "Do you see how the thumb print is on the bottom?"

Feather giggled. "Nobody grabs a bottle from the bottom!"

"Exactly! This was set up to make us think a horrible event took place at this cabin. But whoever did the staging had the skill of a fourteen-year-old creating a haunted house."

"Sophia's cousin? But why?"

"I have my suspicions. I took the shampoo bottle and a sample of blood from the bathtub, also staged. I'm sending it off to a lab as soon as we get back. That should confirm this is all an elaborate hoax."

As they pulled the door shut, Feather whispered, "Tomorrow, we go over everything we know so far."

The sun was dipping below the coastal mountain range, causing Sophia to shade her eyes as she watched them. "You put the key back, right?"

"I did, sweetheart!" Gemini called.

She walked around to the back of the car and hollered, "Could you pop the trunk, Sophia? I put some snacks in there before we left home and I'm kind of hungry now."

The trunk lid opened. Gemini carefully placed her large bag in the trunk and nodded to Feather.

"What is taking so long? Are you two hatching a plot to get rid of me?"

"No, dear. Feather wanted to retrieve the snacks she bought at the convenience store before we left town."

"Got it!" Feather yelled.

When they were all seated and back on the road, Gemini asked, "Do you think we should stop when we get back to town and vacuum all of this gravel off the floor? I know how Brandon likes his vehicles to look pristine, inside and out."

Sophia huffed. "Honestly, Mother. You act like I'm incapable of basic chores. The maid vacuumed the entire car last week."

Gemini turned and winked at Feather.

Chapter Twenty-Eight
Gemini

"Mrs. Reed? We've found some information for you."

Gemini tapped the table with the hand not holding her phone.

She'd been debating what to do about Mick Everson ever since their trip up to Happy Face Lake. When she'd first met him, he acted as though he'd never met Lyle before, but Feather found proof he was there, at least once, with Lyle. Mick even gave her reasons that Lyle may be lying. But now that a member of the Hawkites had died—presumably on a mission for her—she felt uncomfortable confronting Mick.

"That's wonderful, Mick. What did you find?"

There was a pause. "We'd like you to come to another meeting. One of our rules is that we never share outside of the group setting."

At least she would be safe there. The knitting lady didn't take nonsense from anyone.

"When is your next meeting?"

"Tomorrow night. Seven o'clock, same location."

"I'll be there. Oh, and Mick? I feel terrible about Buddy Holly. Can I have his home address, so that I may send condolences to his family?"

"Not allowed. Sorry."

As she dropped her phone into her large purse, she thought about how she might approach Mick about the disturbing scene at the cabin. But for now, there were more pressing issues.

She needed to check on Howard before continuing on to the warehouse. When she knocked on the door, she was surprised by his swift response. He opened the door and grinned. His cheeks were pink and his eyes sparkled.

"Howard! You're looking more like your old self!"

"I FEEL like my old self, Gemini!"

"What brought about the change?"

"My attorney feels there is no merit to this case. The insurance company can insist I made a fraudulent claim as much as they want, but I found the appraisal I had done on it last year. He's drafting a letter with that information and then it will be over."

"I'm heading in to work. Can I bring you dinner?"

He shook his head. "No need. I'm putting together a nice venison chili. Care to join me?"

"Of course. I'll be home by five. Oh, and Howard? You should know, I've been in contact with your college friend from the FBI."

Last summer, Constance Butterfly stopped in

Charming on her way to visit her grandchildren. Howard invited Gemini over for dinner and the three of them laughed and talked until almost midnight.

When it was time to say goodnight, Constance handed Gemini her business card. "This has my home phone on the back, just for special people like you. Even though I've retired, I still have contacts. You may have the need for a lab to process data you've collected, and I can make that happen. If you're ever stuck while working on a case, give me a call."

"Hope she can be of help. See you this evening!"

She breathed a sigh of relief that Howard didn't ask for details regarding their phone call. He had enough to worry about without the description of the gruesome scene at the cabin.

All the way to the warehouse, she tried putting the pieces together. Mick had no idea she would ask him about his group of time travelers, so she could chalk that up to coincidence.

Lyle rarely made trips into Charming. He'd only been to see Leo twice.

"That's it!" She slammed on her brakes, thankful that she lived in a small town without much traffic.

Instead of heading west toward Kindred Spirits Detective Agency, she turned east, toward Charming Acres Assisted Living.

She didn't even bother parking in the special parking spot designated for her by the staff at the care facility. She took the first open space and bound out of her car, for the front door.

"Mrs. Reed! What a surprise!"

Suzanne stood and leaned over the welcome desk for a hug.

"I'm in a hurry today, Suzanne. Can you tell me where Trent is?"

"I can call him to the front if you like."

"Please do."

She tapped her fingers impatiently on the desk while she waited.

"This must be very important. It's not like you to get to business before you stop to see Leo."

She felt a pang of guilt. "I... I don't have time right now. I needed to clear something up with Trent and then I have to get to work."

"Where do you work? Surely you're retired by now."

Was it worth the eye roll to tell Suzanne she was a private detective? Probably not.

"This and that. Odd jobs. Have to keep the mind busy, you know."

Trent appeared at the front desk. He, too, was surprised by Gemini's presence.

"Not used to seeing you out in the lobby. What can I do you for?" he asked jovially.

"Can we speak somewhere in private?"

Trent's expression changed. "We can go into the chapel."

When they were inside, he said, "I sure hope I didn't do something in my care of Leo that you didn't like. He's one of my favorite patients and I try to keep him as comfortable as possible. If you have a problem, please let me fix it before you go to the administration."

"No, it's not about your job, dear."

"Oh good." His shoulders sagged with relief. "What is it then?"

"You introduced me to your friend, Mick. Do you remember that?"

"Yeah."

"That same day, I looked at the visitor log book. Do you know what I found?"

He frowned. "Can't say as I do."

"Lyle was here, visiting Leo. Twice. And both times, Mick was here too. I don't believe in coincidences, no matter how hard I try and convince myself otherwise."

"I'm not sure what that has to do with me."

"It's all too neat and tidy. You told me about Mick's group of time travelers but that isn't something that comes up in casual conversation. I believe Mick, or Mick and Lyle, asked you to give me that information."

He stared hard at Gemini. "Where would you get that idea?"

"Don't play games with me, Trent. We've spent too much time as friends for you to treat me like that. If that's how you want to operate, I'll have no choice but to go to the administration. I can't have a known liar in charge of my Leo's care."

Trent glanced around nervously. "Okay! But please don't say anything to Mick. He did ask me to give you his number. Mick said he knew you were interested in time travel and he could help."

She tapped one finger on her chin. "How odd. I hadn't mentioned it to anyone outside of my agency before that day."

"He paid me two hundred dollars to connect you two. I can give it back, if you want."

He reached into the pocket of his scrubs and pulled out a worn, brown wallet.

She grabbed his arm and patted it with her other hand. "No, that's not necessary. You work hard here and you should be rewarded. Thank you for being truthful."

"Is there anything else? I should get back to work. My break isn't for another hour."

"Yes. I will pay you handsomely if you hear anything else about time travel from Mick or his family."

"You don't have to pay me, Mrs.—"

"I insist. I'll double his donation to you. That way you don't have to incur financial hardship."

Once he'd agreed to relay the information, she headed to Leo's room. When she found his bed empty, a doctor making his rounds called out, "He's getting a bath."

It was for the best. She couldn't wait to share what she'd learned with Feather. They were both making real progress on their cases.

When she arrived, Feather's eyes were red rimmed.

She sat on Tug's lap with her arms clasped around his massive neck.

"What's wrong, hon?" she asked, depositing her purse in her drawer.

"Feath had a visit from her Aunt Tandy. She's a little shaken," Tug replied, gently running his fingers up and down her back.

"Last I heard, she was very firm in her plans to keep you at arm's length. Did something change?"

"You could say that," Feather sniffed. "She went to Candy's grave to leave flowers. When she got there, she found graffiti all over the headstone. Aunt Tandy, along with everyone else in the family, blames me."

Gemini frowned. "That's ridiculous. What did the graffiti say?"

"See for yourself," Feather said, sliding a photograph across the table.

Gemini examined the printed page. "Homewrecker!"

She slid the page back. "What in the world could they mean by that? And why now?"

"I thought about that this morning. My whole childhood, the grown-ups whispered about her active social life. I thought that meant she went to movies. By the time I was old enough to understand, Aunt Candy was in her seventies and whatever relationship she'd had was long over. Because I visited Tandy and asked about Candy recently—"

"Your Aunt Tandy believes you desecrated her sister's grave," Gemini said with disgust. "That's unbelievable. Anyone who knows you knows you'd never intentionally hurt anyone."

"You should have seen it, Gem. Tandy came in here, screaming and yelling. She said she was going to call the police and have your agency shut down. I offered to give her a tour of my factory and a case of Tug Bars. Flavors of her choosing."

"There are definite advantages to having a hot boyfriend." Feather leaned her head against Tug's. "She was flattered by his attention."

"We have our work cut out for us, then. Could your Millicent be of help?"

"That's a great idea! I'll ask her tonight." Feather wiped her eyes with the backs of her hands and stood. "You've got that order to fill for Phit Phil's Gyms by this afternoon. I shouldn't keep you."

"There is nothing more important than you, my love," Tug said, standing as well. "I'll take you to lunch at the Tickled Egg. You've been raving about that place ever since you went with Jayden. That will give me plenty of time to drop off this order. Maybe you should go home and rest."

"I'm fine, Tug. Really," Feather insisted. "Gem, tell him I'm fine."

She hated when they put her in the middle of their conversations. She studied Feather's face and her body language. "She's fine, Tug. She needs a Tug Bar and some juice and she'll be right as rain."

The mention of his product always excited Tug. "What kind can I get you, babe? Olive just finished

Blackberry Bold yesterday. Blackberry with a touch of hot sauce. It's better than you'd think."

"Sure. Bring that to me. And a coffee."

When he was gone, she nodded toward Gemini. "Thanks for that."

"You're welcome. I know that if you went home, you'd feel worse. We need to put our minds to our business, and that will be all the distraction you need."

"Did you hear anything back from your FBI friend? You know, about the finger and the blood?"

"I overnighted it to the lab in Portland, just like she instructed. She put a rush on the order, so we should know something soon." Gemini shook her head. "It helps to have friends in high places."

Her phone had been buzzing in her purse for several minutes. Since she'd just left Leo and she spoke with Sophia this morning, she knew it wasn't an emergency. After the sixth time, she opened her purse.

"Cheese and crackers! This had better be important."

She put the phone up to her ear and immediately heard, "Gemini, it's Lucinda. We need to talk. I'm coming to Charming this afternoon."

CHAPTER
TWENTY-NINE
FEATHER

"Millicent, I promise to listen to your jokes. Two of them."

Feather sat cross-legged in the spare bedroom. She'd been calling to Millicent for almost an hour. It wasn't uncommon for spirits to take their time, especially young children who were easily distracted. Tonight, though, she had important business to discuss with Millicent and she was growing impatient.

"I have a joke for you, but I can't tell you if you won't come out."

She heard rustling behind her and saw Millicent's head pop out from behind the bed. "You have a joke for me, dear Feather?"

Feather had to think quickly. "Yes, I do."

"Tell me! Tell me!"

"Not until you help me with something."

Millicent plopped down beside Feather, her white

pinafore billowing as she did. It never ceased to amaze Feather how lifelike and "living" some entities could be.

"I need to ask you two very important questions. Only someone as smart and mature as you can answer them."

The young ghost studied Feather's face. "I can never tell if you're being serious with me or not, dear Feather."

"Of course I am! Do you see any other ghosts here?"

Feather's chest tightened. Just because she couldn't see them didn't mean they weren't there.

"No, I don't. Ask me your first question."

Feather opened up her hand to show Millicent the gold button she'd found the other day. "The mean man who wouldn't let you out, he left this for me. Do you know whose button it is?"

Millicent's face twisted and "tears" ran down her face. "Why, oh why must you torture me? I was ever so scared."

"I don't mean to frighten you. He left me this clue and now I'm really confused. It looks like a button I've seen before, but I need to make sure. Please, take a look!"

After a short period of contemplation, the child glanced at Feather's open hand before turning away.

"Whose button is that?"

"I mustn't."

Feather sighed. "You can think about it while I ask you the next question. When we were out in the woods, I spoke with someone named Mateo. Do you know who that might be?"

Millicent stood and began skipping around Feather singing, "Old Man Sell, lost his well, made him oh, so thirsty. Old Man Sell found a well, made him oh so jolly."

"I can see this is upsetting you. Did Mateo do something to hurt you? Is he the mean man who wouldn't let you escape?"

Millicent stopped abruptly. "That's not his name."

Knowing she very likely misheard, Feather asked, "You're so smart, Millicent. Can you tell me his real name?"

Millicent resumed skipping. This time, she sang, "Button man, button man, found himself a tree. Button man, button man, made my dear friend flee."

Feather stood. "Are you telling me that the person who owned this button and the man, Mateo, I spoke with in the woods are one in the same? How can that be? The man I spoke with was so nice!"

Millicent stopped. "Mother's calling. It's ham and boiled potatoes."

"No! You can't leave before you've told me everything!" Feather shouted. Instantly she regretted her gruff tone. "I'm sorry, Millie. Don't go!"

The girl paused. "He said you could find him for yourself in the library." Millicent continued skipping and humming to herself as she disappeared through the wall.

"Urgh!" Feather kicked a fuzzy pillow that was

sitting beside the bed. "Why can't I have the kind of spirits who answer questions?"

Her phone rang and she looked down with relief. "Gem? Millicent wasn't very forthcoming, but I did learn, at least I think, that the button belongs to the man I spoke with at the cabin. What did you find out today?"

A smile crept over Feather's face as she listened to her friend. "So it's just as you thought. You're still meeting her tomorrow?"

CHAPTER THIRTY
GEMINI

Gemini sipped her coffee, two sugars, slowly. It was already half-past two. Lucinda said she'd be at Forty Cups by two.

"You need anything else, sweetie?"

Her favorite waitress was at least Gemini's age, or older, but she called her "sweetie" or "young lady" every time Gemini was there.

"Yes, Belva. I'm going to order your pie of the day. What is it today? Please don't tell me it's raisin again. That was cruel. I was expecting chocolate chips."

She winked at Belva, knowing it was a joke Belva told her about another customer who ordered the pie after being told it was raisin pie, and then asking to speak with the manager because it didn't contain any chocolate chips.

"On my honor, Gemini Reed. " Belva crossed her finger over her chest. "No raisins today. I think we've got a piece of marionberry and some chocolate chiffon."

"I'll have the chiffon. Oh, and I'll take that last piece of marionberry for my neighbor, Howard. He's not getting treats from a neighbor anymore. They had a... bit of a falling out."

Belva wrote on her pad and nodded. "Gossip around town is that your neighbor is losing his marbles."

Gemini gasped, horrified by that characterization. Howard was the most intelligent, together person she knew. "His marbles are all present and accounted for. You can tell whoever is gossiping to come to me if they're curious."

Belva turned, ending the conversation. She bumped into Lucinda, causing Lucinda to jump back as if she'd just touched a hot stove.

"Watch it!" Lucinda warned.

Belva shook her head before carrying on with her duties.

Lucinda sat down across from Gemini, looking as white as a sheet. Though her makeup, hair and expensive turquoise scarf draped across her chest were all exquisite, Gemini noted a sense of helplessness in her cousin-in-law.

"What is it you couldn't tell me on the phone? Seems like a long trip for this."

Gemini took a sip of her coffee. "Would you like something? I can get you a menu."

"No, I don't eat diner food."

She resisted the urge to explain that while Forty Cups was a diner, it was also a made-from-scratch restaurant that specialized in fancy sandwiches and salads. Lucinda probably wouldn't believe her anyway.

Belva returned with a piece of pie that stood at least six inches tall. Half was a lightly browned chiffon and homemade whipped cream and the rest was a thick, dark chocolate. She sat it down in front of Gemini with a fork.

"Won the prize for best chiffon at Pacific Piefest five years in a row," Belva said proudly. She sat a paper box containing Howard's pie next to Gemini.

Keeping her eyes trained on Gemini, she asked, "Your friend want anything?" Gemini glanced over at Lucinda who frowned and shook her head. "No, thank you, Belva."

Gemini's irritation with Lucinda was already greater than their last meeting. She didn't suffer fools, or snobs, kindly.

"Tell me what's going on," Gemini repeated, taking her fork and dipping it in the fluffy topping. It was a sweet cream with a hint of... was it nutmeg? She couldn't be sure, but she did know that whatever boring story Lucinda was about to tell, she would be able to immerse her senses in the pie while Leo's cousin spoke.

"Well, since I had the celebration of Lyle's life, his attorney called to ask me to come in. He said Lyle had a will we needed to discuss."

"Uh huh." Gemini dug into the rich chocolate,

savoring the first bite. It was as smooth and rich as she'd imagined. Just melted on the tongue.

"Imagine my surprise when I discovered that Lyle forbade me from selling the lake house to someone outside of the family!"

She was on her third bite of the pie, half-listening. "Can you negotiate a buy-out? Or contest the will? Don't give up yet, Lucinda."

Lucinda used her fingers, adorned with acrylic, tan-colored nails to grasp either side of the table like it was about to take off. "You're not understanding me. This is something he did to spite me. And I'll have to wait five years to have him declared legally dead. This is going to take forever!"

"If he's not legally dead, there's no will to worry about, right?"

"Lyle signed the paperwork. On the day we were to formally take over the property, I developed a horrible illness. I couldn't get out of bed. Lyle said he'd sign the paperwork and we'd get my name on it later."

"And that never happened."

This was making more sense. Lyle wanted total control.

"It shouldn't be his decision in the first place, given this was originally a Reed family dwelling." Lucinda sighed with irritation. "Now someone named Mick is calling me every day, wanting me to allow gatherings on the weekends. He said Lyle told him he could bring friends out."

Gemini dropped her fork, causing chocolate bits to

fly over to Lucinda's side of the table. "Did you say Mick? As in Everson?"

Lucinda nodded. Tears formed in her eyes even as she set her jaw to avoid them from falling. This was more emotion than she showed the day of Lyle's memorial.

"You can fight this. I used to work in my son-in-law's firm and I'm sure he would be happy to help."

Lucinda let out a mournful howl that surprised not only Gemini but everyone seated in Forty Cups diner.

"What a mess." She rested her head on the heel of her hand. "He really hated me. There's no denying it now."

Gemini jumped out of her seat, nearly upending her fluffy dessert, and moved to Lucinda's side to comfort her. "I'm so sorry. I didn't mean to upset you."

Lucinda placed her head on Gemini's chest, like a cat begging for attention. Gemini obliged and patted her shoulder.

"Lucinda, do you know Mick?"

She sat up straight and shook her head. "Never met him. Lyle never mentioned him either. When the lawyer told me his name, it was the first time I'd heard it."

Gemini thought about their disturbing visit to the lake house. She was going to have to confront Lucinda, and now was as good a time as any. "Lucinda, Pedro insisted that Sophia go up to the cabin last week. He created quite a mess, what with the blood in a shower and severed fingers on the table." She paused, ready to gauge Lucinda's reaction.

"WHAT??" Lucinda rose from her seat. "I don't think this is funny, Gemini. Lyle's family has always had a peculiar sense of humor, but at this moment, I'm at a loss to explain why you're imposing it on me."

Gemini reached for her arm quickly. "Wait! Please sit and let me explain."

Reluctantly, Lucinda returned to the booth. "I don't know how you can, but go ahead. Try."

"My Sophia, my co-worker Feather and myself, we all went up to the cabin at Pedro's behest. In the second guest bedroom, I found blood in the shower. Downstairs, the table was set for a formal dinner, only instead of napkins, there were severed fingers in the napkin holders. But I have a contact at the FBI. She had everything tested. The blood in the shower came from a cow, probably from a meat-packing plant. And the 'severed' fingers were nothing more than gag shop props."

Lucinda leaned forward. "You're serious? You found severed fingers? What a sick... I hope you called the police!"

"We weren't sure what to do. Is there any reason you can think of for Pedro to stage this scene?"

Sophia had spoken with him on the way home, and he apologized for what he'd done, but never explained why he'd done it in the first place.

"That is complete nonsense. I'm going to alert the authorities right now."

Lucinda pulled her phone out of her purse.

"Give me one more minute before you call them."

She looked at Gemini, clearly irritated. "Don't you think this is enough for one day? I did just lose my husband."

"I'm trying to wrap my head around all of this. What else can you tell me about Pedro? I barely know him."

"He idolized Lyle. The boy followed him everywhere, even begging to come to our home on his school holidays instead of his own. We've given him as much as our own children over the years, and this is how he repays us?"

"More coffee, honey?" Belva asked.

"Yes, half a cup please," Gemini answered. "Are you sure you don't want anything, Lucinda? They make the best coffee in the entire town of Charming!"

Lucinda's head bobbled like a doll's unable to stay steady. "Okay. Sure."

Belva brought her a cup and filled it. "Cream? Sugar?"

"Neither, thank you."

Lucinda took a drink and raised one brow. Individual brow movement was a Reed family trait. "This is much better than I expected!"

"See?"

Gemini's phone rang and, when she retrieved it, she noticed it was Feather calling. "Will you excuse me for a moment?"

She stood and moved out of earshot of Lucinda,

just in case there was something she didn't want to divulge just yet.

"I'm having a rather strange conversation with Lucinda. What's going on with you?"

"A chat with Millicent. She mentioned the name Horatio. Does that ring a bell?"

Gemini tried to remember all the names of Leo's relatives. "Not off the top of my head. I'll have to look at his family tree when I get home."

When she returned to the table, Lucinda was devouring a large piece of chocolate cake. "I decided I was hungry," she said between ravenous bites.

"My co-worker, who accompanied Sophia and me out to your cabin, called. She was wondering if you knew the name Horatio."

Lucinda wiped her face on her napkin and looked at her clean plate with dismay. "No. But I'll be going through my closets as soon as I return from a trip to Majorca. There should be some family history documents there. Suddenly, I'm not feeling well. Are we done here?"

"Not quite." Gemini smiled at Lucinda. "Can you write down the number of Lyle's boss? I'd like to contact him."

Lucinda's face froze.

"Did I say something wrong?"

"No, it's just... I haven't told anyone that I hired you. I'm afraid his boss would think I wasn't in my right mind. I can't have that when I'm trying to obtain control of the cabin."

Gemini fought the urge to be offended. "Well, I can be very discreet. I promise you, no one will know that I have any connection to you."

Lucinda's lip twitched. "There's one more thing, Gemini. I've dreaded this, but we're at a point of desperation now, aren't we?"

Gemini braced herself for another barb. "What? Do you want me to sign a nondisclosure agreement or something, so I don't tell your country club friends?" She was only half-kidding.

"There is the possibility that Lyle found some disturbing information before he left."

"Oh, dear. What is it?"

"I've already confessed to you that I've been having an affair with my neighbor, George Mint. For the past year, we've been talking about a joint business venture. George and I work so well together, it's been a complete joy."

"That sounds great! What's the issue?"

"I was so excited when we began construction that I invited Lyle to come and see the progress. He called to tell me he was running late, so I wasn't worried. George and I had a moment of indiscretion, and Lyle surprised us."

"Where did this take place, Lucinda?"

"At our restaurant here in Charming. Lyle saw us together at the Tickled Egg."

CHAPTER THIRTY-ONE
GEMINI

"Let's jot down what we know so far." Gemini turned on her fancy electric blackboard and wrote "facts" at the top in bright, pink letters. "Lucinda hired you to find her husband and told you he was having an affair," Feather began. "And then told you SHE was having an affair too."

"When I went to Lyle's office, I discovered a button monogrammed with the letter H, along with some candies that were popular in the early 20th century. They certainly didn't taste that old."

"Gem! That was evidence!" Feather protested.

Gemini continued to write furiously. "Then we found out that Lyle was part of a time traveler's club."

"And Mick too," Feather added. "Mick, Lyle, Jasper and Lucinda's boyfriend George all knew each other."

"Yes, and Jasper owns an antique shop where

another button was found, in addition to the one found at his home."

"There is a spirit at Happy Face Lake who wants us to make things right, whatever that means."

Feather rolled her eyes and leaned back in her chair. "I wish they would offer more concise evidence."

Gemini made another column. "Let's add your spirit troubles here."

"I don't know..." Feather began. "It seems like something I should work out on my own."

"So this is how a real detective agency works!" They both turned around to find Mick Everson standing in the doorway.

Gemini hurriedly shut off the blackboard and turned it to face the wall.

"I'm glad you stopped by," Gemini said. "I need to ask you some questions. Nothing that interferes with your meeting rules, of course."

She gestured with her eyes for Feather to follow and both women moved to their respective desks. Pulling a brown paper bag out of the drawer, she slid it over to Mick. "Thanks for letting us borrow this. I completely forgot to return it. This is my partner, Feather Jones."

Feather reached her hand across the desk. His eyes traveled from her green-tipped hair to her combat boots.

"Did you find anything spooky associated with my trinket?" Mick asked, his voice dripping with sarcasm.

Feather glanced over at Gemini. "No, it was a bust, I'm afraid."

"Trent called me. He said you weren't too happy with our business arrangement."

Feather frowned and waited for explanation.

"I was just about to tell you," Gemini said apologetically. "Mick here paid Leo's nurse Trent to bring us together."

"Why?" Feather asked.

Mick cleared his throat and moved in his seat. "I needed something from Mrs. Reed. It seemed like the best way."

"You could've just asked!" Gemini was incredulous. "Why the cloak-and-dagger stuff?"

"It was too important to leave to chance. Trent likes to brag about you. He thinks the world of you, Mrs. Reed."

Gemini grinned. It pleased her to hear she'd given someone a few moments of sunshine. "And I of him. At least until I learned he took a bribe to do your bidding."

Mick placed one of his extra-large hands on the wall and leaned into it. "No, don't look at it that way. I asked a friend to introduce us. Like a date, in a manner of speaking."

Gemini crossed her arms and leaned back in her seat. "Well, you're here now. Tell us everything."

"Yeah, Trent said you were an investigator and that you never gave up until you got to the bottom of things. That's what I needed, but I couldn't have my family thinking I went to you."

"So you made sure I found out through Trent. And why?"

"Because I'm starting to suspect one of our time travelers is stealing valuable items from different times."

"Like the gentleman you told me about?"

Mick nodded. "And others. Eleanor Roosevelt is acting suspiciously. I wanted to make sure you weren't a fraud before I hired you."

Gemini resisted the urge to feel insulted. "Before I agree to anything, you'll have to answer some of my questions. For starters, my associate and I discovered that you actually knew Lyle Lime. Why did you lie about that?"

Mick's face took on a blotchy appearance. "Yeah, I knew him. We were high school buddies. Before his disappearance, we used to go fishing together at Happy Face Lake. I have my suspicions about what happened to him."

"Oh, really? Please fill us in."

"Lyle and his wife weren't close. In fact, on our last visit, he said she was having an affair and planned to divorce him. I have to wonder if she wasn't responsible for his death."

Gemini bit her cheek. Not that it was completely out of character for Lucinda, but Mick was the only one so far who had outright lied.

There was silence in the room, as both Gemini and

Feather had learned it was the best way to force someone to fill the space with the truth.

"Yeah, Lyle was a friend," Mick continued. "And when he joined the Hawkites, we really hit it off. Since you said you and Lucinda were related, I didn't want to mention that part of the story until I felt like I could trust you."

None of this sat right with her. "What is it you want to hire us to do?"

"Well, as I said before, I've seen some travelers come back with jewels and other artifacts. It's strictly against our rules."

"You want us to investigate them?"

"I want you to time travel and see if you can see if those artifacts are indeed missing and find out who took them."

Eleanor Roosevelt didn't strike Gemini as the stealing type. She was a quick knitter and a straight shooter, as far as she could tell. "That's not something we've done before," Gemini began slowly. "I do tend to get a little queasy in a plane."

Mick chuckled. "You're funny. We give you anti-nausea medication. You'll be fine. I'll set everything up, but first I'll have to run a background check. Routine, of course. Oh, and when you come to our meeting tomorrow evening, please don't mention Lyle or Trent."

She bit her tongue to keep herself from asking why. "I'd like to bring my associate with me. Would that be all right?"

He studied Feather, whose eyes were closed as her lips moved silently. "Are you okay, miss?"

Gemini realized it was the worst possible time to draw attention to her friend. "She likes to meditate," she said quickly.

Feather's eyes popped open. "The person you're hoping to contact is no longer available," she said in a monotone voice.

"What?" both asked in unison.

"You're playing a dangerous game," she said in the same steady tone. "End it now or suffer my wrath."

"She's going to be in the dinner theatre production this weekend. Maybe you've heard of it—Evil in Oregon, the Musical? Feather likes to rehearse all the time."

Mick shrugged. "I'll see you both tomorrow evening."

After he walked out the door, Gemini turned her concern toward her friend. Gently, she shook her shoulder. "Hon, come back to me. He's gone."

Feather turned her head toward Gemini and now it was evident something was seriously wrong. Her eyes stared blankly ahead and there was no sense of recognition on her face.

"My darling girl. I need you here with me. This isn't safe for you. Come back now."

"There is danger everywhere. Stop him now," Feather continued in a monotone.

Gemini stood up slowly and walked out the door. Once she was outside, she ran as fast as her legs would take her to the other side of the warehouse. She was grateful for the early morning walks she'd taken.

Tug was seated on a stool in the large commercial kitchen, placing wrappers on Tug Bars. When he saw the look on Gemini's face, he jumped to his feet. "Where is she?"

"In the office. Please hurry!"

There was no way she could keep up with Tug, so by the time she'd returned to the office, Tug was seated beside Feather, wiping her face with a washcloth. "Babe, it's me. Come back!" he said tearfully.

Whether it was hearing Tug's voice or the trance was over, a look of recognition returned to Feather's face.

"Where am I?" She squinted and tried standing, only to fall back into her chair.

"You're in your office, hon," Gemini replied. "Right here with your Tug and me."

She rubbed her forehead and looked around the room. "The last thing I remember was a conversation we were having with some guy."

"Mick. You told him he was in danger if he stayed on this path."

Tug picked her up and gently laid her on the new couch Gemini had just purchased. "You need your rest now," he said.

Instead of being angry with him for doing this without her permission, Feather seemed appreciative. Tug handed her a cup of water and she drank as if she hadn't had liquid for a week.

"Thanks, babe," she said, squeezing his hand.

"Do you remember anything at all?" Gemini asked somewhat impatiently.

Feather's face was tight and drawn.

"What is it, babe?" Tug asked with concern.

"I was wrong. Lyle isn't dead. He's plotting your murder, Gemini."

Chapter Thirty-Two
Gemini

"Welcome to the two hundred and fourteenth meeting of the Hawkites, Coastal Chapter."

Mick stood in front of a folding table and banged a gavel on a skinny piece of wood.

The rest of the room stood as well. Gemini, having attended a meeting before, explained all of their rituals to Feather on the way over.

"We've got some new business to discuss tonight," Mick said, looking down at a paper in from of him. "Harry Houdini has very generously reserved a space in the last Piney Falls Market of the season."

An elderly man with dark curly hair cupped his hand and waved, as if he were riding on a summer float.

"Tupac ordered a banner too." Mick gestured toward freckle-faced man wearing a cap that read "Aliens don't believe in you either."

Feather leaned over and whispered in Gemini's ear, "If they have a booth next to us, I'll never be able to concentrate! The spirits in this room are loud and angry!"

Gemini nodded. She'd already asked the market manager for the booth closest to the bathroom, without discussing the surrounding vendors.

"Before we begin, we need to acknowledge the passing of one of our own. Buddy Holly was a good soldier who'd taken six trips." Mick cleared his throat. "I've spoken with his wife, who tells me there will be no memorial. She's asked for those wishing to donate to send funds to our group."

The knitting lady, Eleanor Roosevelt, leaned over to Gemini and whispered, "Our group is dropping like flies. We're gonna have to start checking everyone's heart before they leave our timeline, 'else the entire mission will come down to just myself and Marilyn. She jogs twice a week."

Gemini nodded.

"Our next order of business," Mick continued, "is to hear reports from our fellow travelers on their latest missions. Apparently, John Lennon found the donuts of his dreams at The House of the Rising Bun Bakery."

The group chuckled and an Asian man gave the "thumbs up" sign.

Eleanor Roosevelt raised one knitting needle before standing. "I took a ride back to 1902 with Helen Keller."

Out of the corner of her eye, Gemini noticed

Feather rubbing her forearms. A sure sign that ghosts were nearby.

"We stopped in 1846 to pick up some of that jam Elvis raved about."

"Wasn't it great?" Mick asked enthusiastically.

"Sure was. We continued on to the year we'd planned. First thing we saw was—"

"I visited last spring. Oh, the cherry trees. I can still smell them." Someone with a nametag that read Thomas Jefferson interrupted.

"You know the club rules, Thom," Mick admonished. "Everyone gets to speak without crosstalk for five minutes."

Feather leaned over to Gemini and cupped her hand around the side of her mouth. "He's lying. He's too afraid to get inside their time travel machine, so he always insists on taking solo trips and then studies up about the history of that time before reporting back. His mother is so embarrassed."

Gemini nodded.

"Okay, well, if it's all right, I'd like to continue, " Eleanor Roosevelt said, slightly irritated.

"Go ahead, Eleanor," Mick urged her. "We're listening."

"So, like I was saying, we used the coordinates Elvis asked us to use, which took us right here, in Charming. There wasn't much of a town, seeing as how this is a tourist area that only built up when tourists came. Just a few big houses the rich folk used for vacations."

There was a murmur of acknowledgment in the room.

Gemini glanced at Feather, who shrugged her shoulders as if to say, "I don't have anything to contradict that."

"We did find a little general store. I wanted to see if there was something I could bring back for the scavenger hunt, so I—"

"This week it's a glass medicine bottle," Thomas Jefferson interrupted. "Sorry. I'll close my mouth now."

Eleanor Roosevelt turned towards Gemini and mouthed the words, "See, I told you!"

Gemini gave her a nod.

"We walked into this little store and the man behind the counter fit the description of the person we were looking for."

"I'm sorry, what? Are you saying that Lyle is working in a general store? In 1902?"

"He didn't want to admit it at first, but I refused to leave until he told me everything."

The room was so quiet that when Gemini moved in her squeaky folding chair, it made a thunderous echo.

"Eleanor, which of our approved tactics did you use to get him to cooperate?" Mick asked.

"I told him I knew his cousin. That I was going straight back to tell her where he was hiding." She pivoted toward Gemini, causing a ball of pink yarn to roll down the aisle, stopping in front of Mick. "You should have seen his face. You must scare the bageebies outta him!" She chuckled.

Embarrassed and unsure how to respond, Gemini smiled politely. There was nothing she'd heard so far that made her suspicious of Eleanor.

"He told me everything. Lyle Lime is happy where he is. He hated his job and got into a business deal that went sour and the other people involved said they'd kill him if he didn't pay up. Lyle wanted to protect his family, so he went into hiding the best way he knew how."

"This reminds me of the time Elvis and me went to 1900 to find his grandma's prize-winning pie recipe. Do you remember, Elvis?" Thomas Jefferson could contain himself no longer. "You said it was the best trip you'd ever taken."

Mick nodded and frowned. "I do. We should really support our colleague Eleanor right now though."

"It was so funny," Thomas Jefferson continued, oblivious to Mick's anger. "Elvis said we needed to stop at a diner before we snuck into his grandmother's house. It turned out that Elvis had a friend who was also time traveling, sitting right there, eating a turkey dinner. He was as surprised to see us as we were to see him!"

Gemini failed to understand what was so funny about this experience. It only served to make her more skeptical of Mick's abilities to time travel. He must've knocked this gullible man out and taken him to a movie set or something.

"The poor guy didn't research the time period before he made the trip," Thomas Jefferson droned on. "He was wearing torn jeans and a plaid shirt, and the management of the diner thought he was down on his luck and brought him free sandwiches and coffee. Do you remember that, Elvis?" He chuckled, proud of himself for remembering.

Marilyn Monroe raised her hand. "I do! You both couldn't stop laughing about this poor guy's funny clothing choices."

"Did you have any questions, Mrs. Reed?" Mick asked through clenched teeth.

She had plenty. "What was the name of this business associate? Why wouldn't Lyle tell his wife where he was going? The poor woman decided he was having an affair with someone in another century. And what about that? Is there another woman?"

Just like they had at the previous meeting, the group gasped collectively.

"We don't ask more than two questions, Mrs. Reed," Marilyn explained. "We don't want to overwhelm travelers who may still be groggy from the journey."

She was fuming. Whether this was a farce or the real thing, she needed to get to the truth. It was clear it wasn't coming in a meeting setting. Her only hope was that Feather had some entity whispering in her ear, giving her the real story all evening.

When the meeting was over, she stood abruptly

and turned to Eleanor Roosevelt, who was still knitting while she was in a deep conversation with JFK.

"Excuse me, I hate to interrupt, but I've got more questions about your journey. Would you mind meeting me for coffee? I'll buy."

Both members gasped.

Gemini made a swishing motion with her hand. "Oh, I get it. You're not supposed to fraternize outside of meetings. What if we consider this two friends having a hot drink together?"

"Just don't tell Elvis," JFK whispered before walking off. "He'd blow a gasket."

When he'd gone, Eleanor turned to her. "I don't know what else I can say to help you."

"Oh, you'd be surprised what helps. I'd like my associate, Feather Jones, to come along. Would that be all right?"

"I... guess so," she replied with uncertainty.

"We'll keep this a secret meeting, I promise."

Eleanor's expression eased. "Will you be paying?"

Chapter Thirty-Three
Feather

The din of unhappy children and clanking forks made conversation challenging. Twice, Gemini asked if Eleanor Roosevelt and JFK wanted to go somewhere else, but they both refused. Feather worried Gemini would miss out on crucial information.

"So, you were telling us that in order to time travel, you're forced to take some type of medication?" Feather practically screamed. Her head was throbbing. There were so many spirits vying for her attention at the Hawkites meeting that they began shouting at her. By the time she'd "cleared" them, she was left with a nasty headache. Sitting in this noisy place wasn't helping. A lull in conversation when Feather was yelling caused several diners at Forty Cups to turn and stare at their booth.

Both Eleanor Roosevelt and JFK wrinkled their brows. "We don't make that information public. If you're going to insist on yelling, we'll have to leave," Eleanor Roosevelt warned.

Feather glanced at her plate—it was the Second Helpings Platter, scrambled eggs, bacon and home-made toast. There was no way she'd walk away from that.

"Is it possible to travel without being medicated?" Gemini asked, taking a sip of her coffee with two sugars.

"Well, sure it is," JFK, a short, bald man with three chins said. "But who wants that travel sickness upon re-entry?"

Feather leaned forward. "Have you been sick before?"

The fellow travelers glanced at each other and chuckled.

"Did I say something funny?" she asked, slightly insulted.

"No, dearie. It's just that time travel 101 is preparing your body for the effects of time travel. If you don't read through the entire manual and take the test, you can't travel. Elvis's rules."

To Feather's surprise and admiration, Eleanor was halfway through the Use Your Extra Stomach platter. Six pancakes, bacon, eggs, waffles, small potatoes and toast.

"How would we get ahold of one of these manuals?" Gemini and Feather asked in unison.

Gemini patted Feather's leg. "We're forever doing that."

"In our meetings..." Eleanor began between mouthfuls of pancakes, "we call that the timeless connection." She pointed her fork at each of them and pancake bits went flying across the table. "You were probably mother and daughter in a previous life."

While it was a huge compliment to Feather and something she'd think about before sleep that night, she could only imagine Gemini's thoughts. Having a daughter with "gifts" wasn't easy. At least she thought it wasn't. Her own mother never stuck around to tell her.

"How do we get a manual?" she repeated quickly, before Gemini had a chance to answer.

"You'll have to sign the release form."

Feather's heart sank. That would mean another trip to their crazy meetings and more spirits bombarding her with information. "I suppose we'll have to come back next week, Gem," she said with resignation.

"No, I've got one right here."

Eleanor opened her large bag and pulled out two typed papers, slapping them on the table and narrowly missing the syrup container. "Just fill these out and return 'em to a member."

Feather reached to slide the papers closer. JFK used his thick hands as paperweights, keeping them frozen in place. "Before you read through this, we have to make sure you're serious."

"Is there some kind of initiation?" Gemini asked.

"No, nothing like that. We've had reporters try and

infiltrate our organization. It becomes crystal clear when they refuse to read the manual." He leaned back and crossed his arms over his stomach with satisfaction. "You ladies don't seem like press, but you have to know, we'll run background checks. Just to protect ourselves."

Feather gulped. When Mick left their office, Gemini mentioned he was going to do that. What would they say when they found out about her court appearance in her early twenties?

"I... uh..."

"I'll be the only one filling out the papers, so only one background check will be necessary," Gemini replied, squeezing Feather's leg under the table. "It will save you money."

"Oh, Thomas Jefferson got a coupon for fifty percent off one of them online sites," Eleanor said. "He paid for the whole thing himself."

Feather glanced at Gemini helplessly.

"Could we discuss this for a moment?" Gemini asked. "Nothing secretive, it's just that diving in like this is a big decision and we need to be on the same page."

Both Hawkites nodded in sync.

The two sleuths excused themselves and walked to the bathroom.

"Gem, you know I had a drug problem early on. I have a record. If they find that, it might jeopardize this whole thing."

Gemini thought for a moment. "Follow my lead."

They returned to the table, where Eleanor was finishing the last bite of her potatoes. "What'd you decide?" she asked.

"I'll fill out your paperwork, but there's no need for Feather to do so. She won't be reading your manual."

"Oh. I thought you wanted to time travel. You're doing all of this, just to read our manual?" Eleanor asked.

"We're going to time travel. Mick... Elvis invited us to go. Although—" She turned to Feather, acting as if she'd just had an idea. "My poor dear Feather has always had terrible motion sickness." She looked at Feather, who nodded in agreement. "She's very allergic to all of the anti-nausea medications. Instead, I'd like to bring my grandson with me."

"That's highly unorthodox!" JFK spouted.

Feather suppressed a giggle. As if this entire method of time travel wasn't?

"It's never been done before!" Eleanor Roosevelt echoed her cohort. "The rules are in place for a reason."

"I'm prepared to make a large donation to your organization," Gemini continued. "To keep this important program afloat."

"Well, you might change your tune when you find out exactly how much this costs," Eleanor warned. "Your first ride, according to the manual, will set you back one thousand dollars." She stuck her tongue in the side of her cheek, waiting for the bomb she'd dropped to make impact.

It was Feather's turn to smirk. These people had no

idea how much money Gemini had. It was probably for the best.

Without blinking, Gemini replied, "Yes, as I said, my grandson and I will be traveling together. And I'll make a donation on top of that. Shall we say ten thousand?"

Gemini removed her checkbook from her purse. It always made Feather uneasy when she so readily wrote big checks in public. You never knew who might be one table over, eyeing your account.

"Well, yes!" JFK said enthusiastically.

Eleanor placed a hand on his arm. "Hold on. How do we know that check won't bounce?" She eyed Gemini and Feather with skepticism.

"Cash it tomorrow and I'll make my trip next week, after it clears."

"You have to read through the entire manual and take a test. I don't see how you could possibly take your trip before next month!" JFK protested. He picked up the check and examined it closely before running his finger over the numbers.

"I'm a very quick study. Let's set up a day and time and I'll be ready, and so will my grandson."

"You folks seem to have all of the answers. Let me make a call to make sure this is all right. I don't recall a rule against it, but I need to check." Eleanor pulled her phone out of her raincoat pocket and put it up to her ear. "Julius? This is Eleanor. We've got a tender horn here. Assures us she and her grandson will pass the test and be ready for flight by... next week."

Feather detected a hint of disbelief in her voice.

"Unhuh...That's what I told 'em too. Okay." She eyed the women warily before turning away from them. "She's already paid me." Her words were still perfectly clear to those at the table. "Yes, and then some."

When Eleanor had finished her conversation, she placed her glitter-covered phone on the table. "Julius Caesar says he'd be happy to administer the test this Friday."

"Wonderful!" Gemini clasped her hands together with excitement. "We'll be ready!"

"That's only four days. Don't be surprised if you fail!" JFK chided her.

"No need to worry. We'll pass."

Feather wasn't sure what Gemini had up her sleeve, but she seemed very confident.

"And our scheduled flight? When will that be?"

"Calm down, Mrs. Reed. Pass your test and then we'll talk about a date," Eleanor said.

As they left the restaurant, Feather whispered in Gemini's ear. "What possessed you to tell them you and Tug would be ready by Friday?"

Gemini winked at her. "You are the secret weapon, hon."

Flattered and confused, Feather asked, "How am I going to help? I don't know anything about time travel!"

"You have contacts on the other side who owe you favors."

Feather thought about that. Two months ago, she conveyed a message to a widow who couldn't find her husband's favorite socks. The month before, she gave a bereaved father a message of love from his dearly departed son.

"And you want them to do what?"

"They have the ability to see the tests and the questions. You mentioned there were so many spirits at the meeting that you had to shut them off. There has to be at least one of them willing to give you the test answers in exchange for help."

Her eyes lit up. "Gem, that's brilliant!"

Chapter
Thirty-Four
Feather

Feather giggled as she read the book to Tug. "Oh wait, you've got to hear this one." She pulled the covers up to her chin and leaned in close. "All travelers must agree to a body cavity search if asked."

Tug laughed and shook his head. "Really? Do they think people will hide things in their privates to bring them back from another century?"

They'd been lying in bed for over an hour, reading *The Official Time Travelers Manual and Testing Materials*. Gemini said to give her the highlights.

"Are these people all a little off?" Tug asked. "I mean, that Mick guy isn't all there, and from what you told me about your meeting Eleanor Roosevelt and..."

"JFK."

"Yeah, right. Anyway, I don't think anyone in this group has their head screwed on."

She couldn't argue with that assessment. The

manual contained forty steps to be taken and approved by another member before time travel was permitted.

"Tug, you're going to have to memorize the take-off codes."

"I won't have any problem with that."

Tug had an uncanny ability to memorize. In his high school yearbook, he was voted "Most Likely to Become a Human Computer."

"I'm glad it's Gem who agreed to this. I don't think I could keep a straight face."

Tug sat upright. "That does concern me. Do you think that's wise?"

Feather stopped laughing and stared at him with surprise. "Did you suddenly forget she's a capable woman?"

"No, of course not." Tug stared at the magenta sheets. "I think there is strength in numbers, and two people should be there. I don't know who we'd find to replace her, but I just don't want anything to happen to her. I wish you could be there too. If you were, you could spend your time observing every aspect of this whack-a-doodle venture while Gem and I go through the motions of time travel."

"Oh." She hadn't thought of that. "I wish I didn't have an arrest record."

Tug stroked her face. "You were just a kid, and one from a dysfunctional home at that. I hate that a bad decision you made when you were barely an adult follows you around today."

Feather grabbed the hand touching her face and

kissed it. "I was hurting. I didn't know any other way to make it stop."

When she was barely out of high school, she married her first boyfriend. It was mostly to get out of her parents' home, but she dreamed of a world where she had kids and a cute little house. It turned out to be more of a nightmare.

Her new husband quickly lost interest in her. He was selling drugs, and when she offered to sell them at the quickie mart where she worked, he was temporarily attentive. An undercover agent arrested her the very first day. Feather was lucky she still had one cousin who spoke to her. He bailed her out and helped her through the messy legal process.

She glanced at the clock. "I should get going."

"I'm going with you." Tug stood and reached for his shoes.

"What? No, you most certainly are not. You have that reporter coming in tomorrow to write a story on the up and coming business, Tug Bars. Tug Muehler needs to look his best."

Tug shook his head. "I don't care. Your safety is more important."

Feather stood and moved inches from him. "You know how picky some of these spirits are. They might decide not to talk to me if you're there."

He looked as though he was going to argue further, but she held firm, both with her decision and where she stood.

"Okay, but you have to call me. This isn't a great time for anyone to be out and about."

"Promise. You'll get a call on the hour, every hour, until I get home."

Though Feather had great luck finding spirits to speak with in her own home, she was even more likely to find a group of them when she was in the PINK organization meeting room. The idea of spirits only coming out at night was a fallacy, but she couldn't deny the fact that she found them easily accessible after seven.

They were both silent as they went through different scenarios in their heads.

"Got it. One of those chapters you read went into detail about what to do if the traveler needed physical assistance during their journey. While you and I both know Gemini is perfectly capable, none of them do. To them, she's a little old lady who may or may not have problems navigating a time travel machine."

Feather reluctantly left the warmth of the man she loved and her comfortable bed. She'd reserved time at the PINK meeting room from seven until eight. She wasn't the only one who found it the best place to speak with those from the other world.

She unlocked the door and crept carefully through the maze of chairs and promotional material lying around. Finally, she reached the center of the room. After removing her coat, she dropped her arms to her sides and closed her eyes.

"I need help. Grover, I told your wife about the hidden money in your mattress. Bettina, your deadbeat nephew no longer camps out on the lawn of your former home."

She waited patiently. Nothing.

"What about Trudy? I told your husband you knew about his online foot fetish and you'd be watching him."

Still nothing.

"Come on, guys!" she said in an exasperated tone. She felt a cold breeze in the room, though she knew the door was shut.

Feather Weather, do you want to see my invention?

Feather sighed, completely out of patience. "No! I'll let you know when I'm ready for another invention!"

Fine!!!

The room instantly filled with screeching crows, swooping precariously close to Feather's face. She regretted snapping at Daisy. "I'm sorry!" she called, knowing Daisy would pout for several days.

You are the bridge.

"Will you quit with that? I'm here because I need your help!"

You are the bridge, Feather Jones. Without you, evil events will continue.

"What do you mean by that? What am I supposed to do?"

It will become clear. Watch carefully.

Exasperated by the complete waste of an hour, she left the room and slammed the door.

"Oh! Is there bad juju in our room? Should I go home and get my sage?"

She was surprised by the appearance of another PINK member. "No, sorry. I'm just frustrated. I keep getting the same answer without explanation."

"That's because you're demanding."

Feather raised her eyebrows. "What do you mean?"

"Instead of demanding an answer, just sit and listen. It's there, I promise you."

CHAPTER
THIRTY-FOUR
FEATHER

The next morning, Feather set a coffee on Gemini's desk, alongside two sugars and a pastry from the Tickled Egg.

Gemini walked in soon after and stared at her desk as she hung up her coat. "What's this? Did someone die?"

"No, I just like to treat my partner. Isn't that okay?"

Gemini squeezed her shoulder before sitting at her desk. "Of course it is, sweetie."

She took a bite of the cream cheese-filled pastry and stared solemnly at Feather.

"What? Is it awful? I got it from the Tickled Egg. You said Leo's cousin owns the place."

"Exactly the opposite," Gemini replied with full cheeks. "This is quite possibly the best tasting thing I've ever eaten. Part of me wanted it to be awful." She winked at Feather. "But I could make something just as good."

Tug came jogging through the door. He didn't stop until he reached Gemini's desk. He bent down and kissed her on the cheek before producing three roses.

Gemini studied his face. "Okay, now I'm worried. Did my doctor call you?"

"No, nothing like that, Gem," Feather reassured her. "Tug has something to ask you, and he's concerned you'll take it the wrong way."

Tug frowned at Feather and mouthed the word, "Thanks!"

"Spill it." Gemini leaned back in her chair and crossed her arms. "One of you, both of you, I'm not picky."

Tug raised his brows. "Well, we were reading through the Time Travelers Manual—"

"Which is hilarious, by the way," Feather added.

"Yeah, it's pretty funny. I started thinking that we should have a backup plan. Just in case things go sideways."

"Oh? What were you thinking?"

"Well, um..." Tug rubbed the back of his neck. "We —Feather and me—thought maybe you could fake a problem related to... age."

"I've gone into scarier situations alone and never had a single old-person related issue!" Gemini said indignantly.

"We know that," Tug replied. "Gem, we're going to

ask for your best acting job yet. We want you to pretend you're confused by all of the controls and may need the mission to stop at some point. That's if we both see we're in trouble."

The air left the room.

Feather thought quickly. "We're only asking because we may only get one crack at this, and we need to make sure we've thought of everything."

Gemini drummed her fingers on the desk.

"You're right, both of you. And thank you for thinking about buttering me up first. I'd like that every time you have something you want to tell me."

Feather jumped up and hugged Gemini.

"There's just one more thing," Tug said.

Feather's head snapped around. They hadn't discussed anything else.

"What is it, Tug?"

"I read the rest of that manual after you left. We have to have a clean bill of health. This 'air sickness' medication must be something really powerful."

Chapter Thirty-Five
Feather

Tug paced around the desks, barely able to keep himself from bouncing off the walls.

"She'll be here, babe," Feather comforted him. "It's Jayden. She's never let us down."

"There's always a first time," Tug muttered.

When she was unable to garner any help from the spirits, Feather came up with the idea to ask Jayden to help find the test questions and answers.

Gemini took still-warm cinnamon rolls from a pan and placed one in front of each of them. "Well, your spirit friends weren't helpful with the test questions, but were you able to find anything else? You know, I do worry. You've had these terrible dreams, and the fainting and the marks on you when you sleep and—"

Feather shot Tug an angry glance. "You told her?"

Her boyfriend shrugged. "I thought you already had."

"It doesn't matter now, you two. I know. I think

you should tell Jayden about the scratches and see what she says."

"I've heard of spirits who don't understand they're dead," Feather said in between bites. "They are violent because they don't understand their situations. It's probably nothing more than that."

Gemini clucked her tongue. "Makes you wonder if they were this self-centered in life."

"It's not that I'm against cheating on the test, but I don't want to ask anything else of Jayden. She's my biggest supporter. Please promise me—both of you—that you won't say anything about the scratches?"

"She's a very level-headed woman. Someone who runs a giant corporation doesn't throw away valuable people at the drop of a hat. No, I'm certain she isn't the type to cast you aside over one question."

Gemini cut a small piece of her cinnamon roll and put it in her mouth. "Mm. Howard's suggestion to frost with cream cheese icing was a good one."

The door opened and Jayden appeared in a silver catsuit and dark red lipstick. "So sorry to be late, kids. It's always the days you want to leave that a million fires demand your attention." She bent over and kissed Feather on either cheek.

"If you don't want to do this, please know you're not obligated," Feather said nervously.

Jayden smiled and patted her hand. "Gemini mentioned how upset you were. Haven't you figured out by now, you're not getting rid of me, Feather Jones?"

Feather smiled, her body relaxing.

"I just thought that collectively we could figure out the test by reading the manual. It can't be that hard."

Jayden opened her large leather bag. "Actually, the test questions are very technical and hard to follow." She set five typed pages on the desk. "Purposely, I would guess."

Tug picked them up and began thumbing through. "What is the approximate speed of the time machine when entering fourth dimensional orbit?" He dropped the paper and sighed. "How is anyone supposed to know that?"

Feather knew he had that answer, but she chose not to challenge him.

"Believe it or not," Jayden began, "it's very easy. I wrote down all the questions as I saw them and then the answers. It's multiple choice. But look at this."

She pointed a red nail at the first page. "The answers are in a pattern. The first page, the answers go A then C all the way down. The next page, it's B then D. It continues for the next three pages. Whoever wrote up this test wanted to make sure everyone passed."

"I wonder why Eleanor Roosevelt and JFK told us it was so difficult?" Feather asked. She realized everyone was staring at her. "Oh, sorry. Those are the names they came up with to remain incognito."

"When was the booklet published?" Jayden asked.

Gemini pulled it out of the top drawer of her desk and opened it to the first page. "Just six months ago."

"That's what I thought. Your historical friends took a different version of the test." Jayden closed her eyes and the room fell silent.

"Yep, that's it. When the group was formed, the test was written by the founders, Mick Everson and George Mint. Who wrote this one?"

Gemini opened it up again. She gasped. "Lyle Lime. Also known as Buck Rogers."

"All that proves is that he was in the group," Feather replied. "It doesn't give us any hard evidence that he did something wrong."

A quiet fell over the office.

The phone ringing jolted them all out of their respective thoughts. Feather was the first to reach for the phone.

"Kindred Spirits Detective Agency, how can I help you?"

"Get out of the building! Now!"

"What?"

The line went dead.

"They said we have to—"

"Everyone, run out the back way!" Jayden yelled.

They followed quickly, though no one but Jayden had any idea why.

When they'd reached the back of the building, they heard a large crash.

"What on earth was that?" Gemini asked.

"It was a Molotov cocktail, also known as a bottle with a gas-covered rag in it." Jayden bent down and picked it up. "Though our would-be assailants forgot to light it. No one ever confused criminals with geniuses."

Gemini wandered over to the plate glass window. She'd paid extra to have their Kindred Spirits logo etched in the glass. Now it was lying in pieces on the carpet.

"Nothing in your office was damaged," Jayden continued with the sense of calm she brought to every situation. "Besides your window, but that's replaceable."

"Someone called to warn us," Feather said quietly. "How could they know?"

"It's simple, doll. They wanted you to know they're watching."

"Who? You must have some idea!" Gemini asked.

Feather noticed her friend was shaking. She went over and hugged her tightly.

Jayden sat down in Gemini's chair, maneuvering it around the broken glass. "Ever since Feather's accident, I've had a nagging feeling that all of your problems are related."

Tug, who had been placing the larger pieces of glass in the trash can, looked up. "Is it Feather's aunt? The one who smells like caramel corn?"

Jayden smiled. "I have wondered. What's infuriating to me is that my vision has been blocked. That's something that requires work from the spirit side. I don't know if it's someone angry with me, or if they're trying to make sure our darling Feather doesn't solve this mystery."

Feather thought back to the night before, when another member of PINK told her to quit demanding and start listening. She wouldn't tell Jayden until she had something definitive.

Jayden glanced down at her phone. "Sorry, loves. I have to get back. You'll both ace this test. That I have seen."

They waved as she stepped carefully over the glass and out the door.

"I'm going to the park," Feather announced to the surprise of both of her co-workers.

"Now?" Tug asked. "I'm going to call the police and they may need your statement. Is there something we should know?"

Feather shook her head and smiled lovingly at him. "No, babe. I just need some fresh air and quiet. I promise I'll be back before lunch. You guys saw the same stuff I did. I'm sure you'll fill them in."

She grabbed her coat and walked out of the office quickly, before she changed her mind. She drove to the only beach close to Charming that allowed vehicles to drive on the sand. This ridiculous vehicle had to be good for something.

To her surprise, she found she enjoyed the ride. It made her feel powerful. When she reached an area with no other people, she parked the truck and rolled down the windows. She tipped her seat back and closed her eyes. For once, her mind was completely empty.

"I'm listening."

CHAPTER THIRTY-SIX
FEATHER

She could feel the sweat rolling down her back. Feather got out of her car with the knowledge that she'd hit something or someone, again.

"Why do you keep jumping in front of me?" she cried.

She walked to the center of the highway, expecting to find nothing but skid marks. Instead, there was the lifeless body of a man. When she bent down to look closer, he opened his eyes and cackled in a woman's voice. "You are the bridge, Feather Jones!"

She tried to run, but her legs were stuck, glued to the ground.

Feather woke with a start. She glanced down at her arms, which were covered in scratch marks. She looked at the clock. Three a.m. There was a soft, steady snore coming from the other side of the bed.

At least Tug was still sleeping soundly.

Feather threw off the covers and tiptoed out of

their bedroom. She lowered herself to the floor of the spare bedroom and rubbed her hands on her knees.

"Millicent?"

As she sat there, patiently waiting for her young friend, she wracked her brain for the owner of the female voice she'd heard in her dream. It was so familiar, and yet it wasn't coming to her.

She reenacted the events of the last two months. Howard's stolen jewelry, his crazy behavior, the entity that jumped in front of her car...

The hairs on her arms rose.

"My dear little Feather!"

"Millicent? Could you come and sit beside me?"

She heard the sound of Millicent's invisible shoes skipping on the wood floor. The young girl came into view beside her.

"Won't your mother be ashamed?" Millicent asked.

"Why would she be ashamed?" Feather worried that one of her relatives was filling Millie's head with negative words about her.

"You're not dressed. Mother says we're never to show our legs in public."

Millicent pointed to Feather's bare legs, visible under the over-sized t-shirt she wore to bed every night.

"Oh, in my time we show our legs. It's not a big deal."

Millicent viewed her with skepticism. "Now you're teasing me!"

Another day she would gladly have this conversation, but not today. "Millicent, there have been things troubling me. You're so smart, I know you'll have the answers."

"Mother says my spelling is superior to both of my brothers!" she replied eagerly.

Feather knew from researching her death that Millicent had only attended school for three months before her illness and subsequent death. She swallowed hard, trying to push away the sadness she felt for a life ended too soon.

"Someone from your world is playing mean tricks on me. They make me think I've hurt them when I haven't."

Millicent stroked Feather's arm, as much as a transparent entity could. "Poor, poor dear," she cooed. "Is it the bad man who locked me away?"

"I'm not sure. He or she wants me to see their death, but whenever I try, there's no one there."

"Oh. It's not the bad man at all, Feather. It's a lady. She was brought to your side by mistake."

"Who is she?"

"A relative."

The hairs on Feather's neck stood at attention. This time, it wasn't an entity, it was the reality of what Millicent was saying.

"What do they want me to see?"

Millicent stood. ***"Mother's calling. It's time for supper. Tonight it's baked ham and boiled potatoes."***

"Please, just this once, stay with me until I have the answers!" Feather pleaded.

"Row, row, row your boat. Merrily down the stream. They're both coming soon."

Millicent disappeared through the wall.

"Both?"

Despite the conversation she'd had with Millicent the previous night, she needed to direct her attention to something she'd been putting off for too long. Feather Jones had one very glaring weakness: confrontation with the living. Namely, confronting people who hadn't paid for her services.

She promised herself a trip to the Tickled Egg for a pastry as she found the number.

"Jasper?"

"Yes? Who's calling please?"

"It's Feather Jones."

"Oh?" He sounded surprised.

"Jasper, I know you have caller ID." Feather cleared her throat. "I don't have time for games today."

Jasper chuckled softly. "If we aren't to play games, then why are we speaking?"

"Well, number one, you never paid me for getting rid of your refrigerator problems."

"That's because you didn't follow my explicit

instructions. The way the two of you tore out of here, I suspected you stole something. I wasn't wrong."

"You weren't being honest, Jasper," Feather replied, ignoring his last remark. "There's so much you didn't tell me. You're quite the entrepreneur."

She paused. If she gave him enough rope to hang himself, she wouldn't have to tell him everything she knew. It was always good to have a tidbit of information held back.

"I didn't become a wealthy man by bragging about my accomplishments, Feather."

He was going to play hard to get.

"You own an antique store, J and M Antiques. It's the perfect cover to sell the fake jewelry. Somehow you've convinced Zeke and his sweet uncle to go along with you. Do I need to continue?"

Jasper chuckled again, this time much louder. "Feather has done her homework. I do indeed own an antique store."

"What I don't understand is why you've teamed up with Mick Everson. How do you know him?"

"His father and I were business partners at Happy Horatio's Insurance. Mick approached me about taking over his father's interest in the business when the poor man lost his mind. It was all too easy."

There was that name again. "Who is Horatio?"

"What?" Jasper acted as though he wasn't expecting this question.

"Your insurance company is named after him. Who is he?"

"He was a ship captain. Lost at sea during a storm. He was Lyle's great-grandfather, so when I was trying to come up with a name for our agency, Lyle suggested it. He took all of Marv Everson's clients as soon as Mick had his father placed in the Charming Acres Assisted Living."

Feather frowned. Something was missing from this story. "And that's the only reason?"

"I'm tiring of this conversation. You'll understand if I don't continue. There is someone in the neighborhood who has been spying on me. They always take their dog for a walk precisely at 12:15, and I need to be on alert."

It was time for a bluff. "I've already called the police. They'll be arriving at the antique store any time now. Your fakes have caused too much harm already."

"Oof," Jasper grumbled. "How did you know about the ethoesium? It was George, wasn't it? Lyle discovered this chemical while on a safari with Mick. Time traveling is what they told their wives. We realized we could get out of the insurance fraud, stolen jewels and time travel business if we found a buyer. Ko Industries offered us a pretty penny, so we sold. But not before taking some of the tablets used in the testing process. It was the perfect way to get rid of members who were asking too many questions." Jasper chuckled. "Buddy Holly, and last winter Betty Boop."

"Mint?" she blurted, with a surprise in her voice she didn't want. "I mean, yes. He's not very good at keeping secrets."

"How much money would it take for you to remain quiet?"

"You'd have to tell me everything," she replied with more calm than she was feeling. "And I do mean everything."

Chapter Thirty-Seven

Gemini

Gemini paced nervously outside of the makeshift testing center. It was the same place the Hawkite meetings were held, but today a large sign hung on the door that read: "Testing, today only. Quiet, please!"

"You have nothing to worry about," Tug said soothingly. "We've got this. We drilled each other on the way over and we've got the pattern down."

Gemini laced her fingers together. "There's something I've never told anyone other than Leo." She paused in front of him. "I have test anxiety. I used to tell my mother I was sick on test days at school. When she caught on and decided I was pretending, I went to school and promptly threw up all over my teacher."

Tug laughed. "I bet your mom didn't make that mistake more than once."

"No, she didn't. From that day on, I was given

special conditions for testing. I could take the tests while everyone else was busy, so that I didn't feel the pressure to finish at the same time. I was taken to a small room off the principal's office, covered in green shag carpeting. That's what they thought was soothing in my day."

The door opened abruptly. "We're ready for you," JFK said, winking at Gemini. As Tug passed by him, he clapped him on the shoulder. "Big strapping lad, aren't you? We'll have to make sure you don't end up in a rural area on your first flight or they'll commandeer you for farm work!"

Tug laughed and nodded.

The long tables had been removed and all that remained were six chairs and two snack tables.

JFK gestured for them to sit in the two chairs positioned in the middle of the room.

"We'll be observing you both."

"Who is 'we'?" Gemini asked, looking around the room.

At that moment, a previously unseen door opened and three people entered, all wearing Richard Nixon masks.

"These are members of our sister Hawkite group in Seattle. They're here to proctor the test today."

Tug rubbed his hands on his knees. "My grandmother gets very nervous when she takes tests. Is there any way they could remove their masks?"

"I don't think we allow—"

"Good gravy, I was just waiting for that to

happen!" a man's voice boomed as he removed the mask to reveal a red, sweaty, middle-aged face.

"This isn't how it's normally—"

"I'm Lester, but you can call me Charlie Dickens." He held out his hand and attempted to shake Tug's before JFK interceded.

"You may choose to remove your mask, but I won't allow you to touch our pledges. It isn't allowed."

Lester shrugged and sat in a folding chair with a thud.

"If your grandmother is nervous, she can look at Charles Dickens' face. I'm assuming the other two proctors wish to remain anonymous?"

Two Richard Nixon heads nodded.

"Let's get started, then."

JFK set four pages in front of them. Gemini glanced down and noticed that at least the first two questions were the same. She relaxed. Just a little.

"You'll have one hour to complete the exam. We require an eighty-five percent. You won't be allowed to retake the exam for six months if you fail."

"If that little gal is nervous, you're not helping!" Lester said, winking one more time at Gemini.

"Our testers need to be well informed. I don't know how you do things in Seattle, but... oh, never mind."

JFK glanced at an analog clock that had been taped to the wall. "Oh, I almost forgot."

He removed two purple pens from his pants.

"You're required to use our pens. Just in case you've got disappearing ink or something."

Even he seemed to find that ludicrous, Gemini thought. She took the pen which read "Fix ME Restoration."

Something occurred to her at that moment, but it would be some time before she was able to act on it.

"You may begin."

She looked at Tug and nodded.

Fighting the bile rising in her throat, she forced herself to concentrate on the questions. A,C,A,C, exactly as they'd memorized.

When she'd finished, she looked up at the clock. *Fifteen minutes.* It would be obvious she was cheating if she told them she'd finished already. Gemini flipped back to the first page and read the questions for the first time:

1. *When preparing for takeoff, what message do you send your co-pilot?*
2. *How many artifacts are you allowed to bring back?*
3. *How often should you bathe while visiting another time?*

She chuckled after reading that one. Tonight, she would tell Leo about these silly questions.

Gemini felt a tap on her knee and she glanced over at Tug. He was drenched in sweat. Poor dear.

"I'm finished," he whispered. "I don't know how to kill anymore time."

"Mr. Reed, if you have something to say, we need to hear it. Otherwise, we'll have to disqualify you," Charles Dickens admonished.

"My grandson and I are finished with our exams," Gemini replied, rising from her seat. "We studied together for hours and we're both confident in our answers."

She collected Tug's test, mouthing, "deep breaths!" As she approached the Nixon masks, JFK moved in front of her.

"You aren't allowed to approach the proxy personnel. I'll take those."

He grabbed the tests from her hand and turned abruptly.

"If you'll both wait in the hall while we check your answers, we'll be able to tell you today whether or not you'll be traveling with us," Charles Dickens said in a kinder tone.

After they were both out of earshot of the testing crew, Gemini pulled a cloth from her purse and handed it to Tug. She started carrying them when Taurus was a baby and found they had many uses besides cleaning up small child messes.

He wiped his profusely sweaty face and attempted to hand it back to her. "Just keep it for now, dear."

"It was so hot in there! I bet they keep the air conditioning off for these tests so no one feels comfortable!"

Gemini nodded, deciding not to draw attention to his obvious test anxiety. "When we're done here, I'll treat you to a nice, cold drink. Heavy on the ice."

The double doors to the meeting room opened and JFK motioned for them to follow him. By his somber countenance, Gemini wondered if the time travelers had caught on to their cheating.

When they were standing in front of the again-masked group, one of them stood and cleared his throat. "You've both passed—one hundred percent. That's been happening a lot lately."

Both Gemini and Tug let out a sigh of relief.

"It just so happens that we've had a cancellation for the time machine. Willa Cather has strep throat. If you'd like to take your trip tomorrow afternoon, then—"

"Wait!" JFK stood, removing his mask. "They need time to get their affairs in order."

"Are you telling me there is a chance we won't make it back?" Gemini asked, forcing her face to remain serious.

"It was clearly stated in your manual!" JFK retorted.

"Let's keep the emotion out of this. It wasn't on the exam and she and her grandson, by her own account, studied many hours." Charles Dickens removed his mask, followed by the other two proctors. "They are most likely suffering from information overload."

"Sorry," JFK replied sheepishly. "Yes, there is a

chance you won't come back. We've had a few in recent months—I really can't talk about it. If you don't mind traveling so soon, I guess it's all right."

Another proctor, a woman, smiled at Tug and Gemini. "It's time we bestow your travel names. For you, Mrs. Reed, we've chosen Florence Nightingale." She produced a plastic badge on a lanyard from her pocket. On the front were the words "Hawkite, F. Nightingale."

Gemini immediately hung it around her neck.

"And for your grandson, we've decided on Alexander the Great." She handed a similar lanyard to Tug, who also placed it around his neck. He attempted to shake her hand, but she turned away.

"Here's your free t-shirt," JFK said, handing them mauve-colored shirts.

Gemini held it up to look at what was written on the front. "Hawkites, Of Oregon" with what looked like three commas within a circle below.

"You'll both need to sign a waiver tomorrow. Even if your affairs aren't in order, we need a way to notify your loved ones, just in case."

Charles Dickens, who had stepped outside briefly to take a phone call, rejoined them. His previously relaxed demeanor was now tense.

"Sorry, folks. Sometimes this happens," he apologized.

"We're not able to travel tomorrow?" Tug asked.

"You're still going. I just spoke with the boss. He says if you're wanting to travel tomorrow, you'll be sequestered here tonight. It happens from time to time, especially when we're traveling to times of potential mass illness."

"We'll just go home and retrieve a few things," Gemini replied, uneasy by this turn of events.

"The doors have been locked from the outside," Charles Dickens replied. "I'm afraid none of us are leaving until after your trip."

CHAPTER THIRTY-EIGHT

FEATHER

"Feather? I'm surprised to see you here."

Howard opened the door wide and allowed her inside. She'd never been to his home by herself. It was impressive, full of antiques and fancy furniture.

"Wasn't expecting company this morning, otherwise I would have straightened up. Come on in. I'd offer you some baked goods, but my admirer has recently decided I'm frightening and Gemini has been busy."

She glanced around Howard's living room. Neat and tidy. "I just had a chat with someone, and I'd like to ask you some questions. But first, do you still have that tea the restoration people left you?"

"No, I put in a call to them when I ran out, but they haven't gotten back to me. Just the manufacturer's name is all I need."

"My contact has information on that too."

He motioned for her to sit and he did the same. "Do you mean a ghost? You're particular to that type over the living, aren't you? Can't say as I blame you in this crazy day and age."

Feather chuckled. "I suppose that's accurate." She picked nervously at a loose thread on her jeans.

"I've found the best way to tell a person something hard is just to get it out," Howard said with an understanding nod.

"I've had a busy morning." Feather cleared her throat. "First, I spoke with Jasper Montgomery. He was the man who—"

"Had the pickle jar ghost." Howard grinned. "I heard all about him and his briny friend."

"He admitted that he and his friends came up with what they thought was the perfect crime."

Howard leaned forward, placing his elbows on his knees. "Now you've got my attention."

"Mick Everson owns a restoration company. On their initial walkthrough of the home, they take photos of all valuables. When they come back to work, they bring imitation jewelry with them, replacing what they've stolen with a cheap imitation."

"Well, I'll be. They stole my great-grandfather's watch."

"The jewels were created with a cheap and toxic compound called ethoesium."

Howard stood and moved around his living room. "That is known to cause hallucinations, chest pains and eventually death." When Feather stared at him, he added, "I took an online chemistry class, just to keep my mind sharp."

"Oh. I'm impressed you remembered!"

"Don't be," he replied tersely. "This whole time, I had my parents' rings, or what I thought were my parents' rings, hanging around my neck, and they were poisoning me. When I gave them to my attorney for safe keeping, my problems went away." He shook his head. "I've got to hand it to them, it was a brilliant plan."

"The restoration company you hired—Mick's restoration company—I believe the tea they left you contained ethoesium too."

Howard's jaw dropped. "This is stunning. All this time..."

"That's not all of it," Feather continued. "The next phase of their plan involved an insurance agency. Did something change with your insurance company recently?"

"I believe so. Give me a minute." Howard walked away, returning with a letter. He handed it to Feather.

"Dear Mr. Beachmont," she read. "Our office has closed due to unforeseen circumstances. We've transferred your files to George Mint Insurance, where we're positive you'll be well cared for. Please don't hesitate to call him with any issues."

Feather handed it back to him. "This isn't real. They wanted your premiums sent to George Mint, so that when you tried to file a claim, they could say, truthfully, that your jewelry wasn't real."

"And Mr. Mint got to keep my money and the authentic jewelry. Now you're going to tell me how the authentic jewelry was sold through the antique store."

"Yes. What they did with the money, I'm not sure."

Howard rubbed his chin. "This is quite complicated. Not to downplay these men's intellect, but I wonder how they came up with it."

"I spoke with an entity last night. She made a reference to a boat."

Row, row, row your boat.

"I remembered that Lucinda Lime's great-grandfather was a ship's captain. He spoke to me when we visited Happy Face Lake. At that time, I had no idea who Horatio was. He talked about coming out there with his friends. I did some digging this morning and came up with this."

She handed a photo to Howard. "This was on FindMeNow, an ancestor connection site. You can see on the left is Horatio Reed, Justice Magnison, Festus Mint in the middle, and Theodore Everson on the end. They came up with this plan." Feather produced another document, a photocopied page from a diary. "Horatio died before they could implement the plan."

"Miss Jones, you truly are remarkable."

Feather blushed. "I had a little help from my friends." She was relieved Tug had to spend the night away. She hadn't slept a wink between talking to Horatio and searching the internet.

"We need to tell Gemini about this turn of events."

"She and Tug are in the time machine," Feather

replied, feeling a little silly. "He was only allowed to send me a text last night. They weren't allowed to leave."

Howard snapped his head upright. "They're being held there? By Mick Everson?"

She hadn't even given it a second thought. "I'm sure he's not—"

"If any of these men have an idea that we're on to them, Gemini and Tug could be in danger."

While she had told Jasper, wrongly, that the police were on their way, she hadn't thought about what he might do after he hung up.

"I know where this place is. Let's go!"

CHAPTER THIRTY-NINE
GEMINI

"I don't mind telling you I feel like an idiot."

Gemini adjusted thick, black goggles over her eyes. They were so large they almost drooped to her top lip. The only thing keeping them up was the gigantic helmet she was wearing.

"Don't worry, Gem. I won't tell Leo," Tug joked.

They were seated in red velvet theatre chairs. In addition to being buckled in, both wore "vomit bibs" as they were described to them.

"You probably won't need these, but just in case," Amelia Earhart said as she fastened the plastic bibs with a catchall shelf at the bottom around each traveler.

"You know where your controls are, Florence?" a voice said over a speaker just above their heads.

She couldn't get over the names they came up with. Hers was Florence Nightingale, after the famous nurse. Gemini looked down, causing the goggles to fog up. "Yes, I believe they're to my right," she said, hoping she was correct.

"And Alexander, your co-pilot responsibilities will include re-entry braking. Can you show me where that is?"

Alexander the Great. Gemini and Feather had a good chuckle over that one.

Tug reached over to his right side and found what looked like a trunk latch. He gave a thumbs up.

Gemini remembered when Sophia was young and insisted on visiting an amusement park. Leo reminded her that she had a very sensitive stomach and that most of the rides would cause that stomach to move in ways it wasn't intended to.

"All of my friends have gone. Don't you love me?" Sophia had asked.

Leo couldn't resist when she looked at him with big eyes and a slight quiver to her lip. That summer, they bought a three-day pass to Ride, Tide and Slide. It was an eight-hour drive from their home, so they found a hotel with reasonable rates. They planned to hit the water park on the last day.

After the first motion simulation ride, Sophia looked positively green.

"Do you want to quit?" Gemini asked. She would later admit to Leo that she was feeling gleeful at that point. She hadn't wanted to make the trip in the first place.

"No, I'm doing Dizzy Dolly's Day Out next,"

Sophia insisted, walking to the next motion-simulated ride.

"I don't want to watch—" Gemini began.

"Gem, it's okay," Leo said, placing a hand on her arm. "I'll go. You enjoy this lovely summer day."

She had found a nice bench and sat down, removing a murder mystery from her large bag. Gemini was only two chapters into the story when she heard Sophia's plaintive cry. "Mommy!"

Gemini stood and put her arms out. Her daughter came running, embracing her tightly. "What happened?" she asked Leo, though she had a good idea.

Before he could answer, a white cart labeled "Clean Green Machine" pulled up in front of the ride. Three men in green jackets jumped out, each carrying a cleaning device.

A minute later, the crowd came pouring out, no one carrying a happy expression.

"It smells like throw up, Mommy," one boy said, his fingers pinching his nose.

They both frowned as they passed Gemini and Sophia.

"Let's get her cleaned up," Leo said.

Gemini hadn't even thought about her daughter being a mess. Her job was to comfort her only child. She pulled away from Sophia, finding not only Sophia but her brand new pink shirt covered in the remnants of Sophia's grape slush drink.

Gemini glanced over at Leo who was also covered

in the offending liquid. After that, Sophia never mentioned amusement parks again.

"I'm here to administer your motion sickness medication." It was Mick, who had somehow been absent throughout their testing and preparation.

"I really don't need anything," she insisted.

Mick sighed. "It was in the manual that you told us you read. You signed the forms."

Tug took one small plastic cup from Mick's hand and swallowed two pills. Gemini frowned at him and shook her head.

"Well? Are you going to take your pills, or will your grandson be looking for another co-pilot?"

Reluctantly, she took the cup from his hand and put the pills in her mouth before handing the cup back to him. "Am I allowed to wash this down?" she asked sarcastically.

"Of course. That's why we supply you with water."

Mick handed her a bottle marked "Hawkite official water."

"No thanks, I have my own!" Gemini dug in her large bag and pulled out her insulated cup. There was no way she'd take any more than necessary from him.

As soon as Mick left the room, Gemini put the cup to her lips. She knew the trick, as Sophia used it on her plenty growing up. She'd placed the pills under her tongue and, as she was taking a drink, pushed them out with her tongue. Since she was using two hands to drink, the pills slipped from her mouth and into her hand undetected.

"Two minutes until takeoff," a voice said.

"I'm feeling kind of... loopy, I guess. Is that normal?" Tug leaned his head back against the seat.

"It's just your anti-nausea medication taking effect. If you lean back and close your eyes, it will pass."

Gemini looked over at Tug as his head fell back against the headrest. He was passed out cold. Realizing they would suspect something was up if she didn't mimic his actions, she leaned her head back and closed her eyes.

The room was silent.

"They're out," the same voice said.

"How long do we have?"

"It's only about forty minutes until the drugs start to wear off," Mick replied.

"Better get to it, then."

The door to their "time travel" room opened and someone entered. They picked up Gemini's bag and began rifling through. At the last minute, she'd decided against bringing much of anything. On the slim chance they really were going to time travel, she didn't want anything identifying her as someone from the future.

"Fifty bucks, that's it," the voice said with disappointment.

"Look in his wallet."

Gemini tensed. She knew Tug brought all of his credit cards every time he left the apartment.

"No valuables here, but there is a Bank of Charming debit card."

"Leave it. That guy doesn't look like he's capable of saving anything but muscle magazines."

Gemini fought to keep her face from displaying her disgust.

The unknown person left them alone again. After another few minutes, a voice came over the speaker in her helmet. She recognized it as the voice of Mick Everson.

"You've just entered the year 1908. Look around you; there are horses everywhere. You can smell the scent of horse dung in the street."

Gemini stole a quick glance at Tug, whose nose was scrunched up. That was some powerful anti-nausea medication.

"Enter the country store across the street. The kindly store keep, Lyle Lime, is waving to you."

"Hello, travelers! What can I get you today?"

A chill went down her spine as she instantly recognized his voice. She opened her eyes just enough to see the screen. Lyle was dressed as a shopkeeper, a long black apron covering most of his thin frame.

"You're buying sugar, flour and salt to take to your sod home. Tell him now."

"Sugar... not white sugar... do you have coconut sugar?" Tug mumbled.

Gemini shook her head.

"After you've gotten your supplies, head out to the livery stable and pick up your horse and wagon."

Either there was interference in her helmet speaker

or there was a lot of commotion happening in the booth behind them.

She was starting to feel restless, though she didn't dare move. *How long was this going to take?*

"Check your pockets. Your wallet was stolen by the band of roaming thugs. There's no stopping, though. You have to get your wagon home before dark."

Fighting? Arguing? She thought she recognized a voice but wasn't sure. She didn't dare turn her head.

The door burst open, causing her to nearly jump out of her seat.

"Are you guys headed to the moon?"

It was Feather's voice. "I'm sorry, you guys look ridiculous."

"Why are you here? If Mick finds out, all of our undercover work will be for nothing."

"We need to get out of here and then all will be explained," Howard said as he unbuckled Tug, whose mouth was hanging open with a string of drool reaching toward the cement floor.

"Gem, Mick was planning to kill you!" Feather said.

CHAPTER FORTY
FEATHER

"What? How do you know that?"

Feather and Howard exchanged glances. "It's a long story. We need to get out of here now. I found ethoesium tablets on the table," Howard explained. "My guess is they intended to put it in the filtration system as soon as you both were knocked out. As a permanent solution."

"How will we move Tug?" Gemini asked. "You're a little snip of a thing and Howard and I, while very fit for our ages, aren't capable of lifting a man of Tug's size and strength. He's all muscle."

"It will take all three of us." Howard bent down, reaching underneath one of Tug's massive thighs. "Feather, you take his other leg. Gemini, you put one of his arms around your neck."

Feather wasn't sure this would work. One time, when they were out for dinner, Tug had consumed more wine than he thought. He tried to stand and instead fell into the decorative shrimp table. She tried lifting him by herself with no luck. Even the two wait-staff struggled to help her.

"One... two... three... lift!"

They heaved him up and somehow were able to maneuver out of the time travel machine.

"There is more than one person here!" Gemini said through heavy breaths. "JFK, Elvis and Amelia Earhart."

"Gem, are you hearing yourself?" Feather asked, equally breathless.

Gemini giggled softly. "I know, it's ridiculous." They continued moving as quickly as they could, with Tug hoisted precariously between the three of them. Feather would later recall that she had a burst of adren-aline when she knew her boyfriend and best friend's lives were at risk.

They made it to Howard's car and piled in. Howard sped out of the parking lot and drove until they reached the Tickled Egg.

Howard put the car in park and turned his body to view the two women and the sleeping man.

"Scopolamine—it's used to knock people out and make them suggestible," he said, pointing to Tug. "It's likely he'll be out for another hour or so."

"Another class?" Feather asked, now that they weren't in a hurry to rescue their friends. He'd shown her the box as he shoved a pill in the mouth of the "control room personnel," who they'd knocked out already.

"No," Howard shook his head. "A mystery novel."

"That explains the stories people told in meetings," Gemini said, running her fingers through her hair. "How do you know he was planning to kill us?"

"I spoke with Jasper. After I threatened him, he told me the whole plan. Their families had been friends for generations. George Mint told them all about a plan their grandfathers hatched, but they all died in a freak storm while out at sea. "

She took a deep breath. "Between them, they owned a jewelry business, an insurance agency, a restoration business and a large boat."

"The restoration agency, owned by Mick, went to clients' homes to assess damages," Howard continued. "As they did so, they took pictures of all of their valuables. George Mint would replicate the jewelry with cheap materials, namely using a metal called ethoesium. When handled frequently, it can cause confusion, dizziness and give the woman stalking *you* the impression you're stalking *her.*" Howard set his jaw.

"Oh, Howard." Gemini clucked her tongue. "I'm so sorry you went through this. And to think..." Her eyes widened. "Lyle's company makes ethoesium! He was in Chicago for a conference on uses for that very metal at the time of his disappearance!"

Howard nodded. "Our next performance comes from Jasper Montgomery. He took the real jewels stolen from clients and sold them through his antique store to criminals wishing to purchase them."

"That explains why Jasper was so strange," Gemini

remarked. "I'm sure he's handled more than his share of ethoesium."

"And our final player, Lyle Lime himself. He supplied a nice cabin where they could plot their crimes. He sent the letters, directing the unsuspecting homeowners to send their insurance payments to a new address. His group pocketed the money and were able to ensure the true owners would never realize their jewels were gone. They were just cheap imitations."

Howard looked in his rear view mirror. "The lad's still out cold?"

Feather tapped his face gently. Tug's eyes remained closed. "For now," she said.

"When I snooped through his office, I found insurance letters in his drawer. I didn't pay any attention to them. There were envelopes addressed to different people on his desk. I wonder why he left those very obvious clues out. Lucinda could have found them!"

Gemini shuffled through her purse before pulling out her phone. "I'm going to call Pedro right now. He staged that house to look like a murder scene. I'm sure he knows where Lyle is."

They all sat and waited anxiously for the phone to ring. When it did, they all tensed in unison.

"How are you, sweet auntie?" Pedro asked cheerfully. Gemini put him on speaker, so everyone could hear.

"Well, I'm a little confused at the moment."

"Oh? Sophia mentioned you might be having memory issues."

Gemini rolled her eyes. "Pedro, your Aunt Lucinda mentioned several times that you and Lyle were close. I know that you staged the cabin to look like a murder scene under his directive."

"Auntie, you must be confused. I never said that I—"

"You did. Unless you think Sophia is lying to me? I suppose we should let the police sort it out."

There was silence as Pedro contemplated what was said.

"Pedro? Are you still there?"

"I'm here, Auntie. Uncle Lyle asked me to do that, you're right. He's been using the cabin as a staging ground for people who want to disappear."

"Come again? Do you mean time travel?"

"Yes... and no. For a huge sum, people who are in trouble with the IRS or whatever can disappear. They pretend to do the time travel thingy and then Lyle puts them up at the cabin until he can get them out of the country. Lyle paid me well."

"No wonder you haven't gotten a decent job!" Gemini exclaimed.

Feather gasped. "This is so much bigger than we thought!"

"They've been planning it for years, he and his friends. I caught them talking about it when I was just a kid. Uncle Lyle told me I could help him."

"And Lucinda? Is she in on it too?"

"Not that I'm aware of."

Feather snapped her fingers. "I knew there were people watching us at Happy Face Lake!"

"And what about Buddy Holly? Was he killed the same way Mick was going to kill us?" Gemini asked.

"Who?"

Feather leaned through the seats. "Did someone come through recently? On their way out of the country?"

"Um... yeah. Last week."

CHAPTER FORTY-ONE
TWO DAYS LATER

"I just wish we could have solved your mystery too, dear," Gemini whispered as she tiptoed into Feather and Tug's apartment.

Feather didn't want to say anything to Gemini until she'd had a chance to research for herself. "I won't be gone long."

"How is our boy?" Gemini asked, pointing to the closed bedroom door.

"He's still got a terrible headache. Tug probably won't be out of bed while I'm gone."

"That's why I brought some soup and homemade bread." Gemini opened the refrigerator and placed two containers inside. She stood and smiled at Feather. "Take your time, dear. I'm still reading the police report on Mick. It's so hard to understand."

Feather kissed Gemini on the cheek. "See you soon!"

She had two stops to make this morning. She was dreading each equally.

First, she drove to the spot where she'd had her accident. Now that she knew the two cases weren't connected, she wanted to look at the area with fresh perspective.

Her car was finished twenty-four hours earlier. She had to admit, Tug was right. The price was right and her car never looked better. She pulled off the side of the road, beside the tree she'd dented.

Exiting the vehicle, she felt an immediate tightness in her chest. "I'm here and I'm listening. You don't have to do anything else to get my attention."

Looking both ways, she moved to the center of the highway where the entity raced in front of her. She put her hand on the warm asphalt, oblivious to the temperature. She closed her eyes and waited.

"It took you long enough!"

The hairs on her arms stood at attention and she turned back, gazing at the tree.

Leaning up against the trunk was a face she recognized. "Aunt Candy?"

The entity she saw only slightly resembled her aunt. She had the same features as Tandy, but at least two decades younger. But there was a darkness around her, something that she'd not experienced with her twin.

Although she had a million questions, she followed Jayden's directive and just listened. She closed her eyes and took a deep breath, inhaling the caramel corn smell that had become so familiar over the last two months.

"Those boys hired your gal to read their palms. Paid her extra to drive out to their cabin," Candy began.

Her recent massage popped into her head. "Nylah?"

"Yes, whatever," Candy replied dismissively. "Anyhoo, this gal didn't know what she was doing from the get-go. This Lyle guy says, 'Can you bring people back from the dead if we pay you double?' and you know what this gal says? She says, 'Sure I can, mister.' Then they asked her to whip up Horatio Reed and then things went haywire."

Feather kept her eyes closed tightly and her mind open.

"She brought me back instead. What an amateur!"

The dates of recent events ran through her head. She would have to check with Nylah, but it was a fair bet that the first time she started having nightmares coincided with this conjuring.

"It made me sooo angry! I can't go back until you let me. All because of some stupid girl!"

Feather's eyes opened, and she glanced over at her aunt. She was definitely not the sweet person who made caramel corn. This entity was dressed in a short dress with far too much makeup. Almost clownish.

"I don't understand how she brought you back instead of Horatio Reed. Do you know him?"

A hot wind blew, knocking Feather off her feet. She crawled to the side of the road, opposite Candy.

"He was my LOVER!" she steamed. "He only loved ME!"

Feather stood and wiped the soil from the front of her jeans. "Of course he did!" She made a mental note to check with Gemini on Horatio's wife. "How can I help you go back?"

"I've been trying to TELL you! Just like my sister, you never listen!"

Another gust of hot wind blew. This time, she held tightly to a speed limit sign.

"Tell me again," she insisted.

"I came to you, in your dreams, and you didn't listen. I scratched you and you didn't listen. I told you to get together with that little gal and use your powery things. That's what I told you!"

Feather searched her memory. The faceless person on the highway. Hot hands. Melting face. Nope. Nothing about having a séance. "Okay, I can do that. We just wish you back to your place?"

Candy laughed so bitterly it made Feather shudder. "Actually, this has been so fun, I've decided to stay. You're so easy to torture!"

Feather's heart sank.

Feather Weather, DO YOU WANT TO SEE MY INVENTION??

"Not—" She paused and smiled. "Yes, show me your invention!"

Instantly, a tornado formed over her head. Though

Feather's hair was blowing, her body remained planted in place. Candy's form wasn't so lucky. She was swallowed up in the whirling vortex. As quickly as it formed, it was gone. For the first time in three months, she felt peace.

"Thank you, Daisy!"

Feather looked around but didn't see Daisy. "Are you still here?"

"You'd better hurry. I haven't perfected the Entity Eraser yet. She'll be back soon!"

Feather jumped in her car. Without knowing exactly where Daisy's spirit was, she rolled down her window and yelled, "I'm sorry I ignored you, Daisy! You're a good friend!"

On the way over to Tandy's house, she thought about her dreams. Candy definitely didn't look anything like she remembered. Maybe that was why her face never appeared in Feather's dreams.

I've been trying to TELL you! Just like my sister, you never listen!

The scratches on her arms and legs. And her hands must've hurt because Candy was trying to get her attention by showing her what brought her back, the palm reading.

By the time she reached Tandy's house, she was feeling like she had most of the pieces to the puzzle.

This time when Tandy tried to slam the door shut, she stuck her foot out. "I'm not leaving until you hear me out."

"You're just like your father. Never liked him either," she grumbled as she sat down in her recliner. "I'll give you ten minutes."

"I kept thinking it was Candy who treated us so well and you were the one who didn't want to be around us. It was just the opposite, wasn't it?"

Tandy acted surprised. "Why do you say that?"

Foregoing the opportunity to bring up her most recent unpleasant encounter, Feather said, "I remember now. You always told us how Candy was so pretty and funny. Every time we made caramel corn, Aunt Candy was in her bedroom with the door shut. If we encountered her, she growled at us."

Tandy shook her head. "You don't know anything."

"When she died, you wore her clothing for two years. We called you Candy during that time whenever we visited. My parents told us never to ask you why. But I'm asking now."

Tears formed in Tandy's eyes. "Why did you have to bring all this up today?"

"Because I need to know. I promise, I will never darken your doorstep again if you'll just tell me the truth."

Tandy wiped her eyes and stared at a picture of cats on her wall. "She was always the pretty one. The boys loved her. But oh, was she mean to them. Do you know she turned down an offer of marriage?"

"Was it Horatio Reed?"

The color drained from Tandy's face. "How do you know about him?"

"From a... family picnic," Feather stuttered. "Was he a boyfriend?"

Tandy grunted. "You could say that." She took a deep breath. "Okay, I'm only saying this once, and then it's never to be talked about again. Understood?"

"Understood."

"It wasn't Horatio who proposed marriage. It was a nice young man who I thought loved me. Instead, he proposed to her. When it happened, she was sure it was my revenge. It wasn't."

She paused to blow her nose.

"Candy was selling fish and chips at the dock. Horatio was a fisherman who came in at the end of the day. They got along well. One thing led to another and—"

"She had an affair with a married man?" Feather blurted out. "I never knew!"

"No one else did either. When I discovered he was married, with children, I begged her to end things. She refused. That's why I had to take matters into my own hands, you see. I went to his home and told his wife everything."

"You did the right thing," Feather soothed. "For his family."

"I thought so too," Tandy continued. "But the

following week, Candy went berserk. She went to their home with our best butcher knife, planning to kill his wife. Instead, Horatio came home and shot her dead."

The wheels were spinning in Feather's head. "The buttons were from Horatio's coat. That must've been what they used to try and bring him back."

"What nonsense are you mumbling about?" Tandy snapped. "Not your hocus pocus, I hope."

"Do you know what Horatio was wearing the day he killed Candy?"

Tandy shrugged. "He worked part time as a ship's captain for a rich family. A captain's uniform, I suppose."

One month later

"You don't have to worry, Sophia. I promised you I'd be there and I will."

Gemini walked around her home, trying to gather everything she'd need while she listened to her daughter. Of all the days she didn't need distractions, it was today.

"Mother, you're no spring chicken. This is a lot for one person in a day. Sitting in a folding chair and trying to make small talk for hours on end before you drive here is too much."

Gemini felt a twinge of guilt along with relief. There was nothing appealing to her about driving to her old town to watch her naughty grandson throw a fit at his preschool graduation.

When she'd attended his Christmas program, Taurus stood next to a little girl with long, honey blonde hair. Her mother had meticulously curled and sprayed every strand, topping her head with a fancy red-and-green bow.

Taurus had little to no interest in singing the songs he'd learned. Instead, he took strands of her hair and put them in his mouth, sliding them back and forth until he'd removed every bit of hair product and curl.

The girl pushed him away and the teacher frowned, but Taurus never heard the word "no" at home, so he took this as a cue to continue. Eventually, the teacher asked Sophia to take Taurus home.

Gemini was mortified by the entire experience. Parents and grandparents seated beside her whispered, "I've heard about this little boy. Poor Mrs. Smythe goes home and drinks at night because of him."

In the car, Sophia ranted and raved. "How dare she kick us out! Doesn't she understand that young children learn through oral stimulation? How many of the other students are putting toys in their mouths?"

All the while, Taurus was screaming that he hated his car seat and wanted out. When Sophia finished berating his teacher, she turned around and said, "Does Mommy's good boy want ice cream?"

It wasn't an experience Gemini was anxious to repeat.

"Well, if you think I shouldn't drive, I'll trust your judgment." It was hard to hide her glee.

"I'm glad you understand. Brandon will be there precisely at four p.m. to pick you up. Oh, and tell your friends not to ask him to help. You know that Brandon doesn't do manual labor."

Her cheeks burned. There was no way out now. "Yes, I'll watch for him." *Surely their plan would be concluded by then?*

After she hung up and sufficiently cursed about her situation, Gemini looked at the clock. *8:30.*

Today it was of utmost importance that she stayed on schedule. *This is all going to work out, Gemini.*

She ran up Howard's steps and rang the bell.

"Gemini! Come in!" After doing a treatment for heavy metals, Howard had recovered nicely from his incident with the fake jewelry. The police were able to recover his parents' wedding rings and his great-grandfather's watch. They were now locked away in a wall safe.

"No, I don't have time. I just wanted to make sure you remember to water my plants tomorrow. It's supposed to warm up, now that summer is over."

"Of course! What a summer it was. You and Feather took down the largest insurance scam in the state. I only wish we were able to find Lyle Lime. Such a pity he won't face justice for his crimes."

"He's bound to slip up at some point. Don't you worry, Howard. Kindred Spirits won't give up until he's behind bars."

She stepped down his steps and waved.

"Good luck with all of your events!" he called as he shut his door.

Her phone rang. "Jayden? Thanks for getting back to me. Your large acquisition of the company producing ethoesium was—" She nodded excitedly as

Jayden spoke. "Exactly what I thought. I've become a whiz at this internet research!"

8:45.

When she arrived at the Charming Fall Market, vendors were busily setting up their booths. Eleanor Roosevelt was setting out time travel literature in a dark red tent. She waved when she recognized Gemini. "Good to see you!" she said cheerily.

"I'm... so sorry for the way things ended. You all deserved better. Mick Everson will have plenty of time to think about it."

Eleanor put her hands on her hips and grinned. "I sent him a nice blanket that I knitted. It's fluorescent orange, so it matches his clothing." As Gemini walked away, Eleanor added, "Don't feel sorry for us, Gemini. We're continuing the program. This time, we've brought in actual time travel experts to help us. One of these days, you'll see my name in the history books."

Gemini found Feather and Tug at space number twelve, right under an oak tree with leaves still clinging to their deep summer green.

"Gem! I was going to send Tug out for you soon!" Feather kissed her cheek and whispered in her ear, "It's all going according to plan."

Tug arrived carrying boxes marked with different flavors of Tug Bars. "Hi Gem." He kissed Gemini on the cheek before setting his load on the table. "Olive gave me specific instructions on where to place these."

When buttons, stickers, Tug Bars, cookies and

coffee were all in place, they set up their lawn chairs and waited for the crowd to arrive.

A mother and two brown-haired girls approached the table. "Look, Mommy! Ghosts!"

One of the young girls picked up a sticker.

"Take one for your sister too!" Gemini said, enjoying well-behaved children.

"You investigate... ghosts?" the mother asked timidly.

"We do." Gemini could tell she wasn't comfortable discussing paranormal problems in public. It wasn't unusual, especially given they lived in such a small community. The last thing anyone wanted was for the neighbors to laugh at them or think they were crazy.

"Take a brochure and read about our services. You're welcome to come to our office and discuss it any time. We are very discreet."

The woman nodded and looked away quickly.

"You two need some meat on your bones," Olive said, removing her coat and handing them each a Tug Bar sample. "Charmingly Chocolate."

"Can we, Mommy?" one girl asked.

"Yes, that's fine."

Gemini snapped her fingers. "That's what I forgot this morning! I was going to stop and pick up a gift for Taurus's preschool graduation."

"We've got plenty of help, why don't you go now?" Olive suggested, picking up one of Gemini's orange dream cookies.

"I'll go when things slow down," Gemini replied. "But thank you just the same, Olive."

The women found their chairs, Olive pushing hers in a spot that didn't exist between Feather and Gemini.

"Join me in the countdown," a voice said over the loudspeaker.

"Count down with me now. Fifty-nine, fifty-eight, fifty-seven..."

All three women enthusiastically joined in.

"Miss Feather Jones?" a familiar face asked.

She glanced worriedly at Tug. "That's me!"

Gemini popped up out of her seat. "Officer Klump! Nice to see you!"

"Mrs. Reed? Didn't expect to encounter you today!"

"Miss Feather Jones?" his partner asked, ignoring the pleasant banter.

Eleanor Roosevelt stepped closer to their tent, eyeing everyone suspiciously.

Feather pushed a strand of lime-colored hair out of her face. "That's me. What can I do for you?"

He walked around the table and commanded, "Please stand and place your hands behind your back, ma'am. You're under arrest."

Tug sprung up and stopped just short of attacking the officer. "For what?"

Gemini quickly grabbed his arm before things escalated. "Officers, my son-in-law is an attorney and we know our rights. What is it you're arresting her for?"

"Murder."

"Please stand."

She stood, glanced at Tug and nodded solemnly.

Gemini cleared her throat and asked again, "What is the charge, officer?"

"Murder. Specifically, the murder of George Mint."

"What? I never even met the man!" she protested. "Gem! Call your son-in-law! Tell him they found my hiding spot!"

Eleanor pulled out her phone and walked away.

Chapter Forty-Three

"Lucinda? This is Gemini. I wanted you to know, my partner has been arrested for George Mint's murder."

Lucinda gasped. "That can't be! I just... how is that possible?"

"Well, what I know is that Feather had a message from an entity early this morning. She was told where to go, somewhere outside of town. When she arrived, George was there."

"Gemini, he's out on bail. There's no way he would have left town without telling me!"

"Feather told him she knew he was laundering money from his jewelry scam through the Tickled Egg, and the entity told her right where he kept all the cash. I was only able to speak with her for a few minutes, you understand."

"But... but... why did she kill him?"

Gemini sighed. "George wasn't going to let her

leave with that information. He put his hands around her neck and squeezed."

"My George? He's the least violent person I know!" Lucinda sobbed.

"That's when Feather took her fingers and stuck them right in his eyes. He fell backward, and she continued to push him until he stumbled over a tree stump. He was impaled by a wood shard. My poor, poor girl. She was beside herself."

Lucinda was silent.

Gemini looked at her watch. *10:15.*

"In a way, it's a relief," Lucinda said. "First Lyle disappeared and then George was charged with those awful crimes. I'm thinking this is a message to me—men are poison to Lucinda Lime."

"I'm sure the police will be there soon. They'll want to ask you questions. It's a shame things ended like this."

"Thank you, Gemini. You've gone above and beyond."

When she hung up, she ran up the stairs of the police station. "Go time!" she called.

It was warming up nicely and Gemini drunk in the scent of the pine trees as she exited the police car.

Instead of enjoying the sun, however, she had a job to do.

Walking up the steps to Lucinda's home, she found the door ajar. She hoped she wouldn't get lost again.

When she arrived at the doors to Lyle's office, they were open too. Two heads were bent over the spot where Gemini discovered an opening on her first visit.

"Mr. and Mrs. Lime. What a lovely surprise!" she said with sarcasm.

Lucinda and Lyle spun around, shocked to see her.

"What are you doing here?" Lucinda sputtered.

"I came to see the show." Gemini sat in Lyle's leather desk chair. "George isn't dead. He's in jail. When I went to drop off some cookies for Officer Klump, George was leaving. He felt, I'm going to call it remorse, over the people he'd hurt and the time travelers he killed."

"That's highly doubtful," Lyle snickered.

"Oh, he's remorseful. So much so that he told me everything. He agreed to set up a sting to catch you, Lyle. If you hadn't been living in the family cabin, you'd know that already."

"How would you know that?" Lyle asked.

"My friend Feather sensed your presence, for one. The bloody fingerprints were upside down for another. When I was in the bathroom, the one you told Pedro to stage, I found a wet toothbrush and a comb. I'm fairly certain Pedro didn't spend the night after he staged that ridiculous scene."

"Pedro's always been an idiot," Lyle scoffed. "He could have made it much more believable."

"In any case, your presence was duly noted. What I haven't figured out is how long you've known, Lucinda. I am quite certain you asked for my help with sincerity."

"Lyle didn't tell me anything at first. I had a camera set up in here, and during the memorial, I watched you, Gemini. I knew you would lead me to his secrets," Lucinda replied. "After everyone left, I pried this door open," she pointed to the floor, "and found all sorts of goodies. Millions of dollars and a business plan for a nationwide chain of time travel experiences. I knew at that point that Lyle was alive. It wasn't hard to figure out he was living at the cabin." She sighed and glared at Lyle. "You never were terribly bright, sweetie."

"Funded by the jewelry scam, the time travel scam, and, drum roll please," Gemini said with a twinkle in her eye. "The sale of your company, HOO Cares, which produces ethoesium as well as vintage candies, like the Bittersby Chocolates I found in your desk. You sold out to Ko Industries!"

"My, I'm impressed!" Lucinda remarked. "I'm dying to know how you discovered all of this."

"Oh, it came in bits and pieces. Where shall I begin? After we left the memorial, you were angry that I took the buttons, the ones Lyle stole from the Reed family treasure room. Those came from Horatio Reed's ship captain coat. I gather Lyle was in there to dig through Horatio's diary. Am I right, Lyle?"

Lyle smirked.

"I'll take that as a yes," Gemini continued. "At Uncle Buzz's funeral, there was discussion about Buzz's diary and what it contained. Sophia remembers you asking every Reed what they knew about it. To them, it was a joke. But to you, Lyle, it was another business opportunity. An insurance salesman, a painter, a ship's captain and a second-hand furniture dealer all hoping to find their fortune. Instead, they died at sea."

"It's a perfect plan. If one avenue didn't work, we still have plenty of irons in the fire," Lyle said. "And it's not over yet." He grinned at Gemini, making her skin crawl.

"Your plan has a number of flaws, Lyle."

He raised an eyebrow.

"First, using the donan as the symbol for both your time travel t-shirts and the HOO Cares company. Sloppy. Feather found your letterhead in the fire at the cabin. I thought I recognized it from my first meeting with Mick. He showed me the pendant he had made. I'm guessing you have one too, Lyle?"

It's common in Eastern religions. The three 'commas', as you called them, work in a circle that together symbolize Man, Heaven and Earth.

"I had to remind Lyle how much we hated each other." She grinned at her husband. "He didn't take much convincing."

Lyle picked up a bag of money. "I'm leaving. You

two hens can sit here and cackle all you want, but I've worked too hard to lose this now."

"Lyle, don't you dare leave without dividing this equally!" Lucinda warned.

"Calm down, you two. No one is going anywhere. And Lyle, you might want to take a peek inside your bag before you decide to run off."

Lyle opened the bag. Inside were all of the letters he'd sent to insurance clients, telling them that he was now their agent. All to take their premiums to fuel his time travel scam. They were cut to match the size of money.

His eyes narrowed and he attempted to lunge toward Gemini. At that moment, Officer Klump stepped in, grabbing both arms in one motion and pushing him to the ground. "Lyle Lime, you're under arrest for insurance fraud, murder and I'm sure a bunch more."

Lucinda attempted to hug Gemini. "I'm so sorry, dear. This shouldn't have ended like this."

"Yes, I agree." Gemini dusted off her knees and stood. "It's such a lovely restaurant. I hate to see it close. You know, when they're done taking a look at your questionable accounting."

Chapter Forty-Four

The Charming Gazette

The Tickled Egg re-opened last week under new ownership. Phyllis Grant and her son Dan rescued the downtown eatery after the former owners allegedly committed a multitude of crimes.

Lucinda and Lyle Lime are charged with money laundering, insurance fraud and murder. Lucinda Lime has asked a judge to sever her trial from her husband's so that she may testify against him. Both face lengthy prison sentences if convicted.

Local entrepreneurs Mick Everson, George Mint and Jasper Montgomery also face charges for the same crimes. In addition, Mr. Montgomery's antique business is under investigation for passing off stolen jewelry as fakes.

The restaurant has a fresh coat of paint, an updated

menu and complimentary strawberry cannoli for this month. The Grants are excited to serve you!

"I know I say this every time, dear, but this was the strangest case I've had. Your family... gracious. I promise I'll never say another bad word about them. You and Sophia are the diamonds in that mud."

Gemini dropped the newspaper into her lap and squeezed Leo's hand. They were seated in front of his window, watching the ducks swim in the pond. "Poor Lyle and Lucinda. They'll be the talk of the next funeral!"

"Mrs. Reed? You're here kind of early!"

She pivoted in her chair. "Hello, Trent! I brought you some Oatmeal Snappies. The container is in the usual place. We're having an office party today."

He walked over to the window and glanced out at the activity on the pond. "I'm sorry, Mrs. Reed. The last thing I want to do is lose your friendship."

She squeezed Leo's hand for support. "I appreciate that, Trent. We both learned some lessons from this experience. I just finished telling Leo about two of them. The first is that I was far too trusting. Business is business, no matter who the client is."

"And the second?" Trent asked.

"I'll be skipping Reed family funerals and weddings from now on. They're far too dramatic for my tastes."

"I've purchased champagne for those who drink it and a fine vintage of sparkling water for those who don't."

Gemini popped the cork of the champagne and poured it quickly into fluted glasses. She squinted as the sun bounced off their newly-installed window. On her desk sat a brand new picture of Taurus from his pre-preschool graduation. Dressed in a white cap and gown, he was grinning from ear to ear as Gemini knelt beside him. There was a large green stain running the length of his graduation robe. Sophia had insisted that he drink a greens power drink instead of the sugary red punch the other kids were drinking. He waited until his mother was watching to pour it slowly down the front of him.

"I wanna make sure I've got this all straight," Olive said, taking a glass of champagne and handing it to her boyfriend, Elmer.

"Well, you know that George Mint, Lyle Lime, Jasper Montgomery and Mick Everson were running a big scam. They were taking jewelry from Mick's restoration business clients, George was making fakes for the employees to replace and Lyle gave them fraudulent insurance. But that was just the beginning of their deceit."

"Gemini Reed, you act as if I'm a doddering old

fool. Elmer, do you think I'm a fool?" she asked her boyfriend. He shook his head and motioned for her to sit on his lap. After sitting and wrapping her arms around his neck, she turned back to Gemini. "What I wanted to know is what happened with Feather's ghost."

"That's her story to tell, Olive," Gemini replied, taking a small bite of cake.

"Did I hear my name?" Feather asked, licking white frosting off her fingers. "I don't normally like sweets, but this is really good!"

"They have new ownership at the Tickled Egg. They brought in a pastry chef from Seattle," Gemini replied, smiling as she thought about Phyllis's strawberry cannoli. At least now she had guidance. "Worth every penny."

"Olive, my aunt was summoned by accident. Her boyfriend, Horatio Reed, was the mastermind behind this insurance scam. He just didn't have time to implement it because he and his friends died in a boating accident."

Olive nodded. "Does that make sense to you now, Elmer?" she asked. He nodded and smiled. "Elmer's the quiet type," she explained. "Works out perfectly."

"The buttons, Feather, explain those," Gemini insisted, though everyone had heard the story a hundred times. Well, everyone but Elmer.

"Those were Horatio Reed's. They came from his ship captain uniform. Lyle stole them from the Reed family and used one to summon Horatio. The problem was, he only wore that uniform to work when he was planning a rendezvous with Candy. It was their signal. Because Lyle brought the buttons from that particular jacket to the séance, Nylah ended up summoning my Aunt Candy instead of Horatio."

Feather sat down and patted the seat next to her, smiling when her boyfriend sat.

"This cake is amazing, Gemini," he said excitedly. "We'll have to celebrate our re-re-grand opening again!"

Tug, who was now on his third piece of cake, asked, "Gemini, you've mentioned several times that the Reeds had secrets. Sophia talked about it—"

"The diary of Horatio's contained all the family secrets. Sophia and Pedro read some of them as children. In his early days, Horatio robbed a bank. That's how he financed his purchase of the cabin and the surrounding land. Apparently most of the Reeds knew about it, including Leo. Horatio was never caught."

"Enough mystery solving. This is our time to celebrate!" Feather said.

Tug raised his glass and stood. "I'd like to make a toast. To the best baking assistant." He nodded toward Olive.

"Co-executive," she corrected him.

"The best baker slash detective." He looked at Gemini.

She raised her glass in return.

"And the best girlfriend, paranormal detective and —" He paused and set his glass on the desk. Getting down on one knee, he took Feather's hand. "Best life partner. Feather Jones, will you marry me?"

He removed a ring from his pocket and slipped it on her finger.

She jumped up and hugged him. "Yes! Yes! A thousand times yes!"

Violet Vendetta

Sneak Peek

"I want to hire you, but you'll have to follow my instructions. To the letter."

Doing her level best to be polite, Gemini said, "Please have a seat, sir, and we'll take your information,"

She proceeded to close the email she was writing to her daughter, Sophia about a mother-daughter spa day. "Let me just open up the form and we can get started."

It was at this moment that she realized this man was dressed in purple from head-to-toe. That particular fact didn't stand out as much as the thickness of his clothing. Though it was an exceptionally warm day for October, he was wearing a turtleneck and wool pants.

"There we go." A brightly-colored page labeled "intake form," popped up on her screen. "Sometimes the fancy-pantsy internet I paid extra for doesn't work in this ware house. What is your name, sir?"

"Not you. I want her." He pointed across the room, where a pink-haired woman was swaying back and forth while she painted a mural on the wall.

"She's got her ear thing-a-majiggers in."

Gemini stood up and walked over to the other side of the room, tapping Feather Jones on the shoulder. Feather whipped around, her face pinched and defensive.

"ITS ALL RIGHT, DEAR." Gemini over-enunciated.

Feather pulled her ear buds out and glanced over at the tall man. "Sorry. I've been having trouble concentrating. My therapist thought listening to music might help. That, and the mural I'm painting."

She pointed to a pair of violet eyes with dark eyelashes.

He nodded.

"This nice man—what did you say your name was?" Gemini asked.

"I didn't." He replied sternly.

Somewhat flustered by his response, she said, "well...he wants to hire you, dear."

Feather lifted one brow. "Gemini and me, we work as a team. We're partners."

"That's very nice of you, hon, but if he needs your paranormal skills, I have plenty to occupy me. I do have that situation at home."

Feather nodded. "The crazy neighbor?"

This time, Gemini turned beet red. "Something like that."

"Okay, so how are we going to do this?" Feather asked the still unnamed client.

"I will pay you fifty-thousand dollars. Cash."

"What is it, exactly that you want me to do?"

He looked around the room and then at Feather. "I need you to kill someone."

Get your copy now!

Acknowledgments

Each successful writer needs not just one but many people in their corner, helping at all stages of development. Thanks go out to: the Keder Readers for your early reading. David Penpek, for providing answers when I'm all out, Doug Keder, for just about everything, Kyle for technical help, and my entire worldwide family for your love and ever-present support.

About the Author

Joann Keder is an award-winning author who spent most of her formative years (over 40) living on the plains of Nebraska. When she and her husband chose to make a move to the Pacific Northwest, she came to an agreement with her soul that it was time to start novels.

Today, she creates stories about strong, humorous women and the paths they choose. When she's not writing, she and her husband enjoy nature, a good chocolate and spending time with family. Not necessarily in that order.